Robert Cross

FIONA KIDMAN HAS WRITTEN MORE than twenty books, mainly novels and collections of short stories. Her most recent novel, *The Captive Wife*, was a joint winner of the Readers' Choice Award and a finalist for the Deutz Medal for Fiction at the 2006 Montana New Zealand Book Awards.

She has been awarded a number of prizes, honours and fellowships, including the Mobil Short Story Award, the Victoria University Writers Fellowship, and the OBE for services to literature. In 2006 she was the Meridian Energy Katherine Mansfield Fellow in Menton, France. In 2008 she was the Creative New Zealand Michael King Fellow.

Fiona Kidman is a Dame Commander of the New Zealand Order of Merit, a Chevalier de l'Ordre des Arts et des Lettres, and a Chevalier of the French Legion of Honour. She lives in Wellington.

Fiona KIDMAN

The Trouble with Fire

'[Her] stories remind me of those of Alice Munro.
Though they are very much of a time and place
they have a universal dimension.'
— *Booksellers News*

VINTAGE

 The assistance of Creative New Zealand is gratefully acknowledged by the publisher.

A VINTAGE BOOK published by Random House New Zealand, 18 Poland Road, Glenfield, Auckland, New Zealand

For more information about our titles go to www.randomhouse.co.nz

A catalogue record for this book is available from the National Library of New Zealand

Random House New Zealand is part of the Random House Group
New York   London   Sydney   Auckland   Delhi   Johannesburg

First published 2011

Front cover photograph: Allan Jenkins/Trevillion Images
Back cover photograph: Robert Cross
Design: Megan van Staden
Printed in New Zealand by Printlink

For Harriet Allan, friend and editor

Contents

My mother did try to shield my view so that I wouldn't see the leaping flames above the gum trees, the blinding arc of light reflected in the clouds, the sparks which showered the night with dazzling ferocious gaiety. This was the house I had briefly known as home. She wanted to save me from the terror of watching it perish. But of course I saw. I felt the heat of the flames. I heard the confused birds waking as if night were day. Of course I remembered.

from *Paradise* by Fiona Kidman

So, like a forgotten fire, a childhood can always flare up again within us.

Gaston Bachelard

Part I

The Italian Boy

A FARMER'S WIFE

APART FROM THE SOFT FOLDS beneath her chin, there was not a great deal about Meryl that appeared changed. She wore her hair in exactly the same fair bob, flicked under at the ends, as she had when she was fifteen, and her pale eyes were seemingly as innocent as ever. Hilary had seen her once or twice in the years between, so none of this surprised her. Some of her contemporaries were so weather-beaten and misshapen by time and hard luck that she didn't recognise them when they introduced themselves at public readings of her work. They would sit at the back of the room, not people who frequented literary gatherings as a rule, trying to catch her eye. Their expressions, when they came up and said, 'Remember me', during signing time, contained a certain hurt bewilderment when she was forced to admit that she didn't have a clue who they were. Afterwards she was swamped by guilt.

But Meryl was not one of them. Hilary could spot her at once. All she needed was a beret slouched back over her hair to reveal her profile, the smooth complexion and even smile, and they could have been walking arm in arm down a country road together. As well as encounters on Hilary's book tours, they had even sought each other out from time to time when they were younger.

Her visitor had caught her unawares on a Saturday morning while she was putting out the rubbish. 'Surprise,' Meryl had called in a carolling yodel, as she came up the path. 'Betcha didn't expect me.'

Her voice still had the nasal twang Hilary remembered. It reminded her of why, in the end, she had been glad to escape Meryl, why their efforts at reunion had failed so miserably.

In a few minutes, she was sitting at Hilary's kitchen table, asking for sugar for her tea, which she liked 'hot and strong'. 'Just energy shots, I don't usually need sugar, except when I'm working. I'm on my way to a conference,' she explained. 'It's just down the road.' She chuckled. 'You might have taken your name out of the phone book, but I've got your address — remember we sent each other Christmas cards? I couldn't pass this near without seeing you.'

Hilary shivered, this closeness of Meryl like a chill breeze on her skin. It was all she could do not to draw away. 'A conference,' she said carefully. 'Does that mean you're not living in the country now?'

'Oh, I'm still a farmer's wife, Hilary, if that's what you mean. But we country women do have businesses of our own, you know.' Hilary felt that familiar remorse, as if she was being judged for having changed. 'You've kept your looks,' Meryl said, 'but you know you do need your colours done.'

'Colours?' Hilary repeated.

'Colour is my business,' Meryl said. 'I saw you on television the other day talking about your new novel. And I thought, she still hasn't got it. You know I always did have to tell you how to dress. You wore the oddest clothes. Don't you remember, my mum and I used to find you dresses for the dances because yours were such a hoot? It came from being brainy — you couldn't see how you looked for the nose on your face. My mother passed away, did I tell you, she was ninety-seven, and I was blessed to have her for so long, though God took her mind well before that. Look at you, still wearing purple. You're not an old lady, Hilary.'

In spite of herself, Hilary glanced down at the mauve jumper and trackpants she was wearing. As you do, she thought grimly, when you're putting out the rubbish.

'Much too cold for your complexion. You wore that lilac-coloured dress with the diagonals the first time you went to a dance. You didn't listen that time, did you? You must remember.'

'That was a long time ago.'

'It was the night you met Nino.'

'Was it?'

'That Italian boy. Oh, come on, Hilary.'

'I remember the dress,' Hilary said with reluctance. Of course she did. The dress had been one of her aunt's cast-offs, a party dress Hilary had worn for a dress-up game when she was younger, a sheath dress from the era of jitterbug and jazz. Keep it, her aunt had said, seeing as you like it so much. Her mother helped alter it so it fitted her better.

'You look so pretty,' Nino had said that night.

SCARLET WOMEN

THE NIGHT OF THE DANCE was not the first time Hilary had seen Nino, but she never told Meryl that. It began in Alderton, but then most things did. That is where Hilary returns when she least expects it. The town sits prickling behind her eyelids when she wakes some mornings, or when she is on a train in a foreign country and sits lulled by its motion, not knowing exactly where she is, or in the moments before she gets up to speak to an audience, and she finds herself wondering how she got there and where she has come from.

There was one main street, less than a quarter of a mile long, and two bisecting it. A grocery shop stood on one corner and, opposite it, a dairy that sold tobacco and sweets as well as milk and bread, and then came the butcher's shop. Further along was a dress and fabric shop, a salon where Hilary had her hair cut short in preparation for high school and the regulation clearance of the uniform collar. A pity, said the hairdresser, as she lifted the dark skein of hair she held looped in her hand. You could make a silk blouse out of this. Even though it was a summer day when this happened, Hilary's neck felt cold and suddenly naked. There was, too, a hardware shop, a small library that opened on Friday afternoons and a photographer's studio.

And when Hilary remembers the photographer's, she sees herself as a twelve-year-old with her nose not quite pressed to the window, looking at the pictures of young women in long dresses. The farmers' daughters who lived out of town had debutante or 'coming out' balls. They were not seen much around Alderton because they went to boarding schools and only came home for the holidays. When school was over they would disappear to new lives. They wore elbow-length gloves with their fluffy white gowns and swore they were virgins, now ready to be courted by the right man, one they could 'give themselves' to. Plums ripe for picking, Hilary once overheard her father say, with a laugh. The young women were accompanied by black-jacketed partners, sweaty-looking youths plucked from the countryside to escort them to the balls, which took place in the local returned servicemen's hall. (These were not necessarily *the* right men, who might still have to be found in a city, in banking or medicine or law, or even in England, waiting to be met by the girls on their big trip abroad, but these were the men who would do for the moment.)

It was these virgin role models Hilary stood looking at with such longing. Their smiles were wide and gleaming, light was reflected on their hair from the overhead lamps, little twists of tinsel wound around the glittering archways through which they made their grand entrance. Hilary wanted to be one of those girls some day, but already she knew in her heart that it wouldn't happen. Her parents couldn't afford dresses like that. They owned a small piece of land where they were setting up an orchard but it would be a long time before it paid its way. In the meantime, they did odd jobs for other people, worked at picking fruit and gardening. Besides, her mother, a sturdy woman who had grown up Presbyterian, found the idea of these balls ridiculous. Pomp, she snorted.

Behind the main street stood a picture theatre where old newsreels and grainy black and white movies were shown on Saturday nights. Hilary had seen Audrey Hepburn courted by Gregory Peck in *Roman Holiday* and Ingrid Bergman with Humphrey Bogart in *Casablanca*. She cried on the walk home after *Casablanca*, making her father irritable. 'Don't get ideas about that Ingrid Bergman. Don't you know she's living in sin with some Eyetie fella?' he said. Besides, he liked to sing as they strode along the road beneath the starlit canopy of the sky, and her snivelling spoiled the evening's treat.

'What's the point of it all?' he said. 'You cried all the way home last week, too.' This was true, but unjust, because they had heard at intermission that a boy in her class had been killed that afternoon when his horse rolled on him. With the hindsight of all those years, Hilary wonders if her father was just callous — for that is what he seemed to her then — or whether he wanted to shield her from the terrors of death. She remembers how she didn't want life hidden from her, that what really happened was what she wanted to know. On the day of the funeral she had been kept home from school. She didn't just weep when her father complained about her tears, she burst into loud erratic sobs.

'She shouldn't have left him,' Hilary cried, meaning Bergman and Bogart. 'He was the one who truly loved her. None of them will be happy. Her husband'll be miserable for the rest of his life.' And so on. Histrionics, her father said, with a short intake of breath.

Hilary wasn't going away to boarding school. Instead, she would catch a school bus to the Ohaka high school some twenty miles away. The pupils who travelled on the bus had parents who were hard up like hers, or they were Maori or Dalmatians. This was as good an indication as any that she would never have a 'coming out' ball, but it didn't stop her from dreaming about one day falling in love. She had periods and the beginning of breasts with rubbery little nipples that she admired in the mirror every night. She needed clothes, she thought, and lipstick and shoes, not Roman sandals, to wear to the pictures. When the summer holidays came, the last before she started high school, she took a job sweeping floors at Kirk's, the grocery store. Mr Kirk was a short rugged-looking man, used to throwing crates of food around.

'How old are you?' he barked, when she went to enquire about the job.

'Thirteen,' she lied.

'Well, make sure you keep up with the work,' he said, and left it at that.

Kirk's stood on the crossroad, opposite the dairy belonging to Burke's. Kirk's and Burke's. Twin shops. People who were going to town often said they were 'going to Kirk's and Burke's', as if it meant the same thing. Hilary made herself useful, stacking tins the way she saw other staff doing, smiling at customers and showing them where to find golden syrup or matches or floor wax. She hoped she would soon be allowed to serve at the counter. When people from school came into the store she adopted a superior look, as if not having a job and nothing to do for the whole summer was sad.

Hilary had worked at the shop for less than a week when Burke's took on a boy, new to the town, to move the milk crates. At the grocer's shop, some said he was Italian. An Eyetie. Only weeks earlier, Hilary had heard her father use this word and now she saw it for what it was: an insult. But then her father had been to war, and the conflict was still raw. Men who worked in the shop had fought, too. They didn't talk much about it. But in the language between them, a certain contempt surfaced for those who hadn't been, or when they spoke of their erstwhile enemies.

It was hard to guess the Italian boy's age, perhaps fifteen or sixteen. He was tall and thin with a chest that seemed almost concave. His father was said to be opening a fish and chip shop. Well, what would you expect, Mr Kirk had said with a shrug. That's what those people did. He wondered aloud how they would make themselves understood. Refugees, hardly a word of English. Up here in the north, they mightn't get on too well with the Dallies. Sure to be blood on the floor.

In her lunch-hours, Hilary watched the boy from the corner of her eye as she sat on the bench at the edge of the street verge, her feet surrounded by kikuyu and paspalum. His hair was black and too long for the times, his face hollow-cheeked and drawn and there was a pallor beneath his swarthiness. She knew he had seen her. On his third day at Burke's he waved, a covert little acknowledgement of her presence. From then on, she would sit each day picking at her lunch, and wondering how she might speak to him, what other signal she could send beyond a wave.

A girl called Anthea appeared in the shop one day. She was

someone Hilary had hoped never to see again. Anthea was older
than her by three years or so. For a time, when they were still quite
small children, they had attended school together, before Anthea
was sent off to boarding school. She had been a person to avoid,
her tongue was cruel, her fingers like sharp claws that stabbed
you in the arm when nobody was looking, leaving twin bruises. It
was never possible to tell what would attract her malice from one
day to the next. Some sour irritation within seemed to overtake
her, and when it subsided she stopped as if nothing had happened.
Her grandfather, said to be a wealthy man with an English title,
had dispatched his youngest son, Anthea's father, to New Zealand
because he hadn't done well enough at Eton. A remittance man.
Although their house stood not far from where Hilary lived, she
had never seen it, sheltered as it was by a high hedge. Those few
who had described it as a ramshackle cottage. But there was talk of
a splendid dresser, resplendent among camp stretchers and sticks
of cheap deal furniture. A Georgian dresser, a district nurse told
Hilary's mother. She had been called to the house to attend a family
illness. Some fine porcelain cups and saucers, too, remnants from
a former life, some lost refinement.

When Anthea came into the shop, she gave Hilary a long baleful
stare. She had thick wavy hair, a brown mane with rough texture,
and strong chiselled features.

'What are you doing here?' she asked.

'I work here,' Hilary said, and realised, as soon as the words were
out, that she had spoken with too much pride.

'Work,' said Anthea, 'you're just a kid. A brat.'

Hilary stood holding onto the end of her broom handle and said
nothing.

'They don't pay you, do they?'

It seemed best to shrug it off. 'Pocket money.'

'*Pocket* money. You're not worth it. I suppose you've heard I'm going to Ohaka this year?'

Hilary felt suddenly sick. She remembered, then, that Julius, Anthea's older brother, had come back to the town, and for the past year had been travelling to high school on the bus. Julius was unknown to her, someone who had always gone away to school. But now she saw how it must be, that the family had run out of money, and their children were reduced to the local school.

Anthea turned and walked out of the shop. Julius was waiting for her outside. He looked nothing like his sister — almost grown up, tall, with limp fair hair flopping over his high, round brow. His skin strained as if bursting with brains beneath his forehead. Brainy, he looked brainy, Hilary thought. Anthea stood talking to him and they both turned and looked back over their shoulders.

'You should keep away from those two,' said Mr Kirk, startling Hilary. 'They hang around here trying to buy lollies on the cheap. They ran a slate with us, until I told their father they weren't paying. Now I hear they're running one across the road at Burke's.'

'Is it okay if I go for my lunch now?' Hilary asked.

The grocer gave her an old-fashioned look. 'Just don't go hanging around boys,' he said, as if he had read her mind. She had lain awake for several nights planning how she would make an extra sandwich, slip a boiled egg into her brown paper bag. She now knew the Italian boy's name was Nino. She was sure he was hungry. Something wolfish about his expression suggested he had gone without. But when it came to the point, her throat felt constricted. She had wanted to call to him but nothing came out. He waved again and ducked his head.

Hilary didn't make it past lunchtime at the grocer's shop. When she got back, Julius stood talking to Mr Kirk.

'She's only twelve,' he was saying, in his drawling accent. He pointed towards Hilary.

'Is this true?' asked her employer.

'I'll be thirteen in three months.'

'So it's correct, you're twelve now?'

'Yes,' she said. Julius was smiling.

'You'll have the law on to me,' Mr Kirk said. 'Go on, out with you. Out. I'll make up your wages to the end of the week.'

Her father, who had been proud of her venture into work, told Hilary later that Julius had taken her place. But apparently he lasted less than a week.

Nino's family moved away almost as quickly as they had arrived. They were said to be trying to start their shop in another town, one that didn't mind their cracked syllables and halting sentences so much. You couldn't be sure in a town like Alderton whose idea it was for them to leave, but Hilary found herself wondering if Anthea and Julius's family might have had something to do with it. But that didn't seem likely. People thought they were a joke too. Hilary's father said Nino's father had told someone he was a doctor back in Italy, but could you believe that? Who would be starting a fish and chip shop if he was a real doctor? Yet there was a note of sympathy in his voice.

RECOUNT TO ME THE CAUSES

THE CREAM SCHOOL BUS WAS hot and stifling in summer as it trundled past fields of yellow light. In winter, the windows fogged up with the steam from the pupils' breaths. The last to board had to stand, swaying with their hands on the shoulders of those in front to stop themselves falling as the bus whirled around corners. Hilary always had a seat because, with Anthea and Julius, she was the first on the bus. The three of them got on at the same roadside stop and in the afternoon they were the last off. They met each morning when the sun was barely risen, and the last of the dew still rested on the grass. Some days, if he and Anthea were running late, Julius drove a battered old Ford pick-up to the bus stop and left it there with keys under the mat for his father to pick up later in the day. The invisible father, whom Hilary had not seen either. It appeared that he spent most of his time in the invisible house. The three of them, Hilary, Anthea and Julius, stood in the shade of a hedge festooned with furry banana passion-fruit and pink star-shaped flowers. Writers' images, though Hilary hadn't seen this yet, but she would come to it: the erotic fruit with its downy skin, the pulpy tasteless seeds at its heart. Julius said little in the mornings, his blue eyes flat and still.

Although the distance from one town to another was not far, the journey took a couple of hours either way. The bus travelled down little byways where two or three pupils were collected at hamlets: a church spire, perhaps, a store with a bare wooden front, a cluster of houses, a marae. Julius was the school bus prefect. For most of the journey he looked studiously at a book, pausing now and then to rise and stride down the centre aisle, flicking the heads of those he thought were misbehaving, pushing his hair out of his eyes with a look of exaggerated exhaustion. His thin fingers tweaked the ears of Maori boys, in particular, or else he brought down his copy of the *Aeneid* on top of their heads. They hunched their shoulders and sometimes Hilary saw how close they were to hitting him, but he was more trouble than he was worth. At the end of the year he would be gone, and so would most of them, without ever reaching the lofty heights of Virgil. Anthea shrieked now and then with a couple of older girls until it was their turn to get off the bus, then she prowled up and down the bus behind Julius as if she was a prefect too.

Hilary didn't mind the journey. Like Julius, she studied. It was the end of the ride she dreaded. Anthea's fingers hadn't lost their sneaking power to poke and prod. When Hilary protested, Anthea was likely to pull her hair. When she was silent, Anthea called her a frigging little up herself bitch, and wanted to know who she thought she was, too good for the rest of them. This seemed peculiar; there were no Georgian sideboards lurking at Hilary's house.

Ohaka High School was new since the war, built around a quadrangle, its paint still fresh, the trees only recently planted, so that one class could look across and wave to their friends in another. There was a small boarding school for boys. It would have been easy not to take the school seriously, but Hilary did. Cleverness opened doors, and she was fast discovering that she had this. She took the languages course and flourished. Her English teacher was a portly man with grey hair and a moustache, and since the first morning of term, when he had read *Morte d'Arthur* in a voice full of tenderness and meaning, she had loved every moment of his lessons. She liked French and Latin too.

It was in home economics that she faltered. Held on Friday afternoons, the class gathered up girls from different subject areas to teach them basic skills in cooking and sewing. Hilary found her attention wandering, drifting off to her English essay, or nouns and verbs. The home economics teacher wore a tweed skirt and a brown twin-set beneath her apron, or pinny, as she called it. On an afternoon soon after term began, when Hilary returned a blank stare in response to a question, the teacher said, 'Yes, well, miss, perhaps they don't cook at your house. Are you just a tinned vegetable family?' A ripple of laughter spread around the room.

The next week she paid attention. 'Can someone define the meaning of toast?' the teacher asked. Hilary shot up her hand. 'Burnt bread,' she said, before anyone else could answer.

The teacher found this amusing, too, and so did the class. A girl called Meryl put her hand up amid the laughter. The teacher smiled and nodded. 'Bread that has been dried and browned,' said Meryl.

'Thank you, Meryl,' said the teacher. 'A thoughtful answer. Can you elaborate? How is the bread dried?'

'By fire, Miss.'

'Very good, Meryl.' The teacher gave an approving nod. 'Fire is necessary to make toast. Some food can be cooked with heat from other sources, such as heat derived from electricity, but toast must be made against a flame.'

'That was hilarious,' Meryl said to Hilary, as they took off their aprons. 'Burnt bread. You're quite a card. Do you always make jokes like that?'

Hilary saved herself just in time from admitting that it wasn't a joke. She thought she was right, but she didn't tell Meryl this. Bread, burnt lightly, perhaps, but burnt all the same. Instead she said that yes, it was one of her jokes, and they always got her into trouble.

'I'll watch out for you,' said Meryl, in a comforting matronly way.

She was fifteen. She had had an illness when she was a child and was required to repeat some of her classes (it turned out she had already done home economics so she knew all the answers). Meryl had been abandoned by her contemporaries, who had moved on ahead of her. Hilary didn't see this at the beginning. She was simply dazzled by having a friend who was fifteen, a girl with a splendid bosom who knew all the boys in the boarding school. Her married sister had a baby. She knew how babies were born and how many stitches her sister had had in her fanny when they cut it to get the baby out. It was 1955 and the word vagina hadn't entered their vocabulary. Her parents had thought about divorce, because her father used to play around, but now he was on the straight and narrow, although it had left her mother a nervous wreck. Even though, Meryl said darkly, her mother wasn't sure that her youngest brother was really her dad's, but her dad didn't know that. He thought he was the only sinner in the family, and that's the way her mother liked it.

'How can that be?' Hilary asked. 'If she's married to your dad, he must be the father.'

Meryl looked at her and roared with laughter. 'You don't mean that, do you? Is this one of your jokes?' She saw that it wasn't. 'You really are a kid, aren't you? Don't you know how it's done?'

'What?'

'Rooting. Anybody can root. My parents do it all the time, but not always with each other.'

Hilary had an image then of pigs with their snouts in the ground, snorting and snuffling their way under trees, looking for truffles. She had learnt about this in her French class, a diversion from verbs in her textbook *En Route* (although even this title was suddenly imbued with new meaning).

'Yes,' she said doubtfully. She wasn't aware of her parents rooting. If they did they kept it to themselves but it had become a possibility. Suddenly life was more real than the movies.

As Hilary walked around the school grounds with Meryl in their lunchbreaks, soaking up these adult perspectives, Meryl greeted boys from the hostel by name, and was rewarded by smiles and raised caps. There was a particular boy they saw each day, a senior, like Julius, but different in every other way. Bruce had the thick limbs of a farm-raised boy, a big chest, and a crop of pimples that always looked on the point of exploding. Though he had the build of a man, he wore short pants and socks pulled up to the knees. He took the agriculture course, to teach him to be a farmer. When he was older he would inherit the family farm, Meryl told Hilary. Bruce sweated when he came abreast of Meryl. Hilary wondered how she knew so much about Bruce. Again Meryl shook her head with amusement. 'We write to each other,' she said, and blushed. 'Hadn't you guessed? I can't wait for the school dance, he's booked every dance with me.'

'YOU'RE ONLY A CHILD,' HILARY'S mother said, in a scandalised voice, when she raised the subject of the dance, although by now Hilary was thirteen.

'It's a third formers' dance,' she said, 'for people to get to know one another.'

'Will there just be people from your year?'

'I'm not sure,' Hilary lied.

'It's too far away.' Her mother's voice held an edge of triumph.

'Meryl says I can stay the night at her house.' Meryl lived near the school. Hilary hadn't mentioned that Meryl was fifteen.

'But I don't know this girl.'

'This is her phone number. She says to ring her mother.'

Her mother took the slip of paper dubiously. 'That'll be a toll call.'

'Take it out of my allowance.'

It was agreed in the end. Hilary could stay the night at Meryl's and go to the dance.

'Can you wear your gym slip?' her mother asked.

Hilary felt her heart contracting. She couldn't believe her mother would say this. Her thoughts raced back to the girls in the debutante photographs, and how she had put aside that dream as impractical. But this might as well be a ball. She mentally cast her eye over the print florals with Peter Pan collars that hung in her wardrobe.

Her mother looked at her and sighed. 'I suppose you're growing up. I don't think any of my dresses will do.' She brightened. 'What about that dress Auntie Peggy gave you?'

'It's a bit big,' Hilary said, although already she could see the possibilities of the dress. She thought about Ingrid Bergman, but she didn't voice this vision of herself.

'I'll help you alter it,' her mother said, warming to the project.

They spent hours doing this. Her mother was supposed to be picking fruit on the neighbour's property, but she said it could wait. There was lightness, a happiness in the air between them. When the dress was altered, her mother stood back admiring their handiwork, her face glowing, as if she was seeing Hilary in a new light. Her father appeared, and whistled. 'Just no getting into the lipstick,' he said, as if it was a huge joke.

'As if she would,' said her mother.

'You can't possibly wear that,' Meryl said, when Hilary showed her the dress. Her mother said, in a brisk tone, that she would iron one of Meryl's dresses for her; it wouldn't matter if was a bit long. She whipped out a pretty yellow dress with a wide neckline and a full skirt, holding it against Hilary with a measuring look. She had coarse dark hair that curled back behind her ears, and shrewd small eyes. Hilary smelled tobacco on her breath, and old Evening of Paris perfume on her jersey. She wondered whether the perfume was for her lover or her husband, a weathered quiet man, shorter than his wife, who she met briefly as he came in from the milking shed. Meryl's house was more comfortable than hers, with a brown crushed velvet sofa in the sitting room, and heavy embossed curtains, a refrigerator in the kitchen.

In this setting, Hilary saw that her aunt's old dress from the thirties wouldn't do. And yet, thinking of last Saturday, and the afternoon she and her mother had spent together, their hands bathed in the soft fabric of the dress, she was overwhelmed by a fierce rush of loyalty. She said: 'Well thanks, but I want to wear the dress I brought.'

Meryl walked into the dance hall ahead of her, as if they were not really together, even though she had spent the previous hour anointing Hilary's face with rouge and lipstick. She had given Hilary a little Clara Bow mouth. Some girls came up to Meryl and said, 'Well, where *did* she get that dress?' and raised their eyebrows at each other. Hilary flushed. 'Somebody told her it was fancy dress,' Meryl said, and walked off.

The first dance was already being called. Bruce was waiting for Meryl. She glided off in his arms. He held her very close, his big feet adjusting to her step. Later in the evening, when their hips seem moulded together, one of the teachers would speak to them, admonishing them to behave in a proper manner.

'I'm going to marry him,' Meryl said later that night, when they were in bed. As it happened, the following year she would leave school and become engaged to Bruce, but he was not the man she would marry and he wouldn't be the last man to whom she became engaged. There would be more trials and a few errors before that happened.

Not that Hilary noticed much of what Meryl got up to at the dance. For a while, she sat alone on one of the long wooden benches that lined the hall, wishing she could disappear. The kindly English teacher with the grey moustache asked her to step up with him for a round, and this was almost as bad as it got. But something was about to happen that would take her mind off all of this. The supper waltz was announced, the halfway point of the evening, and girls began to take the arms of the boys they had been dancing with, before heading off to the side room where tables were laden with cakes and sausage rolls. Hilary thought she might slip outside and wait for it to be over. But then Nino was standing there before her, his face determined. Nino, the fish and chip boy from Italy, with the black blade of hair across his forehead. As she looked around to see who he was going to invite to supper, she wanted to flee. He held out his hand to her. 'I knew you straight away.'

'Why are you here?' she asked. She felt not so much as if she was in a dream, but as if some inner vibration had begun in her breast-bone and trembled all the way to the pit of her stomach. 'I've never seen you at school.'

He shrugged as if people were always asking him why he was there. As they ate supper and, throughout the evening, as they danced, he explained. After Alderton, his family had gone to Auckland to look for work. But then an uncle had come from Italy and the brothers decided that they could give each other strength. His father and uncle had come back up north, united in a new plan to set up shop in Ohaka, near the high school. Already, after just a week, business was good. 'I hope it stay good,' he said. 'Now I find you. You are the only pretty girl here.'

You ask me what it is like to be Italian, Nino wrote to her. *How can I tell you this? I do not know too much about the history of Italy, even though I am from that country. My family live in Italy, the Germans come and then it is Yugoslavia, the boundaries they are always shifting. One day we lived in one country, the next another, without shifting house. So then we are all Yugoslavia and the Germans go away, but the people who are our neighbours now say we are very bad Italian people. All Italian people they will kill because we are collaborators. That is what they say, but my father was just a poor farmer. We lived all right, you know, not as bad as all that. My father grew food on the land, my mother cooked it, just like your family now. But then they want to kill us and so we run away. We run, many run, very many to America, very many to Australia, not so many to New Zealand. I tell you a secret. I have one more uncle in Wellington who has been here a long time, and he gives us money for the shop. It is a secret because nobody like Italian refugees, they look at us in a bad way. My uncle nearly get locked up during the war time here in New Zealand, but he change his name and pretend not to be Italian. He give us money so we do not go to Wellington, it is money for the shop. We are still afraid, but now the law in your country is better. The police tell us not to be scared. We sell fish and chips to everybody here and that is good. But still I am alone and feel very lonely in my heart until I meet you at the dance. Now I have a girlfriend who writes me letters and I write back to you. Love from your friend Nino.*

On Fridays, when Hilary was in her home economics class, she could see Nino across the quadrangle in the woodwork room. He sat by the window where he could see her learning to make scones and pikelets, and gave her little waves when she looked up. This was now her favourite class of the week. Soon Meryl and the other girls noticed. Nino and Hilary. A couple. He wasn't bad looking, they agreed. She felt grown up and important. Even Meryl was impressed.

Hilary wrote back to Nino at night by torchlight under the bedclothes. She folded her letters up into tiny squares and put them inside *En Route*. They passed their notes in the corridor when they were changing classrooms at the bell. Nino had to walk past the door of her French class on his way to woodwork. She didn't have adventures in her life like Nino's to recount. But she told him about the movies, and about holidays in the south with her mother's family and how she hoped one day to travel a long way across the world. She asked her mother to find books about Italy in the local library. The librarian sent away to the Country Library Service, so it took time, but eventually she had in her possession a handsome book about the great artworks in Rome. *You have a very beautiful heritage*, she wrote primly. *I would like to see the Sistine Chapel and one day to throw coins in the Trevi Fountain.* She wrote some knowledgeable comments about the history of the fountain and the Acqua Vergine, the ancient aqueduct that supplied water to ancient Rome. Then, discarding propriety, she wrote: *We can go there together, and you can show me everything, and when we throw a coin we can wish for our good luck.* Already she had a plan in her head: her own Roman holiday with Nino. She had a future.

I have not been to Rome, Nino wrote back. *I know only the countryside. It sounds very beautiful and indeed I would like to see this city too. I am older than you, but perhaps you know that,* he continued, and here his tone changed. *Your girlfriend is old too. You are still young girl. I like that you look different from other girls, but you must be careful. I think you are a good girl, and you must stay that way.*

His notes didn't come so often after that. She wondered what she had done wrong.

Her mother was fretting about the company she was keeping. She insisted that her friend Meryl be invited to stay with them. Hilary had been resisting this but she knew that sooner or later her mother would ring Meryl's mother and invite her any way.

'Has your friend got a nicer house than ours?' her mother asked, in an injured tone that nonetheless expected the worst.

'No,' Hilary said, and it was true. Despite the couches and refrigerator, and the pull-string toilet, she found Meryl's house oppressive and dark. Her own house consisted of four square rooms and a lean-to for their iron bath, a washtub and copper. But her mother kept the curtains pulled back to let in sunlight and laid the dinner table every night with heavy linen. When she got married, her sisters had embroidered her new initials in the corners of the napkins and given her bone-handled cutlery. Outside, their market garden stretched in ordered rows with hens scratching at the back door, rather than mud and yelping dogs, and the smell of cow dung in the paddock next to the house, as at Meryl's place. Hilary didn't mind Meryl coming at all. But there were things that she had omitted to tell her mother about her friend. About her bosoms. About her age. About her boyfriend. Most of all, she hadn't told her mother that she had a boyfriend of her own. Not that she was sure she did any longer, but she still thought of Nino in that way.

There was nothing for it, the invitation had to be issued. Hilary thought Meryl might not want to come, but she was wrong.

'How about next weekend?' her friend suggested. 'You've got bikes at your house, haven't you?'

Hilary agreed that, indeed, she and her parents all owned bicycles.

'Would your mother mind if I borrowed her bike and we went for a ride?' Meryl asked.

Hilary had lain awake and worried over how she might entertain Meryl. Now everything seemed unexpectedly simple. 'Of course she wouldn't.'

'We won't tell her where we're going, though,' said Meryl, in an anxious voice. 'She might tell my mother.'

'Where are we going?'

'To the beach,' said Meryl. And then it was out. The hostel boys were being taken on a beach picnic that Saturday and would have some free time. Meryl could snatch an hour with Bruce.

'It's a long way to the beach,' Hilary said.

'We can do it in no time.'

Hilary was not so certain. Although tidal rivers snaked towards the town, Alderton sat inland from the sea. The place known as 'the beach' was twenty miles further on at another small seaside village. She had been there only half a dozen times, sitting in the back seat of a car owned by a friend of her parents. These outings took a whole day.

She drew a deep breath. 'All right then. Okay, so long as you promise not to tell either.'

'About Nino? Course not.'

The bicycle ride took even longer than Hilary had anticipated. Although it was early spring, it felt like a summer's day and the sun grew stronger by the minute as the two girls pedalled up and down hills, flying one moment, the next having to get off and walk the bikes. Hours passed. Meryl was worried that she would miss seeing Bruce.

And then, finally, the sea was before them, silky blue, a skein of white sand twisting along at its edge. They were puffing as they rested their bikes against a tree. And there were the boys from the hostel, playing some kind of running game in the sand. Bruce was still waiting for Meryl. The couple clasped hands and gazed into each other's eyes. Theatrical, Hilary thought, and was embarrassed.

'Do you want an ice-cream, Hilary?' Bruce said, his voice dismissive. He waved a ten-shilling note in her direction, and nodded towards a kiosk on the waterfront.

'What flavours?' she asked, thinking she was to buy for all of them.

'Oh, choose what you want.' He gestured her away, and she saw that she was not meant to be there. She felt like a small naughty child. Although she knew Meryl must be starving and thirsty, too, she saw that she would go without for the sake of an hour alone with Bruce. 'Look after the bikes, won't you, Hilary?' Meryl called, as if the bikes belonged to her.

In the end she bought herself an ice-cream and some lemonade to share later with Meryl, and sat down to wait. She wanted to pee, but dared not leave the bikes. She didn't know what Meryl and Bruce were doing, whether they were going to go all the way, as Meryl's sister had done when she got pregnant, or whether they just wanted to talk. Meryl would act scandalised when asked, later on. As if once in our family wasn't enough, and for goodness' sake, Hilary, she would say, there were people everywhere and Bruce's housemaster was on the lookout for them. They had just walked. And held hands.

But they were gone for a long time, and Hilary, sitting alone with the bikes beside the sea, felt a chill in the air, and, looking up, saw that the sun was beginning to slip towards the sea. It was past four o'clock and in an hour or two it would be dark.

IT WAS JULIUS AND ANTHEA who saved them as they struggled up the first hill on the road home. They had been on a jaunt together. Hilary had not been bothered by the pair for some time. Anthea was quiet on the bus these days, withdrawn and almost sullen, while Julius ignored her altogether. It was as if Hilary's circle of friends, her success at school, had silenced them into a grudging acceptance. Now Julius got out of the pick-up truck, and he could have been Hilary's father, he looked so grown up. He was wearing grey slacks and an open-neck shirt. 'Spot of bother, eh?' he said, as he slung their bikes on the back of the truck.

There was no point in arguing, no other way home. Meryl looked flushed and defiant, and Hilary was trying not to show that she had been crying. They clambered onto the tray of the truck with their bikes. Anthea sat in the front, her expression a purring smile, and said nothing, not turning her head to look at them once they were under way. So they rattled along at what seemed an alarming speed, round and round the hills, clutching the edge of the tray, the night rushing past. Hilary decided the safest thing was to lie face down so that she could hold on with both hands and soon Meryl did the same. The wheels were just below their noses, chips of gravel flew up and caught in their hair. The bikes bumped and slithered against them. 'Stop,' Meryl screamed, but Julius didn't hear, or if he did he wasn't letting on. Hilary closed her eyes as tightly as she could and prayed. When she was older she would cling to aspects of belief because, she thought, she was delivered that night.

At the turn-off, Julius let them off and unloaded their bikes. 'Seeing boys, eh?' he said, in an amused adult voice. 'I reckon you owe me, Hilary.'

'I was about to send out a search party for you two wicked girls,' said Hilary's mother, but it was a joke. She had dinner waiting for them. If she found Meryl surprising she didn't say so.

The following afternoon, Meryl's parents came to pick her up, a great excuse for a Sunday drive, they said. They owned a smart green Wolseley. 'Our girls are so close,' Meryl's mother said, as she sipped tea from one of the best china cups. 'Though I must say they're quiet today.' In fact, a certain coolness had fallen between Hilary and Meryl. As the smart car disappeared along the road, Hilary's father said, 'Where there's muck, there's brass,' but her mother pursed her lips. 'They're kind,' she said, as if that was an end to the matter. Hilary thought Meryl's parents had called by to check what sort of people her parents were, her mother in particular, who sent her daughter to dances in old clothes.

On Monday, at the bus stop, Hilary said, in a way that she knew sounded pleading and childish, 'Julius, it wasn't me, I didn't meet any boys.' He was wearing his short pants and school cap again. He gave an aloof smile and didn't answer.

'Well, well, Hilary,' said Anthea. 'Next thing it'll be Waterfall Road.' Waterfall Road, known as Lovers' Lane, ran beside a river near the high school, close to where Meryl lived. Hilary had seen the signpost. Meryl said she would never meet Bruce there, even though it was within walking distance. She didn't want to make herself look cheap.

Hilary felt a wave of terror running behind her heels. Anthea and Julius didn't go to school dances, or have friends, the way other people did. But they knew things, and it occurred to Hilary that as they rode around the countryside together, they gathered up knowledge. They would know, too, what she did at school, and, yes, about Nino.

'How about you buy us a milkshake after school?' said Anthea.

In her pocket, Hilary carried the change from Bruce's ten shilling note, an amount of money that seemed staggeringly large to have been offered so casually at the weekend. 'Sure thing,' she said, as if she was in a movie. 'And a liquorice strap as well, if you want.'

'The change must have fallen out when we were on the back of the truck,' she told Meryl later that day. Who was Meryl to argue? They had agreed to make up and be friends again. Bruce's father sent him a weekly allowance so he probably wouldn't miss it.

The money lasted all that week and the next. At Burke's dairy, it bought jaffas and changing balls, chocolate slabs and peppermints, milkshakes and lemonade, all devoured by Julius and Anthea, and then the money was gone.

'You can charge it up,' said Anthea.

'My parents would kill me.'

'You get pocket money, don't you?'

Hilary agreed that yes, she did. She convinced herself she could wheedle a little extra from her mother, or that she might need an 'extra' textbook.

Julius and Anthea ate their way through her allowance the next week and the week after that, and her money for a school excursion to a visiting theatre troupe: she had to make up an account of it for her mother. At Burke's the woman behind the till agreed to let Hilary put a little on the slate, but just for a week or two.

'I can't buy any more,' she told them.

Hilary and her parents set off to see *Our Vines Have Tender Grapes*, about a farming family coping with adversity in the Midwest, but the film reels didn't arrive in time, and the theatre operator ran *Notorious* with Ingrid Bergman and Cary Grant. Both her parents were stiff-lipped as they left. There had been more scandal reported about 'that woman'. She'd had a sprog with that Rossellini fellow, her father said, and both of them still married to other people. Hilary needed wholesome examples. They should never have let her see Bergman in the first place. And so on, before the credits had finished rolling and the lights came up.

Outside the theatre they met Julius and Anthea as they got into the pick-up. When Anthea saw Hilary with her parents she chanted in a high sing-song voice: 'Chase me Charlie, I've got barley up the leg of my drawers.' Julius nudged her and they both laughed.

'Cheeky bitch,' said Hilary's father, under his breath.

'Hilary, what's going on?' said her mother, as they walked home.

'Nothing,' Hilary said.

'I don't think you tell the truth any more.' There was something stricken in her mother's voice. Hilary was not sure what she knew, but the worst thing she could think of was that Burke's had mentioned her burgeoning debt.

'Have you a boyfriend?'

'No.' And it was partly true. She hadn't had a letter from Nino for weeks, and he hurried when he passed her classroom now. It was many months since she had been held in his embrace at the school dance. Perhaps he had heard about the excursion to the beach. Whichever way she turned, she seemed to be in trouble.

The woman at Burke's told her that she had one week to pay or she was going to tell her parents. Hilary had no idea where she was going to find the money.

Meryl invited her to stay for a weekend, and Hilary was glad to get away from it all. During the week Hilary had seen Nino and he had smiled and waved as of old.

Dear Hilary, he wrote, *sorry, long time since I write to you. We have had bad trouble at the shop, but things are better now. We have to wait for some of the money to come from Wellington. My father afraid it will not come. I work long hours at the shop so my dad do not have to hire someone else. My dad think perhaps I should leave school. Now the money has come. From your friend Nino.*

Dear Nino, she replied, *at the weekend I am going to stay in town with Meryl. How about I meet you along Waterfall Road? Do you know where it is? I will be there at three o'clock. I will tell Meryl I am going for a walk.*

I know where Waterfall Road is, he wrote back.

THAT FRIDAY, HE SAT BY the window next to the quadrangle where he could see her in home economics. He glanced across the space between them and raised his hand, then looked away quickly. Later, she would think that it was a salute of farewell.

Rain had fallen in the night and throughout the morning a misty drizzle came and went as Hilary walked along Waterfall Road. It was little more than a track, and mud squelched beneath her shoes. She was wearing a pale yellow twin-set that used to be Meryl's, and a tartan skirt. An oilskin jacket was slung over her arm.

'You can't go out in this weather,' said Meryl, 'you'll get soaked.'

Hilary had told Meryl that she had a French exam coming up and she needed to memorise her verbs. Meryl gave her a sceptical look. 'You can do your homework in the bedroom,' she said, 'I won't interrupt you.'

'I won't be long,' Hilary said, 'truly I won't.'

'You're weird. For goodness' sake then, take a coat.' Meryl had grabbed the oilskin coat off the rack and thrown it over Hilary's shoulders.

She hadn't protested. She saw what folly it must appear, setting out in this weather, and besides, she and Nino might sit together near the waterfall and talk, and she could spread the oilskin beneath them. She hadn't thought past this. They would talk, they would be close, the way they were at the dance, meaning that they would touch, hold hands. Perhaps they would kiss, and this is what she hoped. She couldn't imagine what would happen next, what ought or ought not to take place.

There were fresh tyre tracks in the mud, but she was past caring and didn't consider them, not until later as she relived her walk to the river. She heard the rush of the waterfall. The trees were dense and dripping above her. She heard a peculiar sound, like a cat's miaow.

'Nino,' she called in a small voice, but her words were carried away against the sound of the water.

It was the pick-up truck she saw first in the clearing. Then it was a tangle of white limbs on the ground. She didn't see exactly what was happening, but it was something she wasn't supposed to see, something she knew was awful. What she would remember most was Julius's eyes staring straight at her, his arm flung over Anthea's head to protect her from Hilary's gaze.

Sobs caught in her chest as she ran back the way she had come, her lungs fighting for air as if she had fallen under the swollen brown river she had glimpsed in her flight.

Meryl stood at the end of Waterfall Road. 'What did he do to you?' she demanded. 'What has Nino done to you, you stupid dumb little cow?"

'Nothing. He didn't touch me. You followed me.'

'Of course I did. Are you crazy, running off after an Eyetie like that? My mother would kill both of us if she knew what you were up to. Are you sure you're not hurt?'

'He wasn't there. Nobody was there.'

'Well, what a surprise. So that's why you're crying — you've been stood up. You're a kid. I knew it all along. I thought you were a smart kid, but you're really, really stupid. Just wait until Nino tells people what you had in mind. Waterfall Road. Bad girls go down there.'

But Nino was not at school the next week, or the one after that. Hilary didn't have the nerve to ask where he was. She supposed he had gone to work in the fish and chip shop. Life suddenly began to change in other ways. Her parents decided to leave the north, and sold up for a song as soon as their property went on the market. They would say to each other, that was one smart customer — he knew that land would be worth millions one day. But it wasn't then, it was just enough to buy a house near Auckland, where Hilary's father would work for a nursery on a regular wage, with regular hours, and Hilary wouldn't have to spend hours each day going backwards and forwards to school. In a way she was disappointed. Meryl was going to leave school at the end of the year, and she had thought that she could make new friends, that she would go on doing well with her French and English, especially English because the grey-haired teacher with the moustache still took an interest in her work, and that some day she would run into Nino again, and whatever misunderstanding had arisen could have been sorted out. Someone had cleared her slate at the dairy a day or so after her walk down Waterfall Road. Julius and Anthea were silent when they saw her.

ARCHAEOLOGY

MERYL FANNED OUT PHOTOGRAPHS ON Hilary's table, pictures of children and grandchildren who looked older than Hilary and Meryl were when they were friends. Wedding photographs, christening pictures, and one of the flowers on Meryl's mother's grave.

When Hilary had admired them, Meryl stood up, saying in a brisk voice, 'Time to get down to business.'

'Business?'

'If we're going to do your colours, we need to look at your clothes. Your hair's nice, by the way. I like the French knot, even if looks a bit retro, but it's bookish, so it works. We'll have a look through your wardrobe. In the bedroom?'

Hilary said, 'Now look here . . .' She thought about texting her husband: I have a stalker in the house, get home as fast as you can. But her visitor was charging along the passage, and it occurred to Hilary that it didn't matter much, that Meryl was a character, like other people in life, and it was easy to escape life if you wrote fiction. She might as well give in, let it happen. Besides, once, long ago, she had been grateful to Meryl, her grown-up insouciance. She felt a stab of remorse for her own lack of charity. Her wardrobe door was being opened, Meryl's hands were flicking through her dresses.

Meryl shook her head sadly. 'So much black. You know, I went on a trip once to Europe. It was ever so nice, though I wouldn't want to live over there. When I got back to New Zealand, I walked into the airport and I thought the prime minister must have died, everyone wearing black. You forget how much black we wear. Like widows. I remember Nino's mother, after the father died, you know?'

'Nino's mother?'

'The Italian boy's mother — perhaps you never met her. Well, you'd gone by the time the father died, so you wouldn't remember her in her weeds. Oh, there's that red dress. I've seen you in that, too; no, it's not right. And green.' She fingered one of Hilary's jackets, and let the fabric fall. 'Green's all right, but you need warmth, more strength in your colour schemes, really you do. Some browns, bright orange, earth colours, autumn tones — you know what I mean?'

'Of course,' Hilary said, recovering herself. 'So that's what you mean by colours? You give people advice about what colours to wear?'

'Not exactly,' Meryl said, 'but I can explain.'

They had returned to the kitchen. Meryl was already at the bench, holding the teapot. 'We could do with another brew,' she said.

Hilary took the pot from her hands. 'Sit down, Meryl,' she said. 'I'll make the tea while you explain. I have to get changed and go out in a little while, so perhaps you could,' and here she groped for a word that didn't seem offensive, 'summarise.'

Meryl opened a little black zippered business satchel and set about sketching some lines on a pad she had taken from it. 'I'm kind of an adviser,' she said, 'but I only sell my services to a few people at a time. I've given you a free treat because we're old friends. But most people would have to go on a waiting list, although they can make a bit of money signing up other people while they're in the queue. And if they follow the advice properly, they can end up as advisers themselves.'

'Giving colour advice?'

'It depends on a person's specific needs. Now in your position, you're always going to need appearance advice. People like you have to look their best. But you could advise people about what books to buy. People who know about books are always in demand. It's a multi-level scheme.'

'You mean I could buy into the scheme?'

'Why yes, I knew you'd catch on.'

'You're talking about pyramid selling?' Hilary said this more sharply than she intended, willing this odd artificial conversation to end, for the woman to leave her house.

Meryl blinked, her face beneath her make-up turning dark red, the familiar blush of her girlhood. Her throat gave her away: it started there. Hilary was afraid that the light eyes would spill.

'You must remember the dress you wore that night,' Meryl said. 'Well, I was only trying to help.'

WHEN HILARY WAS AT UNIVERSITY, she saw Nino one day in Auckland. It was the early 1960s. She wore a black polo-necked jersey and black pants, a duffel coat and a long purple scarf. Her hair floated long and curling around her shoulders. She smelled of cigarettes and coffee, for she had just left some friends in a café. They had been talking about Simone de Beauvoir and *The Second Sex*. Someone was arguing that de Beauvoir's life didn't stand up against her theories, that she listened only to men. Hilary had an essay due and decided to leave them to it. It was a wintry Sunday afternoon, fine although a sharp wind blew off the harbour. A group of young men were idling down near the waterfront, hanging about, smoking and watching girls. She knew they would look at her and she chose to look straight back, and found herself looking Nino in the eye.

'Nino,' she called.

At first he didn't recognise her. When he did, he hesitated, before walking slowly towards her. 'You've grown up,' he said.

'You too.' Hilary couldn't think what else to say. His black hair was slicked up and he wore stovepipe pants. She saw that he was still very thin.

'You live here, too?'

'Yup.'

'Would you like some coffee?' she asked. Her legs were trembling.

'Nah. Thanks, but my mates and I are going to take a spin up the coast.'

One of the mates let out a long low whistle. 'A bit out of your league, aren't you, Nino?'

Nino scowled back over his shoulder. 'I'll be back soon,' he called, and turned towards her. 'Just walk,' he said. 'Up the street.'

So they walked, the two of them heading along Queen Street, a few feet apart, not touching.

'Sorry,' he said, 'cheeky sods.'

'You left school so suddenly. Did you go to work with your father?'

'For a while.'

'Not now?'

'He carked it. I work for a builder. Look, that stuff when we were kids, it was nothing. It was a long time ago.'

'I've often thought about you,' she said slowly.

'Well don't.'

'Did you go down Waterfall Road that day? Please Nino, I need to know.'

'Don't be stupid.'

'You said you knew where Waterfall Road was.'

'Yeah, that's right. That's what I said. I never said I'd go there. Look,' he said, stopping. 'You go to university, yes? You've got it written all over you. So you should, you sure were a smarty pants girl. I was the dumb bastard who leave your note where my father will find it. His English isn't too good, so he give it to our neighbour to read. My father say you were a very bad girl, I should be ashamed to even talk to you if you make suggestion like that. He say I will make a bad name all over town if I go down that road to meet you.'

'Is that why you left school?'

'Ah look.' His voice was weary. 'Too many questions. I've got a good job, nice Italian girlfriend who stay at home with my mother, learn to be a good wife for when we marry, do the cooking. Spaghetti, meatball, minestrone. You make those, Miss Smarty Pants, or do you still make pikelets?' She didn't know whether his contempt was real or feigned. 'The neighbour tell him later on, you are a girl who makes up stories. He hear it from the school. My father is a good man. He has much pain in his life. No more, he tells me, no more bad things in our life.'

They had come to the corner of Victoria Street, where Hilary was turning up the hill towards the university. His expression was suddenly wistful. 'I bet you've got a beautiful cunt,' he said.

HILARY DIDN'T WANT TO ASK Meryl to leave. It was too final, too unkind. Yet she was appalled by what the woman had done — arriving at her house, going through her clothes, trying to sign her up for her wretched scheme. Times must be hard up north. She knew about droughts, and the way people were starting to walk off their land, leaving paddocks bare but for the dust. She remembered the times when her parents' garden had withered and they had had to ask for tick at Kirk's, and how it had once taken them a year to pay it off. Perhaps it was like this for Meryl and her husband. Bad things had happened to them, she recalled, like some outhouses burning down, the loss of farm machinery. And there was a son who had been in an accident. However she ended it, Hilary thought, she couldn't be cruel. She owed too much to the past, the whole story of her own life, which she had the luxury of reinventing to suit herself, the never ending narrative, the lives of others, at her disposal.

'What time does your meeting start?' she asked, willing her voice to be gentle.

'Aha,' Meryl said, as if saved. Her hands were flicking through the photographs still lying on the table. 'That's what I was looking for. Our school reunion. You didn't come.'

'I couldn't make it, I'm afraid. I was travelling at the time.'

'Oh travel, yes, you're a lucky one. But look, see this picture, here's our old crowd. Anthea came.'

'Anthea?'

'Yes, you know, she used to come to school on the bus with you.'

'I know.'

'She came all the way from England for the reunion.'

'I see.'

'She's a dog breeder — can you imagine. You wouldn't have thought she'd have the patience for it. In Devon, I think she said. Labradors. She still looks the same, don't you think?'

Hilary glanced at the picture of a woman with a shock of grey hair, chin raised.

'She looks like a sheep dog.'

'Oh Hilary, that's so mean. She was asking after you. We told her you were famous.'

'And what did she say?'

Meryl looked at her sideways, her expression still guileless. 'She said you liked sticking your nose into other people's business.' She gave a short little rasp of laughter. 'It was a joke, of course.'

'What about Julius? Did Julius come?' Only Hilary knows that he wouldn't have.

AFTER SHE HAD WRITTEN A number of books, Hilary was invited to a writers' festival in Hawaii. On the last evening, a group of writers and academics gathered over a Chinese meal at a big round table. They had all had a good deal to drink and the women were wearing fragrant leis given to them by the festival organisers. Hilary was talking to an historian who taught at an American university.

'So you're from New Zealand, huh?'

When she agreed that she was, he asked if she had ever heard of a professor who worked for a while in his department, a man called Julius.

'Why do you ask?' she said carefully.

'No, you can't have,' he said, 'or you'd know about it. A real scandal. You wouldn't have missed it.'

Hilary tried to explain that what happened in American universities wasn't necessarily known in New Zealand. All the same she was interested.

'Oh, he was a bit of a fiend. Sex for grades, you know the kind of stuff. Perhaps not such a big deal,' the man said. 'You say you haven't heard of him?'

'No,' Hilary lied. Better to say nothing. She had had three glasses of wine, and she was due to fly home the next day. She knew how bonhomie and eternal friendships made on book tours ended almost as soon as you left the departure lounge at the airport. She would say something, too much, and then she would find herself confiding a long complicated story that did nobody, including herself, any credit. Later, she did some research on the internet and turned up Julius's name, but nothing to indicate what had happened, just the date when his career as a history professor had ended. Although it appeared that he was still alive, his career and publications had stopped abruptly. He lived somewhere in California, and Hilary could see it, a gated community in the sun where Julius and his wife (for one was mentioned) could stay safe from the world. A man who took sweets from children. A man with a high forehead and blond hair grown thin.

THIS WAS NOT THE ONLY lie Hilary had told in her life. Before she left school, in the very last home economics class of the year, when they were making small Christmas cakes to take home, she came out with a bizarre lie, so odd and unexpected that she would never be able to understand why it entered her head. She told the girls in the class that she was leaving because she was pregnant.

At first nobody believed her, but Meryl was staring at her with startled eyes. Hilary spun her story elaborately. She was more than two months along, and her parents wanted to get her out of it, it was all they could do, they were so ashamed of her. She would have to go to a home for unmarried mothers. Her mother had already written to a place where she would go the following year. She would miss a whole year of school, and then goodness knows what would happen to her. Perhaps she would go to a school in Auckland if anyone would take her. It was all rather a mess.

'Is it Nino's?' Meryl said, and Hilary saw that she was counting out time on her fingers. 'Is that why he left school?'

'Oh no,' said Hilary, 'it's a boy back in Alderton, someone I've known for years, but you know, these things happen.'

She knew then she had caught their attention. Because it was the last day of term, the teacher allowed them to chatter as they worked. The group believed her. Some looked distressed and patted her shoulders. Meryl was close to tears. Nobody was without response or reaction. She had hooked them.

'You're not telling the truth, are you?' someone said.

She was about to admit that it was all a great lie, when the girl said: 'It's him, isn't it? The Italian boy? We won't tell a soul.'

So then she did tell them it was a lie, and it was harder to convince them of this than it had been to make up the story. Some of them looked angry that they had been fooled and some of them still didn't know what to believe. Her fiction had had greater power than her truth.

But she had entertained them for an afternoon.

Meryl was gathering herself to leave. 'I'm going to ring a taxi. D'you mind if I use your phone? My cell's gone flat.'

'I can run you to where you're going.'

'But you're going out.'

'In a little while. I've got time.' It was Hilary's turn to look away. She had seen the way Meryl's face had lit up at her offer. Hilary found herself again entertaining a flicker of remorse, a wish that she was somehow a kinder, more generous person.

'You were asking about Julius,' Meryl resumed. 'Anthea said you had a crush on him.'

'I *what?*'

'Oh, come on, Hilary. She said he used to buy you lollies and you took it the wrong way. Goodness, Hilary, I don't know what to think, but she did say you even asked him to meet you along Waterfall Road.'

'That was Nino.' Hilary was so shocked she found herself blurting it out before she could stop herself.

'Well, that's what I said. It did get me wondering, though. What you told us that day in cooking class, it wasn't true, was it? I mean, I'm sure it wasn't, of course. I just, well, you know . . .'

'You just wondered,' said Hilary. She saw that Meryl hadn't come to give her advice about her dresses, or even to sell her shares in a pyramid scheme, although that would have been a bonus. After all these years, she still wanted to know what had happened, to excavate the past. Hilary wanted to say to this intruder, with her sad bag of papers and diagrams, and excuses for visiting, that you had to read books to find out what happened next. Like the movies, that was where real life happened. Or not.

Meryl's conference was being held at an Indian cultural building with a façade of minarets and spires, situated in a suburban back street. Hundreds of people were streaming towards it, people who looked tired, as Meryl did. Country people for the most part, Hilary guessed, a few men wearing tweeds, but mostly polyester rain jackets, Warehouse tops and skirts for the women, young and old, people in wheelchairs and on walking sticks, overweight people, skinny people, people with an air of hectic gaiety as if they were attending a gala, muscular men with tattoos and shaven heads, people whose faces wore a kind of callused resignation.

Hilary sat in her car for a moment, watching in her rear vision mirror as Meryl was absorbed into the crowd, greeted by people she knew, shaking hands, here and there bestowing a kiss. Networking, she'd said earlier. That was the point of the conference really, to hear some inspirational talks, and to network. And yes, she'd been to lots of them: they gave her hope, the motivation to carry on. She didn't look back.

The History of It

They came down to breakfast next morning absolutely their own selves. Rosy, fresh and just chilled enough by the cold air blowing through the bedroom windows to be very ready for hot coffee.

'Nippy.' That was Geraldine's word as she buttoned her orange coat with pink-washed fingers. 'Don't you find it decidedly nippy?' And her voice, so matter- of- fact, so natural, sounded as though they had been married for years.

The woman who owned the guesthouse, described as 'boutique' in the guidebook, had laid a fire for them the night before, so that when they retired from dinner the room was warm from its blaze, even though a hard frost had settled in the paddocks beyond. Two chairs had been set in front of the fireplace, as if she expected them to settle down with the liqueurs she had provided — a Drambuie for Duncan and a Cointreau for Geraldine — while they talked over their day.

'Have you got children?' she had asked when she served dinner.

They were her only guests, which did not seem to trouble her, although places for another fourteen people stretched away on either side of the vast kauri table. The house had high ceilings, built in imitation of the Tudor style, but more than a hundred years ago, so it was historic for this part of the world. From the verandah of their upstairs room they saw gently rolling hills and sheep nuzzling close to the fences. On the other side of the house, native bush pressed close to the edge of the carefully cultivated garden where, the woman said, over two hundred roses were planted. If they came back in late spring they could see the riot of colour for themselves.

Geraldine declared the dinner perfect; the woman, whose name was Hazel, had made her own horseradish sauce to accompany the beef, cooked to exactly the right shade of rare. Everything was natural, the vegetables all grown here on the property.

'So how many children did you say you had?' she persisted, when Geraldine praised the food.

'Five,' said Duncan firmly. 'We have five children.' His eyes met Geraldine's for an instant.

Hazel exclaimed extravagantly then over Geraldine's figure, how she had kept her looks, and asked the ages of the children. Hazel herself had a tightly packaged body that suggested constant battles with her weight, short blonde hair styled in crisp upward flicks, lips a light shade of fuchsia. She could have passed for fifty, but Geraldine thought her older, perhaps sixty.

'We've come to have a weekend away from the children,' Duncan said lightly.

Hazel apologised then, said of course, and what was she thinking of, but later when dessert was cleared away she couldn't resist bringing out some pictures of her grandchildren. They were round and cheerful-looking, standing beside ponies.

'They come here now and then,' she said wistfully. 'Not often enough.'

'I'm sorry,' Duncan said to Geraldine, when they were seated before the fire. 'My friend recommended it for the quiet — he comes here when he wants to do a lot of reading.' Duncan's friend was a bookseller who believed in keeping up to date with his wares. Duncan managed a research unit in a government department but he spent his lunch-hours browsing in bookshops; reading was his great pleasure, although he admitted to a modest interest in the arts. Mostly he read non-fiction, preferably biography. He had just finished one on Shakespeare's wife that cast her in a more complimentary light than previous biographers. He liked the many details it provided about Elizabethan farming and the making of malt ale. Duncan had considered life as an academic, but it had not worked out that way.

'It's perfect,' Geraldine repeated, in the way she had praised the beef, as if stating the obvious, and none of it mattered. She was curled in front of the flickering fire, wearing nothing but a necklace made of fine rolled gold that followed the shape of her collarbone. Her long, carefully crafted hair fell across her shoulders. She stretched her arms above her head and stood.

'You look like a painting,' he said, reeling off a list of the masters, starting with Rubens. 'Or an Evelyn Page, perhaps — the woman standing in the boat. The New Zealand painter,' he added. He was still dressed, his liqueur half finished.

'All these painters and writers — how can I possibly keep up with them when I have five children to look after?' she said.

'I shouldn't have said that,' he said.

'No,' she said, 'probably you shouldn't.' She knelt on the chair so that her knees were either side of his. The bed behind them had a canopy of white above it, soft and floating.

'Ravish me,' she said.

He carried her to the bed, and groaned as he undid his clothes. 'I shouldn't be doing this,' he said. 'I shouldn't be here.'

Geraldine reached over to the night table and picked up his

cellphone, her fingers travelling over the keys to check that it was switched off.

Towards morning, she got up from the bed and opened the windows because, although the fire had died in the grate, the room was still so hot she said she couldn't sleep. Outside, sheep bleated in long concerted aaa-aahs as the beginning of their day drew near.

Geraldine slept then, face down, one arm flung over Duncan's chest, as if she were used to the shape of him in sleep. When she woke up she declared herself famished for more of him, and for the breakfast she could smell wafting up from the kitchen, in that order. When at last they dressed the room was freezing; outside they could see that fog had rolled in, creating a lace-edged blanket fluttering over the paddocks. A strange hush had fallen, so that the sheep sounded muted and far away. Geraldine laughed and stamped her feet and made Duncan hurry his dressing as she had, in order to get warm, refusing to close the windows or turn on a heater.

After breakfast, when Hazel asked them if they wanted to confirm their booking for the second night, Geraldine said yes, yes, of course that was what they wanted, it had been the most wonderful night and she loved the house, every inch of it. She was still smiling, laughing over some joke Duncan had made, not a funny one really, but as she buttoned her orange coat, everything in the world seemed amusing and possible. The coat was a Jane Daniels, made of fine merino wool, meticulously cut.

'Perhaps I'll call you later in the day,' Duncan told Hazel. He had taken out his wallet. 'We should check on the children.'

'The children, of course. Five of them. Really, if you're coming back, you don't need to pay me now.'

'Four,' Duncan said. 'Well, two of them are mine,' he corrected himself hastily.

Hazel noticed that he was counting out cash. 'Of course,' she said easily. 'Of course they are.' Something like disappointment had gathered around her eyes. Disillusionment, Geraldine thought. Hazel met people like them often enough and was kicking herself for not having recognised them earlier for what they were.

In Duncan's car, Geraldine said, 'You lied about the children — see where that got us.'

'What was I supposed to say?'

'You said five! We have two each. Well, I have two children.'

'It was just a number.'

'Don't you ever use my children as an excuse to change your mind,' she said. The tyres of the car were crunching over frost as they jolted down the rough driveway and out of sight of the house.

'All right,' he said, 'we'll stay somewhere else tonight.'

'Oh, don't feel obliged. I thought you liked last night.'

The car paused on the edge of the country road as he looked for oncoming traffic. He dropped his head on the wheel for a moment. 'I did. The best time.'

'You think it isn't hard for me, too? I'm supposed to be at a school reunion, for God's sake.'

'That woman will have the car's registration.' His voice was morose. Geraldine had suggested taking her car but he thought his green five-door more appropriate. More ordinary, he might have said.

'Oh, damn the car. She doesn't care about it. I don't care.' The bumps had dislodged a miniature soccer ball from under the back seat. He glanced behind him.

'I can't stand things rolling about in the car. Can you fix it?'

'I'm not your bloody wife.' They were quarrelling for the first time. Later she would think she should have known then, that in shifting the boundaries of what had gone before, they had begun their descent.

'Aren't you scared? What if you lost your kids?' he asked.

'Hardly likely.' All the same, she ran her hand through her hair, clutching it in an anxious knot. 'My children are near enough to grown up.'

'Well, mine aren't.'

'I don't want to talk about my children any more,' Geraldine said. 'Besides, this was about us being together for a weekend. Who mentioned forever?'

But for a time, when they had recovered themselves, the idea took hold and enlarged itself. Forever. Perhaps.

A MAN WAS STABBED IN the city. The police were looking for a youth in his late teens, dark-complexioned, of medium build, last seen wearing a grey hoodie. And a weapon, believed to be a kitchen carving knife. If people were stupid enough to get into fights they got what they deserved, Geraldine's husband said as he glanced over the newspaper. Her husband was an industrial designer whose company exported millions of dollars worth of goods all over the world. He had the competitive edge, he often said, and Geraldine was glad that Duncan couldn't hear him say things like that. Geraldine lived with her husband in the central city, in an apartment in a converted warehouse with exposed bricks and giant pipes in the ceilings. They had two Hoteres, a McCahon and a Frizzell hanging among their paintings, although Geraldine hadn't mentioned this to Duncan. Sometimes, just lately, it seemed to her that an air of emptiness pervaded the apartment. The boys went to boarding school during the week and came home at the weekends.

'I don't like these things happening in the city,' Geraldine said to her husband with a shiver. 'He was killed for his iPod.'

'They'd been fighting,' Geraldine's husband insisted. 'Another loser.'

'Anyone can get stabbed,' she said. 'I worry about the boys.'

A flicker of concern crossed his face. 'They need to watch out for themselves. Keep an eye on them,' he said, as if this resolved the matter. 'And you watch yourself in town. Don't go out in the mall on Friday nights.'

This was an absurd thing to say because Geraldine didn't go out alone on Friday nights. She would be going somewhere with him, to dinner at a brasserie, or at a colleague's house, or with the parents of their children's friends, occasionally to a theatrical performance of one kind or another. Because her husband was a minor corporate sponsor they had complimentary tickets for opening nights at the ballet. They sat in one of the rows at the opera house reserved for the prime minister and the leader of the opposition, who came in when the rest of the audience were seated. Geraldine would be wearing something severe and simple with a low-cut back that showed her shoulder blades and a floating stole in a colour to match her dress. 'Hello,' they would say, in subdued intimate voices, and people would lean across the rows to shake hands. 'Good evening, Prime Minister,' her husband would say, because privately he disliked her, although Geraldine would call her Helen, as if they were friends.

Geraldine and Duncan had met in the bookshop where his friend worked. Geraldine had gone in to buy a guide to the classics for one of her sons, who was struggling with the topic at school. The bookseller had called Duncan over and suggested he was just the man to find something that would help. 'How old is he? Sixteen? He needs Robert Graves, of course.' The shop had got busy and Duncan's friend was occupied, so they searched for the book together. 'Voilà,' Duncan had cried, pouncing on the book and flourishing it aloft, like a scholar who has just made a find. 'Or should that be eureka?' Afterwards it seemed natural to have coffee. The bookseller, a round man with a beard, eyed them benevolently when they left the shop, as if he had just arranged something important.

She would wonder if the bookseller had already become Duncan's confidant, if he knew more about him than his tastes in reading. That Duncan was dissatisfied with disposables and weekend sports runs, badly cooked meals and the way even a good salary didn't seem to run to all the things that families needed these days. These things he told her about later, although in a glancing way, indicating that he knew it was bad form to talk about the wife he was betraying. Not, he hastened to add, that he hadn't known what he was signing up for when he married; it was just the reality that was hard. He'd possibly left his run a little late.

These were admissions he would come to. But on that day, the one when they met, they had simply found themselves laughing a lot over nothing very much, and exclaiming about their chance encounter, and how you never knew what was just around the corner. She found herself saying, 'Have you ever had an affair?' just like that, as if these words were springing from the lips of a stranger. Their laughter became uneasy. She bit her lip and shrugged, looking at him sideways, and he blushed and said, 'Nothing much more than a bang at the Christmas party', and God, he could be fired for stuff like that, and anyway it was a mistake and he was sorry it had happened. The woman had left, which was both a relief and made it worse at the same time. 'You know what I mean?' Letting her know that what she was suggesting was not beyond the bounds of possibility.

He didn't look the way she imagined a scholar would look. He was a lean, closely shaven man with rimless glasses, a bristle haircut, a slight dimple in one cheek; once he might have been athletic. He had fancied an academic life but it hadn't worked out. Instead, he was an office manager. The bookshop became the place where they met once or twice more before sloping off to Starbucks to drink coffee. She wasn't sure how many times exactly, because when he suggested they drive out in their separate cars and meet somewhere, she had already decided. It was simply a matter of when, although this was not as simple as Duncan had made it sound at first, because he had to organise to have his car on days when his wife was not using it. Summer was at its height, white daisies with yellow eyes filming the hillsides, agapanthus floating like tethered blue balloons above them when they lay down. When they walked back to their cars, they smelled of grass and pollen, semen and heat. Later, after the weather changed, they began to talk of a weekend away, some place where they could sleep a whole night together in the same bed — or, in a reckless fantasy, two nights even. This would take a long time to arrange. Meanwhile, their meetings were as necessary as eating and sleeping, as nourishing as red meat.

In a way Geraldine supposed that what her husband said about the man who had been stabbed was true. There was a dark side to the town and it wasn't very far away, just up the road and around the corner in Newtown, where people lived cheek by jowl in cramped council flats with washing hung out on the verandahs. She had seen them when she took the children to the zoo, places where leaks showed in rusty lines down the sides of the buildings, and dusty flights of steps led up from the streets to rooms with torn curtains in limp disarray at the windows. The occupants were often Maori or Polynesian, or men wearing turbans and women in the shadow of their burkhas; others talked aloud to themselves and laughed at nothing in particular, as if, perhaps, they lived in halfway houses.

She also had seen the low life that lurked in the shadows, some of it up close and far too personal. Of late, she had become more familiar with the area when she made her way to the town belt reserve to park and wait for Duncan in his lunch-hour. Depending on the weather, they made love on pine needles at the edge of the grass, or in the back of her car, their feet awkward against the door. 'We can't go on like this,' they said, using all the clichés that people say to each other when they haven't the slightest idea of an alternative. And: 'We can't not go on.' One afternoon, when Duncan should already have been back at work, a face appeared at the window. It was a man with a shock of faded yellow hair and a rough beard, leering and lurching on unsteady feet.

'Give him some money and tell him to go away,' Geraldine said, pushing her handbag along the floor of the car with her toe so that Duncan could take notes from it. He opened the window a fraction and stuffed a rolled hundred through, while Geraldine sat up and pulled her skirt down.

'Cheers, mate.' The man laughed. 'Nice bit of bush there.' He nodded in Geraldine's direction.

'We're going to get caught,' Geraldine said. Her voice was sharp and frightened. 'My picture was on the social page of the paper last week.'

Duncan had seen that, of course: Geraldine and her husband at a diplomatic reception for successful exporters. 'I doubt if that man looks at the paper.'

'You don't know. Perhaps he sits in the library when he's got nothing better to do. You see people like him there all the time.'

'He won't remember. He's pissed out of his brain. Christ, Geraldine, we can't go on like this.'

'You said that before.'

He sighed then. 'I thought you weren't afraid.'

'Well, I am now. The car — he'll remember the car.'

'He won't have taken the registration.' Trying to make a feeble joke of their earlier indiscretions. Of course the man, pissed or not, wasn't going to forget a flame-red Audi shedding hundred-dollar bills on the edge of the town belt. It wasn't like Duncan's own car, parked further down the road, full of plastic balls and ready to be turned over.

'Perhaps we should let it go,' she said. She was digging her fingers into the sides of the seat to stop her hands shaking.

'Is that what you want?' Thinking back, she recognised something almost hopeful in the way he asked the question. Some tired chime that said he was ready for the affair to end.

'Let's see how it goes. I'll call you soon.' He leant over and kissed her cheek. 'You're gorgeous,' he said as he slid out of the car.

She didn't care for the way he said this: it was too easy, too pat.

'I can't rescue you, you know,' Duncan said the next time they met, although she had spoken little of her marriage, simply mentioning that at times she was lonely and that she had a lot of money but it didn't really make a difference, especially if you were used to it, as she had been all her life. Many months had passed since the beginning of it all. Soon it would be spring and then summer all over again. They had agreed to meet for coffee rather than drive out the way they usually did.

'Are you sure it's not you who needs to be rescued?' Geraldine retorted. Already she felt an ache of loss, thinking back to their first meeting between the rows of spines and dustjackets in the bookshop, somewhere close to the bestseller stand, the way his friend had thrown them together. As if they were characters in one of the novels he sold, their lives ordered to suit the plot.

'Keep your voice down,' he said.

'Since when has that bothered you?'

'Since now,' he snapped. 'Look,' he started over, 'I know this is hard. It's not what I want. But you know what you said: we're going to get caught. Think about it. Let's be careful for a bit.'

Only she thought it wouldn't happen. When it did, she wondered at her own surprise. People didn't get caught by accident, not as a rule. She had heard this from friends. It was the kind of thing they might tell her after a session at the gym when they were fired up and uninhibited. They hadn't always talked to her like this and she supposed that somehow she looked or acted differently, that they noticed the way she lowered herself tenderly onto the exercycle some days, or touched her breasts lightly while she dressed as if remembering a caress. It wasn't necessarily a planned moment, they said — some instant when one or other of the lovers said, 'Now, now is the time to get caught' — but the signals and warnings had already been planted at home. Something had changed. A crisis was about to occur. The messages were as clear as Post-it notes on a fridge door. Listen and watch, and you'll find out. Only fools didn't read messages. And, her friends said, it almost always happened when the love affair was drawing to a close, a message that enough was enough. A phone call overheard, a text message intercepted, a hotel bill or a condom in a jacket pocket. Nothing subtle.

'I'm sorry,' Duncan said when he phoned her, 'I've got no idea how it happened. I didn't mean to leave my phone where she could find it. I wasn't expecting a message from you right then.' There was something accusing in the way he said it.

This was how she came to be standing near the sea at Island Bay on a blustery day in August. She had some books of his. He had a bracelet of hers. They would exchange them at a place where they were not in the habit of meeting. 'Somewhere where I won't be tempted,' he said, only Geraldine didn't believe him.

She sat on the sea wall and smoked a cigarette, her first in years.

The wind was a northerly, violent and harsh, flicking ash in her eyes and flattening her hair around her cheeks. The cigarette tasted sour and she tossed it away as she drew her orange coat more closely around her shoulders. Across the road stood a small low building on its own, housing an art gallery that showed a regular selection of quality works. She had been to an opening there with her husband. For a moment she considered crossing over and browsing while she waited for Duncan, then decided she might be noticed, perhaps remembered. She turned, intending to go back and wait in the car. But the waves drew her towards the edge of the sea.

As she stood there, the elements rising around her, it occurred to her quite suddenly that she was out of it, this situation she had brought on herself, and that she was safe and free again. Some shift was occurring, like a boat slipping its anchor. There had been an expectation that Duncan would change her life, offer some prospect of enlightenment, evidence of things she had glimpsed but not recognised. But all that had really happened was that she was constantly afraid. She thought, I don't even like him. In her head she said to herself, I've had a sheltered life and I'm ready to move back into it. She saw freedom of a different kind beckoning her. There was nothing to stop her doing things that might interest her: going to the theatre more often, learning a language, taking up charity work. She might even take a course in the arts. All of that had been there for the taking, and she hadn't seen this.

Out in Cook Strait a mountainous wave was lifting and rushing towards the shore, causing her to step backwards. A young man, hardly more than a boy, wearing a thin cotton hoodie, hurried along the sand with a stumbling gait. He seemed not to notice Geraldine, stopping close by her and lifting his arm, an object poised above his head. For a moment she thought he was throwing a stick to a dog, but she was close enough to see that it gleamed in the dull light.

The object wheeled through the air, landing close to the edge of the water, and she saw that it was a knife. The young man ran towards the breakers to pick it up and in doing so almost banged against Geraldine. Water lapped over his trainers. After an instant's hesitation he turned towards her, the knife raised again above his head, his expression frightened. His face was speckled with pimples and patchy stubble. There was a grey pallor around his mouth. She began to run, screaming as she breasted the rise leading to the road. She was faster and fitter than the boy. People who had been browsing in the gallery emerged, rushing towards her.

Duncan arrived, too, at that same moment.

'Duncan,' Geraldine said, weeping as she collapsed against his shoulder. A man in an anorak who had been walking his dog wrestled her attacker to the ground, dragging the knife from him, using only one hand to break his grip because the young man was weak and pathetic, trying to flee when he saw all the people coming at him.

And, in a short while, the police had arrived, and Geraldine and Duncan were both witnesses. More than that. Geraldine was now, as the newspaper described her, the victim of an attempted second murder with the same knife that had stabbed the man in the city.

'It could have been worse. The boys weren't here,' Geraldine said. She knew how lame that sounded, but she had to say something, now that truth lay all around her in the silence of the apartment.

'You think they won't find out?' her husband said with deep bitterness. 'Oh, don't be naïve. I don't want their names or mine dragged through the newspapers. I'll get on to a lawyer to get you name suppression. The best person money can buy.'

'I was in the wrong place at the wrong time,' she said faintly.

'Quite often, by the sound of it.'

The lawyer came and spoke to her at length. He would support her all the way in court, he assured her. It was difficult to say whether he could have her name suppressed when she gave evidence — it was not as if it were a sexual violation — but he would do his best.

'What about Duncan?' she asked him.

'What about him?' the lawyer said. Geraldine's husband was sitting opposite in a deep leather chair, observing her closely.

'I thought,' she began, in a faltering voice, 'well, because he's why I was there. It'll come out. In court.'

'How many people know about this . . . this friendship of yours?'

'I don't know,' she said, twisting a tissue in her lap. It was a long time since she had been a schoolgirl. Geraldine remembered her headmistress, blonde and elegant, who spoke with a refined and carefully modulated voice. She called the pupils her 'gels', but when they erred there was no avoiding her gaze. 'The man in the bookshop. The woman at the guesthouse. Her name was Hazel. A man at Newtown.'

'A man at Newtown? Who?'

'I don't know. We — well, that is, I — gave him some money to go away.'

A look of dislike settled over her husband's face, the long face with folds at the corners of the mouth, which she had once loved.

Duncan's wife appeared at their apartment. When she announced herself on the intercom, Geraldine said: 'You can't let her in.'

'Why not?' her husband said. 'Don't you want to see the competition?'

'She's not.'

'Well, let's take a look anyway,' he said. 'I'm curious.'

The wife was much younger than Geraldine expected. She had a thin, lightly freckled face, and fair sticky hair pushed back behind her ears. 'I knew,' she said, 'even before I found your soppy text. I do the accounts, I count every penny. I thought I was helping him, watching the money. His first wife left him over money. Well, I said, I'm a good bookkeeper, I can keep an eye on things. I noticed straight away when he started taking out cash.' She said this in a light, breathy voice.

'I didn't know Duncan had been married before,' said Geraldine. Only she did. She understood now.

'I'll make up the money to you,' Geraldine's husband said.

'You will not,' the woman said, lifting her chin. She might look stupid, she told him, but she wasn't.

Geraldine's husband said that no, she didn't look at all stupid to him, far from it. The woman said she came from Taita. She'd lived there all her life until she met Duncan when she went to work in his office. 'I was good at school,' she said, with defiance in her tone. 'I was proxime accessit to the dux.'

'I can see you've got what it takes,' said Geraldine's husband. 'I think it's very brave of you to come here like this. Although I'm not quite sure why you have.'

'I got pregnant with Duncan,' she said, as if he hadn't spoken. 'Straight off at the office Christmas party. I suppose that sounds real old-fashioned to you,' she said, addressing Geraldine. 'Anyway, I could have got rid of it but Duncan was all for getting married — it was quite a surprise, I can tell you. My mum said it might be for the best — he's got a pretty good job, even if he does throw his money away on tarts.'

'Please,' said Geraldine's husband.

'You can have him,' the wife said to Geraldine. 'I don't give a shit about him. I've got two kids now — well, perhaps you know that — and he's got another one he's still paying for. I'd rather go home to Mum.'

'If I can help in any way,' Geraldine's husband said again.

Another woman came to see them. It was difficult to see how she had found the address, because Geraldine still had name suppression. 'The victim did not wish to be identified,' the newspaper reported.

This woman was overweight and missing some teeth. Her hair straggled over the neck of a red crepe blouse that had seen better days. The defendant in the coming court case was her son. They came from Taumarunui, she said, the centre of the island, near the railway lines. It was a good town; her boy never got in any trouble there, only when he came to the city. That's the way it was with so many of the kids. 'We told him, don't you go away down there. You meet all sortsa rubbish in the city.'

'He stabbed a man,' said Geraldine's husband.

'They say he did but nobody knows that, eh. Now he's up on this new case but how can he get a decent trial? Look at you,' she said to Geraldine. 'He never even touched you.'

'What do you want?' Geraldine said, much as her husband had to Duncan's wife.

'To get him a fair hearing. Drop this case. Someone else give him the knife. He was just getting rid of it for a mate.'

'You should tell the police.'

'Well I did, Madam Muck. They're still doing the DNA — he might be all right if it wasn't for you. You and your boyfriend know he never laid a finger.' The woman began to cry then, heavy tears sliding and gathering into the trail of snot forming beneath her nose. 'He's a good kid. You've got boys?' Her eyes rested on a photograph, a family picture taken at a lake with their boat in the background. 'The legal-aid man said he might get out on bail. You got no idea what it's like in jail for boys.'

Geraldine's husband stood to show her out. 'If you said something,' the mother said. 'Like he never touched you. He told me he just didn't see you. It might give him a breather.'

Shouting echoed from the lift lobby when Geraldine's husband led the woman out.

When he came back he dropped heavily into his chair.

'Perhaps it's true,' Geraldine said.

'The boy?'

'He mightn't be the killer.'

'For fuck's sake, Geraldine, he was disposing of a weapon.'

'But we don't know.'

'Who cares?' he said. When he had composed himself again he said, 'I loved you. I really did. I gave you everything.'

'Everything? Is that the answer? You just buy things?'

'Well,' he said, 'it's what I had.'

They decided Geraldine would stay. Between them, she and her husband agreed that this was best for the boys. For them all. Things could be smoothed over, they would pass. For the moment her husband couldn't bear the thought of touching her, but perhaps in time he might because, he said, he had always fancied her so much. This admission surprised and pleased her more than she might have supposed. A date had been set down for the boy's trial. Her husband had a conference to attend in Stockholm and afterwards he would stay on and look at some new design trends in Europe, but he would be back in time to support her when she gave evidence. He was happy that he could travel and meet new people, his time occupied. When he returned, this would be just another matter to be dealt with. They could begin again after that.

By the time he got back the young man had died in a prison fight and the trial was called off. The DNA results had come through and it seemed that someone else might well have used the knife on the night of the killing in the city.

His weeping mother was pictured in the newspaper. 'I don't know how it all come about,' she said. Geraldine believed she did, and wished it wasn't so. The history of it all, the death of a boy. These things would haunt her.

Preservation

If you had known us when we were girls, Sabrina thinks, Jan is the last one you would have expected to land up in prison. With a name like hers, Sabrina was bad girl territory, or so people imagined, and for a time they were not entirely wrong. She and Elsa and Jan, always together, a clan of their own that others would have loved to join but never could. They hitched up their gym slips to the edge of their bums, and chewed gum in class and smoked on the boundary fence that divided their girls' school from the boys' one next door. Jan was the one who managed to stay out of trouble.

Yet here Sabrina is, with her hair, wispy and greying, piled up on her head, glasses sliding down her nose, as she scans the newspaper for art-house movies, waiting in the prison car park for Elsa. Her grown-up son has gone away to university, so she and her second husband Daniel have time to devote to their jobs, Sabrina as a policy planner in a government department, Daniel as an engineer. (What policy does Sabrina plan? It varies as she moves around departments, edging up the career ladder. At the moment she is planning trade deals.) They have money and friends and time to live well. Why has she come here, she wonders.

'You don't have to do this,' Daniel had said at breakfast. 'Well, look at the weather.' Saturday morning is special time for them.

A tall man, with riotous curls and an infectious grin, Daniel likes jokes and cult movies and making surprise breakfasts for her at the weekend. Later, they shop together: a ritual. He was disappointed that she ate in haste, distracted and about to go out. 'It's not as if you're in touch with her very often.'

'I do have to go,' she said. 'It's hard to explain.' She realised that he had never met Jan, understood that he was worried about this expedition of hers.

Outside, it was a grey April morning and, indeed, the sharp chill of winter had already descended on Wellington. In the night a southerly wind had blown leaves from the copper beech in the garden. The wind had bowled her along the motorway, and now a sleety rain is falling on the asphalt of the parking lot beside her. She shivers and pulls her mohair jacket closer, glancing up at the stark building, the steel bars of the prison. Perhaps Elsa won't come.

But even as Sabrina is thinking this, Elsa's smart yellow Citroën pulls alongside.

Elsa, like her, has turned out to be respectable, only more matronly. Elsa stays home and minds grandchildren, and cooks endless meals, though, as she says, she does like to keep herself 'looking nice'. She goes to her hairdresser in the city every other week, and shops in boutiques. It's quarter of a century since she taught school. I guess I got lucky, she will say whenever they meet. Fortunate to have a husband with a good income, his job as steady as a rock even in a town like this, where for so many people it's in one office door and out the other. An accountant is worth his weight in . . . though herself she wouldn't wear gold, she prefers silver. It's not that Sabrina sees herself or her life reflected in the way Elsa lives hers now, but there is a history from the days of sleepovers and fat scones and hot chocolate, of ballet practice in tutus, of Girl Guides and music practice, of regular bedtimes and cut lunches, of homework schedules and summer holidays, a history that has traced itself in their own domesticity, however varied it may look on the surface. Their rebellion was temporary, a rite of passage on the way to their grown-up lives. Our mothers will go ape-shit, they had said, and when it happened, they'd move onto something else. Like university, eventually. Their mothers uncrossed their fingers behind their backs.

Jan was different in almost every way, and Sabrina has wondered since how it took her so long to see this. Jan was simply there. At school she passed exams without seeming to notice what happened in class, or without reading her textbooks. While everyone else was deep in study, Jan would sit as if in a trance. It was only later she revealed what they should have noticed, that she had a photographic memory. All the same, it seemed Jan was part of all that they did, only, looking back, Sabrina sees this wasn't so. Rather, she was the person who gave them permission to get up to their pranks, the one who listened to them plan their misdemeanours, dared them when their courage faltered and, later, covered their tracks. Sabrina smiles at herself when she uses the phrase 'gave them permission', as if she is some latter-day counsellor, a jargon freak like Jan's mother, Leonie. She was weird, not like other mothers. She and Elsa never said this to Jan, but they knew she thought so, too, noticing how she liked to stay over at her friends' houses but never asked them back to her place.

They did meet Leonie once a year while they were in high school. When it was Jan's birthday, they were summoned to gather at a Chinese restaurant, the same one in Courtenay Place every year. 'My mother wants you to come,' Jan would say, her face rigid with embarrassment. They said yes, of course, and thanks, that would be fine. When Jan wasn't there, they would say 'Le-Oh-nie, oh my God' and raise their eyebrows. It was the only time they were unkind to Jan, and she would never know, and, after all, they did turn up. How could they not, because if they didn't Jan would have to do it on her own.

Leonie was one of those women who liked to party hard, wore platform shoes and maxis, and talked about women's liberation. She worked as a reporter, a media-hen she called it, and cackled at herself, her toughness, her fearlessness in tackling the big stories. Each year she would have a different man with her, although the uniform didn't change much — flared trousers, sideburns. They had names like Eddie and Norm and Ted, and they all worked for one or other of the unions. They smoked over dinner, because you could do that then, and drank red wine, and complained that they couldn't order spirits.

The year Jan turned fifteen, Leonie brought along a photograph of Jan as a baby. Jan was blonde and dimpled, and the dimple in one cheek had stayed with her. In the photograph, Leonie had straight hair dangling to her waist, and wore a poncho over a long flowery dress. How we change, she had said, passing the picture around for everyone to admire. That was the sixties, you know. Jan would hunch down in her chair and look as if she wished her mother would die. Jan was dux of the school in her year, the first of them to graduate, the first to get a real job, as a flight attendant it turned out.

'My daughter, a trolley dolly,' Leonie said to Sabrina when she chanced upon her in the street one day. Her hair was permed in a very big Afro and she wore round spectacles.

'I'm surprised,' Sabrina said, although she thought anyone as pretty as Jan, and as clever, could do much as she liked.

'She says she doesn't have to use her brains. It figures — she was always lazy.'

'I'm sure she does,' Sabrina said, thinking that, after all her talk about women's liberation, Leonie was being sexist. She, herself, had an appreciation of feminism, now that she went to university and suffered jokes about her name. Her parents had named her after a British pin-up star with enormous breasts. They had done it as a kind of a joke, they told her, shamefaced. Sabrina, the pin-up one, had visited the town where her mother grew up, and she'd thought it great that someone got so much attention. They were sorry. They would understand if she changed it; they were only young themselves when they had her. As acts of contrition, they gave her brothers plain staid names. But Sabrina has hung onto her name as if it's a lucky charm.

'I talked to her about it as a political concept,' said Leonie of Jan's job. 'But she says she hasn't got time for concepts.' Leonie was almost spitting the words. 'I thought you of all people would understand.' At the time, Sabrina was struggling with political science.

'Sort of,' she said, and it was the nearest she and Leonie ever came to understanding each other. Afterwards, she wondered about Jan's trances, and hoped she could deal with emergencies on aeroplanes.

Jan was the first to get married, too, something she has done only once, and the first to get divorced, although this is something Elsa has never done, and Sabrina believes that she is happy with Daniel and can't imagine she will repeat separation. Jan never had children. Not her scene, she said once.

And now Leonie is dead, and Jan is locked up, and there is nobody to see to her mother's funeral arrangements.

The car park is filling up as Elsa ducks out of her car in the rain, her expression distraught. 'Sabby,' she says, climbing into the passenger seat. Beneath her raincoat her cashmere sweater is tight over her ample breasts; her dark pleated skirt doesn't conceal that she is getting stout. 'What on earth is this all about? Did you know Jan was in here? I never saw anything in the paper about Leonie dying.'

'No, but remember Jan's got a different surname to Leonie. I can't even remember what it is. Perhaps we've missed it.'

Elsa sighs heavily. 'How did we ever get in tow with Jan?'

'I think Jan got in tow with us,' says Sabrina, half laughing at the memory of the way Jan was always at their heels when they first went to high school. By that time, she and Elsa had known each other forever. There was something adoring about the way Jan spoke to them. Sabrina thinks they were flattered. Jan was sensational — the way she looked, the way she came top in everything — and yet she chose them. 'She was a good mate.'

'I feel awful for her,' Elsa says in a small miserable voice.

'Well, we're here now. We can do it, can't we?'

'I haven't told Ross,' says Elsa. Ross is her husband. 'He wouldn't like me coming here. Thank God he didn't pick up the phone when she rang yesterday. I thought it was a hoax at first.'

Jan had called them both the day before. A recorded message had come on the end of the line, a flat cold man's voice saying: 'You are about to receive a phone call from a prison inmate. Press one if you do not wish to receive it, otherwise hold the line. Your call will be recorded and may be used as evidence in court.' And then there had been a click and a rustle, and Jan's voice. She had a special dispensation to phone people because of her mother's death, she explained. As a rule, she had to have people she rang approved of first, but this was different. Besides, she said, there weren't all that many people she could ring. You know how it is, she had said to Sabrina, in that kind of drifting voice she sometimes used at school when she wasn't paying attention. Her brother had been brought up by their father, and Lord knows where he is now; they don't keep in touch. She can't even let him know that their mother is dead.

She had pulled herself together, hurrying on to explain that she needed to see Sabrina and Elsa urgently. It was visiting hour the next day; if they could come she'd be grateful, because her mother was a bitch most of the time, as they knew very well, but she couldn't let her be disposed of without someone in charge. Disposed of, that was the phrase she used. 'I'm banged up,' she said and laughed, or that's how it came across. Because of the circumstances they are allowed a special dispensation to visit at short notice. They will have to carry identification, but their names are already down on the visiting list.

'We'd better get on with it,' says Sabrina, turning to face the wall of wire fences. 'Come on, Elsa, they won't keep us in there.'

Elsa shivers, adjusts her fine floating navy scarf. It's decorated with tiny pale tan-coloured elephants; one of her daughters-in-law had bought it for her in London. 'Click click,' she says, which is what they used to say, from the times they played knucklebones together.

It is not getting into the prison that is so hard, though that is bad enough. Somehow they had thought they would be different, that because they were two respectable women hurrying to their friend's aid, they would be, if not exactly welcomed, at least swept through the doors in a discreet manner. Instead they must stand together in a wire enclosure and speak their names into a microphone, while they wait for what seems a very long time until a gate slides open. There is no sign of human presence until they are inside the doors. They must sign documents, show their drivers' licences, put all their belongings in a metal cupboard and return the key to an officer behind a grille, walk through a metal detector like the one at the airport, only the guard on the other side who scans them and frisks their pockets is less friendly. Sabrina wants to protect her crotch but is reminded sharply to keep her arms extended level with her shoulders.

They are instructed to sit on stools attached to tables dotted around the room. The stools are different pastel colours, like toys in a playroom. Families are gathered round the tables, waiting for prisoners to appear. Guards stand in line near a counter. One of them calls Jan's surname, and a minute or so later she emerges, wearing a baggy fluorescent-orange jumpsuit. Her hair falls in a long single plait down her back and her face is without make-up and more bloated than they remember, but then it's a while since they met. They reach out to hug her, and for a moment it is allowed, then they must all sit down.

'Bit of a shock, eh?' says Jan. There is an uncomfortable silence.

'Why?' says Elsa. 'Why are you in here?'

'Oh, a bit of fraud, or that's what they said. It's all right, I haven't bottled anyone or done drugs — well, not that anyone's nailed me for.' She laughs again, it's a shock to hear that it sounds just like Leonie's laughter, deep and smoke-laden. 'I was doing a computer job. You know, transferring money from one account to another.'

'I don't understand,' says Elsa.

'Why I did it?' Jan looks at her squarely. 'It was easy, Elsa, that's why.'

'We're so sorry about your mother,' Sabrina says.

'Yes, well, it wasn't what I was expecting. The old whore. It was only last Saturday she was here.'

'She's been visiting?'

Jan hesitates. 'I was her cause. Finally. It pissed her off my whole life that she had to look after me. I guess I was more interesting in here.'

'I'm sure she loved you,' says Elsa in a helpful, hopeful voice.

'Love. Oh, shut up, Elsa.' And Jan's eyes fill with tears. She leans her elbows on the table and pushes her fingers into her temples. 'I'm not sure we see love in the same light. It's not something we talked about in school.'

Elsa looks puzzled, and Sabrina doesn't know where this is going either.

'We talked about it all the time,' Elsa says hotly.

'You and Sab talked about boys but it's not the same thing.' Jan is crying openly now, her shoulders shaking. 'Oh shit,' she says, 'I didn't mean to do this. Yes, you could say we made up, even though she left it a bit late. She saw me in here. You know, she *saw* me.'

'It's okay,' Sabrina says, 'really it is.' Her own ditsy happy mother, who had loved her father and all of them, and had given her a silly name, had died in a hospice more than a decade ago. It's the only unforgivable thing she ever did to Sabrina's father, and to Sabrina, too. Sabrina knows what it's like to wake up in the mornings and feel absence in the air, the mystery of loss that is there like some tangible object, that takes minutes to recognise, that has to be quelled before the day begins. She sees the way it is, that Jan has loved the mother she could never please. 'What happened?'

'Heart. She was a bit out of breath last week. That's all. Anyway, are you two going to do the honours for me?'

And then Jan unfolds the plan. Leonie is in a funeral parlour. There hasn't been a notice in the paper, so first of all they need to see to that, and then she wants her mother to have a proper funeral. There's a lawyer who has told her there's money for it. Jan doesn't know if she'll be allowed to go or not, but she's got her fingers crossed. Before the funeral there must be a viewing of her body. Leonie still had old friends and they'll need to say goodbye. The viewing part is important, something Leonie was in the habit of doing when people died. She liked funerals. For the viewing she must have a nice dress.

'I'm sure she's got nice clothes in her wardrobe,' Sabrina says. 'She always had lots of clothes.'

'You have to get past this lawyer first. Apparently the house is all locked up. Anyway, she'd let herself go, not like the old Leonie. She told me last week her latest hairdresser was so over her. That's probably what killed her — she'd run out of new hairdressers to try.'

Jan wants them to go to a particular boutique and pick up a dress that Leonie had told her about on that last visit. It was, as she described it, the most gorgeous dress she'd ever seen: a label dress, black with a puffed skirt and a peacock at the waist, with feathers trailing down the front. The kind of dress she would have loved to wear when she was young, and now never would, or not in this life. Leonie in her true colours, an exhibitionist at heart. All that gear she got togged up in. The fems never really took to her — she was too much of a girl. And a boys' girl at that. But she will wear it, Jan says fiercely, just this once. She has got one of the guards to phone the shop and ask them to hold the dress. It's waiting for them to pick up. She is so relieved the dress is still there, but at the price, this is perhaps not surprising.

'How much?' says Sabrina.

'Two thousand three hundred,' says Jan without a flicker. 'Will your credit cards stand it? You can go halves. It's only for a couple of days.'

'Hullo,' says Elsa, on a sharp intake of breath.

'You lay her out in it, and then you take it back after the viewing. They can pop her in something else when they close the coffin. Be sure to leave the label on when you take it back to the shop.'

'Oh no,' says Elsa, 'no, you can't do that.' Elsa's mother had been a corsetiere in a department store. She'd told Elsa about the way customers did dreadful things and tried to return clothes that were grubby and you could see they'd been worn. Undergarments at that. Filth, her mother used to say. We wore rubber gloves to deal with some of that stuff.

'I'm not asking you to pay for it,' Jan says. 'Just treat it like a loan. Somebody in here told me how it's done.'

'But it's not right,' says Sabrina.

So Jan reminds her then, reminds both of them. How they always said they'd stick together. About the night they stayed over with those boys, and she'd told their mothers they'd been at her place, and the way Elsa's mother had rung to check, because she didn't really trust Jan, and besides they weren't in the habit of staying at Jan's place, and her daughter was such a good girl, and Jan had sweet-talked her into believing they were all asleep already, and told her what they had watched on television, only it was Jan who had sat by herself and watched that programme, not knowing where they were, or even that they had gone out with the boys, and lain awake all night worrying that she should really have told Elsa's mother in case they'd been raped and murdered. She says all of this in a flat relentless tone, not really looking at them, just going on and on. She raises her eyes to Sabrina. 'She liked you, you know.'

'Did she?'

'Yep, she wished I was like you.'

In the end, Sabrina says that, yes, it's true they weren't angels and they can do this thing she's asking. 'We could actually pay for the dress,' she says, 'so then Leonie can go up the chimney in it. Couldn't we, Elsa?'

But no, Jan tells them, that's not the plan, and haven't they listened to a word she's said? She wouldn't ask them to part out with big bucks like this — that's not her style, not with friends. It's just a simple favour. 'For God's sake, Elsa,' she says, looking at her stricken face, 'you never used to return those lipsticks you flogged at the chemist's.'

Elsa says, with a sudden spurt of resolution, 'All right then. Okay, we'll do it.'

'They said I could see her. A couple of the guards will take me down tomorrow evening. They've promised me that, at least.'

Visiting hour is over, time for them to leave.

'Over to you now,' Jan says, standing up 'Remember, get it in the paper. If I don't make it to the funeral, say one for me. No hymns. She liked Julie Felix — choose something of hers. The one about going to the zoo tomorrow, she'd get a laugh out of that. Eddie might do the eulogy. He was her favourite boyfriend.'

Sabrina reaches over and gives her another quick embrace. 'Take care, Jan,' she whispers.

'I'm okay,' Jan says. 'If you keep your head down, it's not so bad. The food could be worse.' She turns and leans her cheek into Elsa's. 'You'll be pleased to know I've got a friend who works in the laundry. She makes sure I always get my own knickers back from the wash.' She walks to the far side of the visiting room, a guard moves towards her, she waves and disappears.

The rain has cleared, and they stand in a patch of weak late morning sunlight, although the whipping wind is like pain slicing through them. Elsa begins to cry. 'We must be crazy.'

'She drives a hard bargain. I guess you learn that if you're inside.'

'Sabrina, I want us to do it in cash. No credit cards, all right?'

'Ross?'

'He pays my card.'

'Well, I pay my own.'

'All the same, it would be better if we did it all in cash. It's like leaving a calling card otherwise.'

Sabrina pulls her coat around her more closely. 'I'll bring it this afternoon when we go to the funeral director's. You can get the money all right?'

'Of course.' Elsa is impatient. 'I've got money of my own. But you do see my point about the card?'

'Double click,' Sabrina says. She does see. Elsa is showing common sense. Already Sabrina has decided that this is something Daniel might be better not knowing either, although they pride themselves on the honesty of their relationship. Sabrina was a practised liar in the dying days of her first marriage, and she has sworn never to lie again. Truth is so easy when you have nothing to hide.

As she drives home she wonders if there is some crime involved. On the face of it, she can't see that there is. It's a lot of money to blow on a dress. Besides, they've made a promise. Not that Jan need know if they broke it and just paid. Like saying *Le-Oh-nie* in that mean schoolgirl way. Only she probably did know. And then, she thinks, why not? It's not such a big deal, a simple enough transaction. People return things to shops all the time. As Jan pointed out, it's the things she and Elsa haven't returned in the past that she ought to feel bad about. She had stored away that part of her life: small wickednesses and betrayals of her friend who stayed at home and watched out for them like an anxious young mother, the kind Jan would have liked to have had for herself.

'All right,' she says to herself again. 'Okay, Jan.'

THE FUNERAL DIRECTOR IS A natty young man. He wears a brown suit with a brown button-down collared shirt and a black tie decorated with orange poppies. He knows the circumstances, he tells them, and coughs discreetly. Their friend has told him that a suitable dress is being brought in. When they hand it to him, he enthuses — the prettiest lying-in dress he has ever seen. Sabrina explains that it is not to be burnt with Leonie; they will hold it for her daughter, who wants to keep it for sentimental reasons. It's too beautiful to be destroyed, and he says, oh yes, yes, he does understand that, entirely agrees, and it's not unusual for people to be slipped out of their clothes once the curtain comes down. No trouble at all. Sabrina has the price tag in her wallet, still on its cord.

They retire for a short decent interval to the waiting room while he dresses Leonie. They sit in deep armchairs and read magazines about royalty and English country homes. 'Perhaps it's just as well,' Elsa says. 'You can't imagine Leonie being one of those old ladies with talcum powder hair and clip-ons.' Her own mother is going that way, her memory not so sharp. 'Goodness knows what I'll do with her. I've been looking after kids all my life and now it'll be her I suppose. Not what Ross and I were planning.' Her face softens. 'Sorry, Sabby,' she says. 'I know you miss your mother. I can't believe it's ten years.'

'That was the last time we were all together, do you know that?' Sabrina says. 'The three of us, you and me and Jan at Mum's funeral. I'd forgotten how long it was.'

The undertaker calls them in. There is Leonie, in a satin-lined casket, her face younger than they remember it, her hair fluffed around her face. The black dress, with its silk ruffles, is settled around her, the peacock's head made from knotted leather nestled between her breasts, the tail feathers which, except for two or three real ones, are actually little appliqués of felt sewn with sequins, fanned across her knees. Sabrina remembers a moment when a peacock illuminated her life. She and Daniel were on their honeymoon. He had elected to stay in a bush cabin, although she would have preferred something more glamorous. Daniel liked the outdoors, which sounded charming, but the camp kitchen was basic, the bed hard and the duvet had been used by others. She had woken on their second morning, and crept out of bed while her new husband still slept. But then she had lifted the curtain to see what the day was like outside. On the branch of a tree near the window she saw a peacock. He sat picking at a berry, his splendid shining tail sweeping before her, filling the window frame with colour. In this moment of radiance, Sabrina saw a sign, a promise of happiness, and she hasn't been disappointed.

'You'll be here when your friend comes to view her mother?' the undertaker asks. 'I understand she'll be here about five.'

As one, Sabrina and Elsa shake their heads. They know Jan doesn't need them here.

'We'll see her at the funeral,' they say.

But Jan isn't at the funeral, and they aren't really surprised. Sabrina supposes that, even if she were allowed, Jan wouldn't want her mother's friends to see her tethered to a guard. The undertaker has told them that the viewing went very well, and that Jan's escorts, as he described her guards, had allowed her to stay a long time. She had been able to bring a friend from the prison. They had spent some time with Leonie, then Jan stayed with her for a while by herself. She loved the dress on her mother, said it was exactly right. Sabrina thinks Jan would have said goodbye then; it would have been enough.

For, after all, it's not such a great occasion. Twenty or so people attend, hard-bitten older reporters for the most part, and some union people. Eddie makes a lugubrious speech to the effect that Leonie was a great laugh and tough as old boots with a heart of gold and his very good mate. All the old clichés, and bit of cover-up too. His wife, standing in the front pew, is a tiny woman with a nut of a face and knowing eyes.

The undertaker hands them the dress, wrapped up in tissue paper, and they shake hands with him.

Back at Elsa's house, Sabrina gives Elsa the tag and Elsa, who is more adept at folding things, reattaches it. She is wearing her kitchen gloves. 'You can't be too sure,' she says. It's Sabrina's job to return the dress. Elsa had picked it up; now her part is over, as she says. Done and dusted.

The shop's manager is indignant, although she tries to be polite. She studies the dress from every angle and finds it perfect. She asks if she can give Sabrina a cheque, given that she 'doesn't appear to have a credit card', and when Sabrina says no, her friend paid for it with cash and that's what she wants back, she has to wait for a long time while the woman goes to the bank along the street. The notes are counted out with crisp fury.

In the days that follow, Sabrina frets about the dress. Perhaps it has been sold and now some other woman might be wearing it. There seems something deeply unpleasant about this possibility. In her lunch-hour she slopes up the street to the shop and takes a quick look round to see whether the manager is at the counter. When she see the coast is clear, she ducks in and looks on the rack, but the dress has gone. An attendant at the other end of the shop looks up and sees her. 'If you've changed your mind, that dress is sold,' she says.

So Sabrina knows it's not as easy as that: everyone in the shop knows who she is and remembers. She and Elsa meet so that Sabrina can give her her money back. She tells Elsa about her second trip to the shop. Elsa blanches a little, says they must forget it now, because there's nothing they can do about it, and they don't need to draw attention to themselves. Who knows, they might be on security cameras. Really, it's not a crime. 'You have to let it go, Sabby,' she tells her. 'Click click?'

They talk about going to see Jan. Both of them have written to her and described the funeral. Sabrina has even tried to make her account a little comical, describing the way Eddie's toupee had slid over his ear while he was giving the eulogy.

Weeks pass and neither of them hears from her. They wonder about going to see her again, but it turns out to be complicated. They have to get permission to visit, and be on Jan's list of people she wants to see and when they enquire it seems that Jan hasn't asked for them again. Elsa is annoyed that after all the trouble they've been to, Jan hasn't bothered to write.

THERE IS A DINNER PARTY. There are dinner parties all over this city every night: diplomacy, solid silver cutlery and crystal; business, private rooms in restaurants, some talk, a deal cut and home by ten o'clock; culture, artists or writers or film dudes (but rarely a combination of the three) take over the whole restaurant and shout their way through a main and several bottles of wine. And there are the weekend dinner parties in old houses that have been elegantly refurbished, with dark wood panels and high ceilings, shelves full of books and a handful of good pictures on the walls, wine glasses that don't always match, dress casual, six or eight people gathered round a table, gossip. Always gossip. These are the ones Sabrina and Daniel like most. They go to a dinner party given by an architect called Mark with whom Daniel often works in the construction business. Mark's business partner is recently separated from his wife. He's brought his new girlfriend, a tall rakish woman with tousled red curls, who works in television make-up. Mark's wife doesn't approve of Hortense, the make-up artiste (this is how she describes herself), and the atmosphere is cool until the third bottle of wine, when Daniel and Sabrina catch each other's eye and they're both thinking that they need to cut this woman some slack.

'Tell us about your job,' says Sabrina. 'It sounds really interesting.'

Hortense is a little drunk by then, and glad to have their attention. She tells them about some politicians she's made up, and who has had work done on their faces. You'd be really surprised at some of the men who've had the cut, she tells them, and names a couple. Mind you, men are easier than the women. Some of the women she gets through are real bitches. Power bitches, she calls them, talking on their cellphones while she's trying to do their blusher. How the hell do they expect her to keep it even? And then it's all her fault. Unless they're having a bad day and then they want all her attention, expect her to be Mother Teresa. Holy shit, she says, and Mark's wife begins clearing away dishes, with a bit of a rattle and clatter, but Hortense doesn't notice.

'I mean shit,' she says, 'I had one in the other day, who'd got this new dress. She was a mess, had a rash on the back of her neck that she was trying to cover up. I said don't worry, they can't see your back on telly. She started to bawl. The rash was right around her neck and on her arms, and other bits of her, too, that she'd rather not mention. She told me she had a new dress that she paid major money for, and every time she wears it, the same thing happens, and she gets a fever as well. At first she thinks it's all in her head, but the night before I saw her, she'd passed out at a dinner party at one of the embassies, face down in the dessert, and you know what everyone was thinking. Pissed. She said she'd never live it down.'

'It must be in her head,' says Mark's wife. 'How could a dress do that to you?'

'Well, it seems it's got feathers on it so she wondered if it was some kind of bird sickness.'

'What sort of feathers were they?' Sabrina asks carefully.

'Oh, I don't know. She was just one of those silly cows who get hysterical over nothing, I reckon. Who knows whether it was her dress.' Hortense is looking for her glass to be refilled.

'Like tui feathers? Or peacock's or something?' Sabrina is trying to keep her voice casual, even indifferent.

'Oh, I'm blowed if I know,' Hortense says. 'I never thought to ask.'

'So who was she?' Sabrina persists.

Hortense pulls up short, as if her head has cleared. 'I can't tell you things like that. It'd be more than my job's worth.'

'She sobered up fast enough when it suited her,' Sabrina says on the way home.

'Well, she's right, she can't talk about her clients.'

'She mentioned those cabinet ministers.'

'That's different,' Daniel says.

'I don't see that it is.'

'How would you like it if it was you?'

'She probably made up the part about doing that woman's make-up,' Sabrina says. 'She probably just heard about her. I mean, she would have told us if she knew. You could tell she would.'

'You're making too much of it,' he says in an injured way, as if she has just spoilt the evening. Of course it already is spoilt.

Only, the next week he dines at a restaurant with some business-men who are going to put money into a project he hopes to get involved in, and when he comes home he tells her he's heard the story again. 'Remember, the one about the woman who passed out with her face in the lemon meringue.'

'I don't remember that it was lemon meringue.'

'Whatever.'

'Did they say who it was?'

'I missed that.'

'Daniel.'

Somebody tells her the story over the water distiller at work. 'Do you know who it was?' Sabrina asks. She is desperate to know.

The woman telling the story rolls her eyes. 'Somebody well known, she goes on television. Well, that's what I heard. She's quite high up.' Though what she is high up in is still not clear. The story has become more about the woman passing out than about the dress and the rashes, which Sabrina thinks is just as well.

'I have to tell the shop,' Sabrina says to Elsa on the phone. They have been in touch more often than in years.

And Elsa says no, Sabby, don't do it, or if she must, just leave her out. Sabrina says: 'We could write the shop a note.' Because by now she has looked up embalming fluid and knows that it contains formaldehyde, ethanol, ether — a proper cocktail of solvents. Leonie had been preserved in toxins.

'Look,' says Elsa, 'the woman won't wear the dress again. She'd be a fool to.'

'You don't know that for sure. She might think it was a coincidence.'

'A dress like that? Well, you wouldn't want to wear it too often anyway. It's not one you'd forget.'

But Sabrina can't let it rest. At night she lies awake, flooded with what she supposes is deep moral panic. When she was a child she used to have sleepless nights, thinking, Please God, let me off this time and I'll never do it again. She is thinking exactly the same thing now, with a variation that goes something like, Give me another chance, and I'll grow up. She has decided she will go in and tell the shop manager, although first she must tell Daniel, and then goodness knows who else. Her lawyer, perhaps. It could be a crime, after all. Inflicting a noxious substance on an unsuspecting victim. She must tell, because at heart she doesn't think she's a bad person.

When Daniel comes home in the evening, she can't find the right words. While she's getting dinner he pours a glass of wine for each of them and sits on a kitchen stool.

'What's new?' she asks.

He looks so happy and at ease with his day, that she thinks another time might do to tell him. All the same, she begins: 'That woman with the dress that freaks her out. You know the one I mean? It makes her faint at dinner.'

'Oh that,' says Daniel. 'The story gets worse. I meant to tell you, someone told me at work yesterday. The woman told a friend who was an industrial chemist and he offered to test the fabric. Turns out the dress had been on a corpse. How gross can you get?'

Sabrina agrees that yes, it's about the worst story she's ever heard, and how did it happen, and what did the woman do about it, and is she all right?

But Daniel doesn't know the answers to any of those questions. Presumably she returned it to the shop, he says.

'It would be covered by insurance,' Sabrina says. She has to believe that part. And she sits there thinking, Saved, saved. At least the woman won't wear the dress again.

This is what she says to Elsa the next morning, and, as it happens, that day they both receive letters from Jan. They are written on cheap lined paper, with the address care of the prison on the back and they say much the same thing. Thanks for everything, they're a couple of dolls. She and her friend hope to get out about the same time. If probation will let them, they will get a place together. That would be the best thing of all.

Friend, says Elsa, what does she mean by friend? And then she goes quiet at the end of the line. She hadn't realised.

'I guess we should have,' Sabrina says.

'Perhaps we've got it wrong,' Elsa says doubtfully.

'She sounds okay, that's the main thing,' Sabrina says. Relief floods her, fills her nostrils, makes her hands tremble. Relief and release. And yes, redemption, there's that, too. Love, so various, has discovered them all.

'We should get together,' Elsa says, her voice vague. 'After the school holidays, perhaps.'

'Soon,' Sabrina replies. 'When I've done my annual report.' She is preparing to leave trade behind. With luck, she'll get an arts job next.

Yes, they agree, yes, soon.

Extremes

There was every reason Rachel could think of not to have a baby and none in favour, although the small lump of tissue growing inside her was already a presence she knew she could come to like. She wished that the baby's father was someone with whom she could live happily ever after. She wished that he wasn't married to someone else already, and only last year, in a ceremony that the newspaper had dubbed 'our town's wedding of the year'. His wife had worn a sleek satin gown, and had five bridesmaids, some of whom were Rachel's friends, too. Most of all, she wished that when he'd had his hand between her thighs at the bank's office party, she'd had the strength to say no, that she'd screamed for help. Except she didn't want help, she wanted Mark's length sliding inside her, and it wasn't as if she was a virgin and didn't know what was happening, as they whimpered and shuddered among a pile of ledgers in the back room behind the staff cafeteria. 'We must be mad,' Mark had muttered in her ear. 'Thanks, kid, I really needed that.' His wife was seven months gone and he was so frustrated it was killing him.

'We shouldn't have,' she'd said, and she was crying already, partly from the wine she'd drunk, and partly in the sweet aftermath of having come so perfectly with him. And that was something new, something she hadn't done with anyone else.

'Steady on,' he'd said. 'Hey, steady on. It wasn't that big a deal, was it?'

And when she'd said that yes, it was, couldn't he tell, he'd said perhaps he could see her home, and they could get another one on, but they mustn't make a habit of it, as if it was her fault that it had happened, and that they needed to make sure that nobody saw them leaving together.

In the end, he'd pecked her cheek before she got out of his car, without anything happening, sour reserve seemingly descended upon him. Lying in bed, she had thought how he was wasted on his wife, and touched herself where he had been. It was a month or so before she began wishing all those things that couldn't be reversed. She wept in her bedroom, not daring to sob in case her mother or sisters heard her.

Her mother was a tall blonde called Penelope, who Rachel resembled, or so people said. Penelope came from old money in the south, she intimated, as if she had a farming background, although there was no farm and it was actually trade. Not that Rachel thought of any of this as she was growing up; that would come later. Her father was the one whose family farmed, in Taranaki; the son who had made his escape. My parents bred children in order to have more hands to milk cows, he would say — not the life for me. In photographs of him when he was young, he was a dark crafty-looking child. He had never looked back, a lawyer who was always winning his cases and making headlines in the local paper, bulky now, his iron grey hair settled on his head like a finger perm, only of course it wasn't. The house where they all lived, Rachel and her parents and two sisters, was a low ranch-style place surrounded by gardens and a grass tennis court. Penelope had her work cut out keeping things ticking over, as she would tell people, especially with a trio of daughters to keep in order. 'A bit of a burden, three clever girls,' she would say, as she poured cold lemonade into tall glasses, between games of tennis. It varied, who was in and who was out at Penelope's gatherings. There were some, like Lesley, who had simply been uninvited after her daughter vanished. 'An office party baby,' Penelope said, raising her eyebrows in a knowing way. 'Poor Lesley. I don't suppose she ever saw it.'

It. An office party baby. (Not even the Christmas party, just a party for a retiring accountant, who Mark had now replaced.) Rachel had had her pregnancy confirmed by the family doctor, the same doctor who had delivered her and her sisters, the one her mother claimed had gasped with pleasure when he first examined her breasts. 'Oh I had nice knockers then,' she said, 'a pretty good pair.'

'Well, young lady, you're going to have to do something about this,' the doctor said to Rachel. 'Will the fellow marry you?'

'I don't know,' Rachel said. Only of course she did.

'Your mother know you've skipped your period?'

'Not yet. You won't tell her?'

The doctor said that no, he wouldn't, but she'd better not leave it too long. Her mother was a sharp woman. He smiled then, a gentle affable smile.

The girls' bedrooms opened onto a low verandah that ran the whole length of the house. On clear nights, her father would go outside and smoke there, a glass of wine in hand, waiting for Penelope to join him. Perfect. They had perfect lives, Penelope said, but you had to work at perfection. Rachel knew her mother worried about her. Her older sister was engaged to a doctor she had met at university; she was coming home in the holidays to plan the wedding. Her younger sister was always coming top of the class. Dark-haired girls, like their father. Working in a bank wasn't really what Penelope expected of her daughters, a service industry, however you looked at it, unless you were a manager, which of course was unlikely if you were a woman. The job was only meant to last a year while Rachel worked out what she really wanted to do, but it had stretched into nearly three. Rachel shone at maths when she was at school but in Penelope's view, counting out other people's money in a red brick bank on the corner of the main street was hardly the best application of her talents.

In the spring evenings that year, Rachel put her head under the blankets and tried to hold her breath so that her parents wouldn't catch a hint of her erratic breathing, her crazy heart beating, as she held her hands over her belly. The air in Rotorua was very still, heavy with volcanic sulphur, the moon like floodlights on the garden, that chemical smell and the scent of the nearby pine forests piercingly, achingly sharp.

DOREEN'S HUSBAND, SAMSON, SMELT THAT same deep pungent tang rising from pine needles, even closer, while he scanned the treetops for a hint of fire. It was 1976, the beginning of the fire season, and high above the forest he sat in a tower watching for tendrils of smoke. It was easier at night to detect the start of a fire, any spark like a lighted match in a dark room. Samson had been a fire spotter for twenty years. He worried that the new techniques of detecting fires, like infra-red, might put him out of a job, but so far he was still being sent up the tower at Rainbow Mountain. Here, in the thermal area, where steam rolled out of the earth in unexpected places, a spotter could be fooled into believing there was a fire when there wasn't, so as he saw it, it was a specialist's job. In America, in the old days, news of a fire was dispatched by carrier pigeons. The idea of owning a cage of birds for company was appealing. Here, you just phoned up headquarters.

In the summer, he would stay for six weeks at a time, living like a hermit, alternating twelve-hour shifts with periods of deep exhausted sleep. People thought it was an easy life up there, sitting and watching for something that might never happen. A Dharma Bum they called him and laughed, as if he was a character in a novel, and he knew that a man called Jack Kerouac had written his job description into the record. He could see how he must look like a beatnik, his hair matted and tangled, his beard heavy, But people couldn't know how he loved his work, how the treetops were like a sea, changing and shifting all the time, depending on the time of day and the weather — blue green in some lights, bottle green in others, a faint lime tinge in early morning, dense black outlines at night. In the winter, he thinned the trees, and tried not to think about the fact that eventually they would be felled and turned into paper. It was enough to put a man off wiping his bum.

All the same, sometimes, towards the end of a stint in the tower, when days had turned into weeks, he found himself imagining fire, almost wishing it to happen. He had seen forest fires in his time although under his watch they never got out of control. One nearly did, and he remembers this mysterious and beautiful conflagration, short-lived though it was, with something akin to longing.

Samson had known Doreen since he was nineteen and she was sixteen, and that was not far off quarter of a century, and already they were grandparents. Now that the children had grown up, Doreen worked in a bakery shop in Tokoroa. Toke, they called it. We live in Toke, near the forests. Doreen iced Sally Lunn buns with white icing and raspberry buns with pink, the Sally Lunns first, so she could add cochineal to what was left over from the first batch of icing. The baker's name was Mr Isaacs. It was not that he was exactly formal, but he was older, and Doreen and the two girls who worked in the shop always called him that, although they called his wife, who did the accounts and the ordering, by her first name, Mary.

Doreen told him in detail about her job, because now she had an interest outside home, and he had heard enough of the kids to last him for a lifetime. She felt responsible for things going well, because she was in charge of tasting, and also for the way the front counter was run. She took orders while the two girls made the egg sandwiches. Doreen checked their mix, tasting a spoonful to make sure there was enough mayonnaise, and not too much parsley. Some of the customers, and it was mostly men who drove trucks, weren't keen on green muck in their sammies. That's what they said to her, and she said, 'We'll see to that, for sure.'

'You should just leave it out,' Samson said.

'Well, some of them do like it. Joe Blake gets mad when we leave it out.'

'You mean Joe Paki? Drives for the firm?' He was talking about the logging company.

'His name's Joe Blake.'

'Blimey, where did he get his fancy ideas from? He was Joe Paki when I went to school with him. Didn't he marry some girl from Auckland? I expect that explains it. I'm not that fussed on parsley myself.'

Doreen just shrugged. She got a buzz out of working in the shop, the girls were company for her while Samson was away and the money was great. Her savings account was growing and every now and then she showed it to Samson. When there was enough they would visit their eldest son, who had gone shearing in Western Australia. Neither she nor Samson had ever been to Australia, never boarded a plane. Not long now, we need a bit of adventure in our lives, she would tell him.

Doreen was the thrill in his life, the one who could quench his secret thirst for flames. These days, when it was time for him to go home, he tried to get there during the day, so that he could clean up and shower properly before she arrived. He didn't look like a bum then, although he kept his white-blond hair collar length and a little loose and wild because Doreen liked it like that. Then he would pretend he wasn't there when she unlocked the front door, until the moment she walked into the bedroom, and he was lying there on the bed as naked as the day he was born. She screamed the first time, and swore at him, son of a bitch, what if I'd got the axe from out the back, but then she'd laughed. They hadn't got up until the next morning, and she was so done in it was all she could do to go to work. This had been going on for a few years, and he knew she could tell when he was home now, had learnt to check the garage to see if the ute was there, but she still pretended it was a surprise. These days they got up in time for dinner and then they watched television until it was time to go to bed properly. She didn't have the stamina any more, she said, with a lazy laugh. Remember I'm forty.

She didn't seem forty to him, plump and hearty perhaps, but then she had always been solid. I eat too much at that damn bakery, she said sometimes.

Forget it, he said, you're just right. They had had this conversation a score of times. She would wrinkle her short little nose at him, pushing her bandeau up on her head. Ever since she was in high school she had worn her curly, almost frizzy, fair hair the same way, the wide white bandeau clipped to her head with hairpins.

It was during one of Samson's stand-down times that a call came in the evening to say that someone was laid off sick, and he was needed up at the tower sharp the next morning. Doreen had taken the call, and without even asking him had said he would do an extra shift. He couldn't understand this. It wasn't like her. She'd always let him make the decisions, and this was his job, not hers, she was talking about here. Perhaps it was working in the bakery: she'd got used to telling those girls what to do. It felt odd, though, as if some piece of his life had been jolted out of shape.

When he had come home the week before, he'd done their trick, their 'thing' as he called it, and she had turned on her heel at the bedroom door. 'I'm not up to much today,' she said. And that had been that. She was sorry, she said later, she had a really heavy period, clots as big as side plates; perhaps she was getting the change early. Only he didn't think she had her period because, as a rule, he could smell her when they lay in bed and there was no smell; she just lay on her side with her back to him, and would not let him put his arm over her. In the morning, her face was grey, the way it was when she was pregnant. But that was a long time ago. The first baby had come when she was eighteen, and the last when she was twenty-four. Later that day, sitting up among the treetops, he supposed he must have imagined it.

Then he saw it, a sudden snake gleaming in the trees. Wildfire, or that's how it looked to him, because it was close to the tower and one of his favourite trees had exploded nearby, then the flames leapt a firebreak and began snatching others in their wake. He made a hurried phone call, before clambering down from the tower. This was against the rules, because spotters were supposed to stay at their post and report the progress of the fire, but he couldn't resist it, he needed to save the trees.

THE PLACE WHERE THE TWO women were to stay was a narrow terrace house, so close to the neighbours that you could almost touch the walls next door, a house that land agents probably described as full of character, but the charm, if there was any, didn't translate into comfort. The room where they were to sleep was narrow and on the dark side of the house. Their two single beds were covered with beige candlewick spreads. Above one stood a bookshelf with books that the children of the house had apparently discarded. *Dorothy's Little Tribe*, some Ethel Turners and *The Little Red Schoolbook*, an odd combination. Or perhaps the books belonged to their mother, Viv, who had met them at the airport off the Rotorua plane. Dishevelled and apologetic, she was dressed in a navy blue suit with a straight skirt and padded shoulders. She was sorry, she said, but she got held up at work and she knew they could do without waiting around at the airport at a time like this. Were they okay? She asked this often, which, they tell each other later on, is stupid. On the way from the airport, Rachel had to ask her to stop the car because she needed to throw up, but they were in a no stopping zone until they got past the roundabout at Cobham Drive and by then it was almost too late. But Rachel had had practice at eating toast under her mother's watchful eye in the mornings, and slipping to the bathroom between bites, so she managed to hold on. Doreen had dark circles under her eyes. She hadn't slept the night before, she told them, and she was just so damn tired.

Viv was one of the Sisters Overseas volunteers who picked up pregnant women from the outlying areas and delivered them to the Sydney flight that left Wellington at six in the morning. At midnight on the same day, they were picked up from the incoming plane. SOS sent groups on Tuesdays and Fridays. This was a better arrangement, so they could support each other after their terminations. Some day, Viv said, we'll win the battle and get legal terminations in New Zealand. After that there were awkward silences. The SOS woman did not ask questions. As they had driven through the suburbs,

Doreen said in wonder: 'I thought it would be nicer than Toke. I thought Wellington would be different.'

There was nothing awful about the house, but it felt damp and the absence of light in the rooms seemed oppressive. Nor did Viv appear to have much time for housework. Piles of boys' clothing, washed and unwashed, took up space on most of the chairs. Viv sighed, and swept them aside to make space. Some smudgy paintings hung in the sitting room. Doreen studied them with curiosity.

'Did your children do these?' she asked Viv.

Viv looked at her, almost speechless. When she saw Doreen was serious, she said, 'They're quite expensive, actually. My husband got the house in Kelburn when we separated. It's pretty flash, he thought he'd got the better of the bargain. I got the pictures, but they're sky rocketing in value. Who knows, I might get the last laugh yet.'

Rachel didn't like the paintings much either. Her mother had Austen Deans landscapes in her blue and white sitting room. But she saw that busy, weary Viv belonged to a whole different kind of world from the ones that she and Doreen, in their different ways, knew and understood. Her mother's friends were smart, in their own eyes, but they would be scornful of people who admired modern art and got involved in causes like sending girls off to have abortions in Australia, and read the kind of books Viv did. Education, in Penelope's eyes, was a step towards professional status for a man and a better marriage for a girl. Rachel sensed that the enlightened Viv would take a poor view of this.

For the past two months Rachel had watched Mark with a fierce, urgent gaze full of longing, admiring his ginger hair, the way it curled back from his forehead, his light hazel eyes, the rust of freckles across his face. She was sure she was in love with him, and certain he could only return it, even though he barely acknowledged her presence in the bank these days. It was understandable, of course, what with his wife expecting any moment. She wondered if both the babies would have hair the colour of his. But he must know how she felt. Nobody could have made love like they had and not understood that they were right together.

Mark had said, when she told him, 'Don't look at me, it's not mine.'

When Rachel said that yes, it was his, he said everyone at the bank knew she was a right little player. Why else would he have made a pass at her. He bet it could have been any of half a dozen blokes she'd had it off with.

'I've only had two others,' she said. 'That wasn't even this year.' And then she had begun to cry, while he sat without moving, except for the drumming of his fingers on the steering wheel. They were parked at Sulphur Point, the hot volcanic edge of the lake, where the ground was a dirty yellow and gulls wheeled over the rubbish tip that lay beyond it. 'I thought I was pretty careful,' he said. 'I pulled out.'

'You did not,' Rachel cried. 'You couldn't get enough.'

They started down the track of an ugly quarrel then, and in the end he sat defeated, and asked her what she was going to do about it.

When she was silent, looking out the car window, he said, 'You don't expect me to do anything, do you?'

'My parents will find out soon,' she said.

'Jesus. You're not going to tell them about me?'

After a while, she agreed that, no, she probably wouldn't tell them. His mother-in-law played tennis with Penelope.

'I'll see what I can find out. There must be somebody who can fix you up.'

'I expect I'll die of sepsis.'

'Shut up, bitch.'

'Don't talk to me like that.'

'I said shut it, Rachel.'

The day after that, at work, he gave her a slip of paper with a phone number in Wellington. 'My sister gave it to me,' he said stiffly. 'Only you didn't hear that.'

THE FIRE WAS EXTINGUISHED ALMOST as fast as it had started, or that's how it appeared to Samson, because there was no time to stop and think, just the whirling smoke to contend with, the scorching beautiful flames, the beating of the ground until his arms felt as if they would break, and then he was back up the tower watching for hot spots while the fire crew finished off the job. He expected a reprimand but his boss came in and said, 'We've got it covered, Samson. You want to get home now, get yourself cleaned up, grab some rest.' He was needed again the next day, so he had got off lightly. The boss reckoned that the fire looked like arson, and if someone had got away with one, they would want more, and Samson knew that was true. He could understand that. His hands holding the steering wheel before him were blackened as he drove home. There was a curious lightness in his head.

VIV VOLUNTEERED TO MAKE PASTA, were they all right with that?

Doreen didn't think she could face anything to eat, thanks very much, but Rachel was suddenly famished and tried some lasagne, and would have had a second helping except that Viv's two teenage sons had arrived home and were starving. The boys looked at them sideways, knowingly and with what Rachel figured was dislike. In the course of the conversation it surfaced that Viv and her ex shared the boys week and week about.

Viv said, 'Just ignore the boys in the morning. They'll be asleep on the sofas in the sitting room. We'll sneak past them just after four.'

'I think I'll turn in now,' Doreen said. 'If we're going to be out of here at four.' Doreen knew about early starts at the bakery; she knew that you needed sleep to cope with the day ahead, but she didn't tell the others this. Her face was blank and stony.

'You're welcome to watch some television if you like,' Viv said.

Rachel saw that the boys wouldn't like anything of the sort. She said, hastily, that she would go to bed, too. She and Doreen undressed with their backs to each other, without speaking. Viv had left electric blankets on, for which Rachel was thankful; it was so much colder here in Wellington than at home.

When the light was off she lay on her side, waiting to hear the other woman's breathing deepen into sleep, only it didn't happen. An awful stillness had settled in the room. The muffled movements of Viv and her children lay beyond the closed door, and, in the house on the other side of them, the sound of a quarrel could be heard, a woman shouting at her children to go to bed. But within the room, it was as if a vacuum had formed. Both she and Doreen were trying to hold their breath. Rachel gritted her teeth and thought, *Do not cry.* At home her parents would be out on the verandah. She imagined Penelope saying to her father, thank goodness, Rachel has finally come to her senses. She had had friends in for coffee the morning before Rachel left, and she had almost sung with the good news. *Rachel has left the bank. She's off to Wellington to see about her courses at university next year.*

This was more or less true. Rachel had left the bank the week before. There had been a leaving afternoon tea for her, and a present that the staff had pitched in for: a set of French hand cream and matching talcum powder and soap. The manager had made a speech, saying what a useful member of staff she had been, and how the customers would miss her, and that there would always be a place for her behind the counter if she decided life in the city didn't suit her.

Earlier in the week, Mark had given her eight-hundred dollars and changed some of it into Australian money for her. She should count herself lucky, he said, because you had to show your airline ticket at the bank to get foreign currency; that was how he found out about his sister, the silly bitch. A pair of silly bitches, if you asked him. At least his sister had got married a few months afterwards, and if Rachel had any sense she'd find herself a man. There should be plenty in Wellington. It was a relief to him that she was getting out of it. She was too weary to remonstrate with him any more, he could say what he liked. None of it made any difference now. A part of her was still making excuses for him. He had had to find the money in a hurry, and had no idea how he was going to pay the mortgage for the next couple of months. Just what he needed, with the baby coming. Rachel had some money of her own; she could have got the rest from her parents, only she would have had to explain, make something up. Mark thought this was too big a risk. It was worth finding the money to get it sorted, he said. In return, she had promised to leave the bank, get as far away as possible. She'd put off thinking about university but now she promised herself she would.

She choked on a sob in the narrow bedroom of Viv's house. The polyester pillowslip was already wet from her steady silent tears.

In the darkness, Doreen said, 'We'll be all right,'

'I'm frightened,' Rachel said.

'Yeah. I'd never been on a plane until today. That was bad enough. But what about this big one tomorrow? All the way to another country.'

'It's not that,' said Rachel, who had been on several planes before. 'It'll hurt, won't it?'

'Not much, I reckon. It won't be so bad as having a baby. It half kills me. I've had three, all boys. I couldn't go through that again.'

'Is that why you're having your abortion?'

'Go to sleep,' Doreen said, her tone sharp. 'You need to rest.' Very soon Rachel heard her breathing turning into shallow snores.

In the morning, the whole suburb was blanketed with fog so thick it was almost impossible to see even the street lamps ahead as Viv drove them towards the airport, inching her way along at a crawl. She had tried to phone the airport but all the lines were busy. 'Oh my God,' she said, several times. 'What if the airport's closed? What if the plane can't get away?'

'Can we go the next day?' Rachel asked. She was nauseous again.

'It's possible. I hope not though.'

'I should get back to Toke tomorrow,' Doreen said, sounding panicked.

'Try and stay calm,' Viv said, although she didn't sound any calmer than Doreen.

The closer they got to the airport, the more dense the fog appeared. When they got out of the car it felt tangible, like a shawl thrown around their faces. They learnt at the counter that the earliest the plane might leave was midday, and by that time it would be too late for the women to go to Australia, have their operation and board the evening flight back to Wellington.

SOS managed to arrange for flights the next day. Doreen was in two minds as to whether she would go or not. She and Viv held an urgent private conversation among the milling chaos of people who hadn't been able to board the flight.

Doreen was very pale when she returned to Rachel's side. 'I have to go to Sydney,' she said to Rachel. 'I don't have any choice. It's funny, isn't it, you forget that it's real, you forget why you're here.'

Viv drove them back to the house. 'Go back to bed,' she said. They knew she meant keep out of the way of the boys. Later, when the house was quiet, and everyone had left, Doreen said, 'Let's get out of here, go to town. I might as well see something while I'm here.' The fog had rolled away, and the sky blitzed the house with sunlight. Overhead they heard the roar of a big plane.

As their bus carried them into the city, Doreen began to relax, asking Rachel if she'd had trouble getting the money, because that had been the biggest drama for her, and how could you be sure the people in the bank wouldn't talk about her going away? Rachel said that it was more than the tellers' jobs were worth. And then she found herself telling Doreen how she had worked at the bank and everything that had happened to her so far, and how she was supposed to be in Wellington looking at university courses.

Doreen grimaced when she heard about Mark. 'You *worked* with him? It never pays to get your meat with your bread, Rachel.' Although she was more cautious, she did tell Rachel that she was twelve weeks gone and if she didn't go to Sydney tomorrow they wouldn't take her at the clinic. It was just as well she had had some savings, she added, and that was all she was going to say on the subject.

The city was busy and the shops looked full of promise. They peered in clothing shops and wished they had their normal figures so they could try things on. 'Not long now,' Doreen said, and squeezed Rachel's arm. At the beginning of Lambton Quay they came to a milliner's shop, full of the kind of hats you could wear to the races.

'We can try these on, at any rate,' Rachel said. 'C'mon.'

The woman behind the counter asked if they were shopping for a special occasion, and Rachel said that yes, they were, a real celebration. She chose a hat with a short brim and a garland of ruffled ribbon around it. 'Gorgeous,' said the assistant. Rachel found a big lacy navy blue picture hat, its front brim pinned back with a pink gauze rose, and handed it to Doreen.

'Off with that bandeau,' she ordered, and in a moment Doreen was shaking her fair hair loose.

'You've got lovely hair,' Rachel said. 'Why don't you wear it like that all the time?'

Doreen put the hat on, staring at herself in the mirror. 'I can't believe it,' she breathed.

'Mother of the bride, I take it?' said the assistant.

Doreen looked shocked and took the hat off. 'I'm sorry,' she stammered. 'We shouldn't have bothered you.'

Outside in the sunlight, she was still shaking. Rachel put her arm through the other woman's. 'I wouldn't mind you for a mother,' she said. 'Honestly.'

'You would,' Doreen said, her voice short again.

'Oh, go on,' Rachel said, 'it's kind of funny. One extreme to the other.' A lunchtime demonstration was in progress, university students protesting about war, unemployment, apartheid — it was hard to tell what it was all about, because the placards carried different messages. Doreen and Rachel had arrived at the entrance to the cable car that carried people up the hill to the university. Doreen had lightened up again. 'We should go up there,' she said. 'I've heard about this cable car, it's like the one in San Francisco or somewhere. You could tell your mother you really had been to the university.'

As the red cable car clattered up the hillside, Rachel felt suddenly exhilarated. Next year she would be living here, among all this bustle. She would do a science degree, and wear jeans and sweaters each day, with a bag full of books slung across her shoulder. The brick bank seemed far away.

AT FIRST SAMSON THOUGHT DOREEN was just late back from work. He wished she was there waiting for him, not because he wanted her to jump into bed with him — something told him his little joke, their private 'thing', was over for the time being, perhaps for good — but because he wanted to tell her about the fire, about the suspected arson and about how he had beaten the flames. He wanted her to put gauze bandages on his burnt hand, the way she had for the kids when they were little, and dab cream on his face. Doreen knew what to do, she always had.

Instead he attended to it himself. There was a quietness, an absence, about the house that felt remarkable, and he felt fear wash over him for the first time that day. Yet everything around him looked normal, untouched, in its place. Doreen's car was in the garage. The cat prowled around his feet, hungry and discontented.

At seven o'clock, he picked up the keys of the ute and drove into town. A sense of urgency had overtaken him.

The lights at the bakery were all out but still he banged on the door and called out. When nobody replied, he thought about going over to the Isaacs' house to see if they knew where she was. But that didn't seem like a good idea. A man should know where his wife was. And then he thought that this was one of the first times he had come home earlier than he was expected. Sure, he had given her 'surprises', but they weren't real ones, except for that once. She always knew what day to expect him. Perhaps she had gone to visit a friend. Maybe she did this sometimes, when he was away. He wondered if there were more things he should have asked her about her life.

Back at the house, he found Mary Isaacs, the baker's wife, feeding the cat in his kitchen. She dropped the spoon when she saw him. 'What are you doing here, Samson?' she said, straightening herself.

She was a wiry woman with white hair and big quick eyes, but now she looked scared of him.

'I could ask you the same.'

'I heard about the fire,' she said. 'Are you all right?'

'Where's my wife?'

Mary said that Doreen had gone to see a doctor in Rotorua — nothing to worry about, just a little lump she had discovered — and Mary had told her just to go right away, so that she could get it cleared up. She couldn't get an appointment until late in the day.

'Look,' Mary said, 'she didn't want to worry you, Samson. I told her to stay overnight.'

'Why didn't she take her car?' he asked, perplexed. 'It's not serious, is it?'

'I'm sure it's not. She must have got a lift.'

'Well, who did she go with?'

'Look, Samson, I can't tell you that. I might have got it wrong.'

'She wouldn't have gone on the bus?'

Mary took a deep breath. 'Oh, now you mention it, I think she did,' she said, and walked out quickly. Later, she told Doreen, I walked out of that damn house of yours too fast.

POTTS POINT. KINGS CROSS. THE riot of old houses, and eccentric-looking people in the street and young men with needles hanging out of their arms and women leaning against doors, vamping at strangers. Sydney Harbour, as dark blue as posters Doreen had seen of the Mediterranean Sea, she said, and so much more exotic than she'd imagined. She gazed around her, eyes full of wonder. Rachel had been to Sydney before, although not here at the far fringe because her parents didn't think it a healthy place to take a young girl. Her hand was still sore from being squeezed by Doreen's on the plane. She had given a small shriek on take-off, and sat fidgeting and frightened when they came in to land. Doreen clung so hard that her wedding ring felt as if it was cutting Rachel's palm.

But now, as they travelled through the city, driven by a person from the Contact organisation who met the women when they arrived in Sydney, her face had become strangely still, almost peaceful, as if the ordeal was over. 'I might as well have a good look,' she said, 'I don't expect I'll get here again.'

'Of course you will,' Rachel said, because it was just something to say, and reassuring Doreen seemed to have become her duty, even though her heart was full of terror and a longing to turn back.

'I don't reckon so. Not now,' Doreen said, closing her eyes for a moment. Just as they were about to leave Viv's house that morning, something odd had happened. A phone call with a message for Doreen. Nobody was supposed to know where they were, except for a relative or friend to get in touch with if there was a real emergency. (Rachel hadn't given her name to anyone. Only Mark knew where she was and his was the last name she would have put down. She figured that if she didn't return from this trip, sooner or later someone would track her down. The friendly family doctor, whose referral letter she had in her purse, would have told Penelope she was pregnant in three seconds flat.) The call for Doreen had been from someone called Mary. She had asked Viv to give Doreen a message: *Samson came home early.*

Rachel couldn't help overhearing, because Viv was puffy-eyed and shooing them towards the car when she told Doreen. Two early mornings like this would kill her, she said. When Doreen got the message, she appeared to hesitate again. Then she had shrugged, and said, 'I might have known.' She had followed Viv and Rachel out to the car.

Rachel put her hand on her stomach and tried not to think about why she was here, about how much she wanted this baby, and how she could have loved its little silky gingery head, cradled in the crook of her elbow.

As if reading her thoughts, Doreen said, 'I'll take care of you.' She appeared totally recovered from her earlier panic.

And then they were at the door of the clinic, with its sterile white rooms, and men and women in white coats, their voices soothing. Before long Rachel was asleep and when she came round from the anaesthetic, there was a big bloodied wad of gauze bandage between her legs, and her body felt empty, drained of everything, as if she was just an idea of herself hovering above.

RACHEL AND DOREEN DIDN'T HAVE seats side by side on the plane going back to Wellington. Doreen was sitting several rows back. She looked normal, just as she had the day before. Two other young women were delivered to the check-in by the Contact people; they looked as white and barely able to stand as Rachel.

'You'll be all right,' Doreen said again to Rachel. 'Just hold on. It's only three hours and you can have another lie-down.'

She disappeared towards the back of the plane. A stewardess took a blanket out of an overhead locker and put it over Rachel. 'Press the button if you need any help,' she said quietly.

A young man, perhaps in his mid-twenties, stacked his bag above and took his seat beside her. He had fervent brown eyes, and a short back and sides haircut, although these were details she didn't observe closely that night. The lights in the plane blurred before her, like the lights in the operating theatre, dim haloes, frail and shadowy. Halfway across the Tasman Ocean, she found herself shivering and calling out for water. The man pressed the call button.

When the water came, he held the cup to her lips, because her hands were shaking so much. 'It's all right, Rachel,' he said. 'I know what you've been through. I see it all the time.'

'How do you know my name?' Rachel's teeth were clenched together.

He laughed easily. 'Your name's on your bag. You're not very good at travelling incognito, are you?' He introduced himself as Joshua. He was a typewriter salesman who crossed the Tasman on a regular basis, checking and ordering new stock from a Sydney warehouse. 'Everyone can pick out you girls on this flight. Don't worry. Give me your hand,' he murmured. 'It's all right, I won't put it under the blanket.' Rachel did as she was told, hypnotised by his voice. 'Jesus loves you,' he said. She felt a huge wave of drowsiness wash over her. From far off, she heard him say something about sin, and that she could be forgiven, if she followed the Lord's way from now on.

'This girl needs a doctor,' Joshua said to Viv, who had moved forward from the crowd when Rachel appeared through Customs. He had gripped her arm in the queue so she didn't fall over. He was holding onto the overnight bag.

'Oh shit,' Viv said. 'Thanks a bundle.'

None of it was as bad as it first appeared. The Sisters had a doctor on hand who examined Rachel and put her to bed at her house for the night. The haemorrhaging abated by the morning: she didn't need a transfusion, which was the big fear everyone had about the girls on the SOS flights. When she went to pick up the rest of her things from Viv's place, Doreen had already left.

Her period was really bad, she told Penelope, when she arrived home on a later flight. She would go to bed and rest up a bit. Yes, she had liked Wellington, and the people at the university were great and she would enrol for next year. In the meantime she would get a temporary job; perhaps one of the banks would take her on in Wellington. 'No, Mum,' she said firmly, 'I don't plan to make a career in banks. I promise I'm going to do a science degree.'

This might have happened then, if Joshua hadn't arrived one afternoon the following week. Rachel had gone to town to pick up a few odds and ends: a card to send to Viv, some cotton tops for the summer that was nearly upon them, new panties because her old ones were mostly ruined from all the blood. She shopped at the other end of town from the bank. The birth notice for Mark's new son had been in the paper the day before. Mark and his wife 'welcomed a strapping cute guy. Mother and baby well'. Rachel walked into her mother's blue kitchen, her arms laden. She had bought a bunch of irises for Penelope. She thought she owed her something, even if her mother didn't know it. An apology, perhaps. Penelope stood at the bench, wearing a gingham print blouse, a blue denim skirt and canvas slides, her face dark.

'You might like to introduce me to your friend, Rachel.' She was incandescent with anger.

Joshua was perched on a stool at the breakfast bar, his grin wide and white like an advertisement for toothpaste. He looked like a well-groomed teddy bear, not at all evangelical. His suit and striped tie were the same ones he had worn on the plane.

'You followed me,' Rachel said.

'I had to make sure you were all right. I explained to your mother how we'd met, that's all.' His smile was very sure. She saw then how intense his eyes really were. 'You met on the *Sydney plane*,' Penelope said. 'A likely story. Is he the father?'

When Rachel said no, of course he wasn't, and Joshua had tsk-tsked and said that he was a man who had saved himself for marriage, Rachel gave Mark's name. Penelope clutched the bench, strain lines appearing like cords in her smooth neck. 'You'd better get lost,' she said, 'before your father gets home.'

Rachel's older sister was practising the piano in the next room. Rachel hadn't known she was home. It sounded as if she was playing the Wedding March, although perhaps she imagined this. Whatever it was, it was tiddly-pom music. Soon her younger sister would be here, throwing her books on the table the way she always did. And, after that, there would be drama and tears, all the lovely order of her mother's perfect house collapsed in ruins, her sister's wedding spoilt. Sooner or later, before the night was over, Rachel would have to walk out of this house, whether ordered to or not.

'I don't think that's Christian,' Joshua said. 'Rachel can be saved.'

'Really?' answered Penelope. 'So save her then.'

'YOUR MISSUS HITCHHIKING?' SAMSON'S MATE said to him at the Cosmopolitan Club. He'd gone in to have a drink and steady his nerves before he went to see Mary Isaacs again. It was three in the afternoon. First he felt a fool that his wife had gone to the doctor's and he didn't know about it, but other people did, and second he was crazy with worry that there was something bad wrong with her. The night before he had turned the house over, and now realised that certain things were missing. Like her savings book. Their savings. He had rung their daughter-in-law in Auckland and asked if she had heard from Doreen, and when she said no, he had said, as casually as he could, 'Oh, that's right, she said she was going up to Rotorua. I forgot.' He guessed there was no point in ringing the other boys. He didn't think she was missing, not with Mary Isaacs prowling round his house, feeding his cat. His hands felt raw and worse than earlier in the day.

'What are you on about?' Samson said. His mate was half cut. It was his week off, and he often went on the piss around lunchtime. Samson thought him a fool because piss took the edge off things, blurred your vision. He worried sometimes that his mate might not spot a fire the way he would.

'I heard she took a truck ride up the line with Joe Blake.'

'Oh yeah, she mentioned something about that.'

'Oh, did she now?'

'What about Joe?' Samson said at last. An image of Joe Paki in his logging truck swam before him, a big man with a barrel chest covered in thick black hair, copper skin, a gold tooth in the corner of his mouth. 'Mate, you got yourself a girl's job up there in the trees, I reckon,' he'd said to Samson one time when he saw him. He never had liked the bastard, even when they were at school.

'Yeah, well, mate,' the other man said. 'Forget I said it.'

'No way, man. What about Joe?' Samson said each of these last three words with slow emphasis.

'Nothing to it, mate. She and Joe are pals, aren't they? I guess he was just giving her a lift.'

Samson downed his beer and walked outside. The air was clear and crisp. Soon the day would be closing in. He glanced down at his bandaged hands. He no longer felt any pain.

He got in the ute, and drove to the bakery. Mary Isaacs was behind the counter, standing in for Doreen. 'Tell Doreen I hope her lump is all right now,' he said. 'Tell her I've gone up the tower.'

'IT'S ALL RIGHT, I'M LEAVING,' Rachel said, the afternoon Joshua turned up, although she would think later that neither of them meant what they were saying, that somehow they could have made up the quarrel and their lives could have carried on, if not in the same way, at least with understanding for each other. Her mother had had a shock.

'I told you, I'm going to Wellington,' Rachel said.

'I can give you a lift,' Joshua said. 'It's on my way.' As though it was just a trip to the shops.

When her mother said nothing, Rachel turned and followed him out. He was already in his car, the motor idling. She hesitated.

'You'll need some clothes,' he said. 'I can wait.'

This was how she found herself travelling south with a man she barely knew. She had gone back inside without speaking to her mother and thrown some clothes in a suitcase. As she put the bag in the back of his car, she looked around at the garden and the wide verandah of her parents' home. She couldn't believe she was doing this. If only her father was there, he might put a stop to it, but he was away in Auckland on a case.

Joshua kept driving until they came to Taihape, where he pulled in to buy food. It was too late to get anything but hamburgers and milkshakes. They sat in the car in a side street, and when they'd eaten, Joshua closed his eyes and leant over to kiss her. His breath smelt of vanilla, and he didn't open his mouth. When she poked her tongue out experimentally to push between his lips, he took her wrist and shook his head.

'We should get married,' he said.

Rachel was shocked. She only wanted to marry Mark, but she couldn't think of anything else except to agree.

A pastor conducted their small wedding in a church hall that looked like a schoolroom. Daddy was very disappointed, her mother said on the phone. Rachel could see the way her lips would be tightening. She wondered what he had been told. Could Rachel imagine how difficult this would be for Penelope to explain to her friends? When Rachel didn't respond, Penelope told her anyway. She would say that Rachel always was different and now she had committed her life to God and to Joshua, and that she had been thinking for a long time about doing missionary work, and she and her new husband would be off soon to New Guinea. This was, in fact, what Joshua said when he phoned Penelope to discuss the marriage. Only first he had to give up selling typewriters and become an elder in his church. They would practise abstinence during this time so that when they became one person, Rachel would be as chaste as a virgin. This last part wasn't mentioned to Penelope.

Rachel took a job filing invoices in a government department in Wellington, travelling into town on the train each day. She and Joshua lived in a complex of houses in Lower Hutt, occupied by members of his church. On Sundays, they attended church meetings in a hall and sang and clapped their hands above their heads, shouting 'Praise the Lord'. The women wore headscarves and did as they were told, at least in public, but in private they had their own ritual tasks set apart as women's work. One of these was examining each other for signs of fertility. Rachel knew her bed had been turned back some nights when she got into it. She sensed their floury domestic hands in her sheets, believed she could smell the rank thickets of their armpits. Rachel hated being near these women. They suggested she was not trying hard enough. Was she really submitting to her husband, or was she wayward? Perhaps it was time she stopped going in to work among those heathens. Rachel thought, If you only knew. She and Joshua had not consummated their marriage, although he had begun to fumble wordlessly around her legs at nights. Some days she thought about dying, about some way out.

One night, he said, 'Help me.' She rolled to the far side of the bed, feeling sick from his touch.

A letter arrived for her at work the following day, readdressed in Penelope's handwriting. Her mother had written to her once or twice in the two years since she married Joshua, impersonal little letters with accounts of the garden, a picture of her older sister's wedding and another of her younger sister receiving a prize. No mention of her father. It was strange to see her maiden name crossed out, alongside her married name. She felt as if that part of life had ceased to exist.

The letter was from Doreen. A picture of a chubby dark child with a mass of curls fell out of the envelope. Doreen had written: *I often think about you. I hope everything turned out good for you. As you probably guessed, I kept my baby. I guess I got lucky cos she turned out a girl which I always wanted. I thought Samson, that's my husband, might kill me, but he never said one single word. He is a fire spotter and he stayed up the mountain in the tower for six weeks after I got back. There was a wildfire in the forest that day I went to Australia, which is how Samson found out that I'd gone, cos he came home when he wasn't expected. When he came back down for Christmas, he was calm and never said boo, not even when his kid wasn't blond, like the others. Her other dad isn't around to say anything. He got killed when a log slipped off the cradle on his truck not long after the baby. I'm real sad about that but perhaps it's all for the best. I called my little girl Sydney, by the way. Some people say, how come you gave your girl a boy's name but that's what I wanted to call her, you even get film actresses named after cities these days.*

Anyway, kid, take care of yourself. I guess we both got what we wanted that day. Funny the way things work out. Love Doreen.

Rachel gathered up her bag and coat and left the office. 'I'll be back soon,' she said, although it was against the rules to leave the building. She walked quickly along Lambton Quay. Students were heading for university. They didn't all look happy or careless; in fact some of them looked tired and poor, as if they had been up at all-night jobs, or preparing for exams. But they looked freer than she felt. They looked to her as if they had *got what they wanted*. She closed her eyes and the ugly scene in her mother's kitchen swam into focus.

Instead of returning to the office, she took the cable car up the hill to the university and enrolled to do her science degree. She didn't go home that night. She phoned Joshua and told him she wasn't committed to him at all. She had also seen a lawyer about having their marriage annulled.

Later, she met Elliot, an architect, and when she was thirty-five they had their first son, although it had been difficult for her to conceive, and then a second, who arrived with ease the following year. She and Elliot hadn't married. Rachel had decided she would never marry anyone again, and this didn't bother Elliot.

AND HERE IS A WOMAN called Sydney in the sitting room of Rachel and Elliot's house, one that had featured in *House and Garden* magazine. More years have passed. Rachel is a lean sinewy woman, a marine biologist, lightly tanned from working outdoors. In her spare time she gardens and helps refugee teenagers learn to read and write in English. She and Elliot travel all over the world, looking at beautiful buildings in cities as diverse as Chicago and Kuala Lumpur and Paris. They have holidays in the south of France and drink wine and hang about in cafés and watch people going about their lives. Their sons are tall and slim. The first one is in his third year of law, the second just beginning a degree in building sciences.

Sydney sits on the edge of a leather couch, looking at her feet, then glancing around her with what Rachel thinks is a feral look. Her copper-toned skin is devoid of make-up, her hair caught in a trail of dreadlocks that fan from an elastic band across her shoulders, as if she is a teenager, although Rachel knows she must be in her mid-thirties. She is dressed in baggy jeans and an old T-shirt. Circlets of tattoos embroider her arms.

Michael, the older of Rachel's sons, wanders through the sitting room. 'Right there, Ma?' he says, trying to disguise his curiosity.

'This is my son Michael. Michael, Sydney.'

'Hi there, you doing the ESOL course?'

Sydney's expression darkens. 'I'm not some nigger,' she says.

'Of course not,' Rachel says, flustered. 'I do help some people with their English.'

Rachel wonders whether she should try to explain her refugee work, but she suspects that that would make it worse. She sees how far apart her and Doreen's children are, that the gap between them is extreme. And a phrase comes back to her, from that day when she and Doreen went to look at the shops in Wellington. Mothers. One extreme to another. Rachel no longer knows what extreme really means. That's a bit extreme, Ma, her boys might say to her, but extreme is a place inhabited by other people, like refugees who have been through the hell of war, or like kids who are lost in their lives and can't find their way back. Rachel has found her way back.

'I wouldn't have thought Doreen would know where to find me these days. It's been a long time.'

'Mum? She died when I was twelve. She got cancer.'

'I'm so sorry,' Rachel says, apologising again. 'How on earth did you find me?'

'Easy as. Your sister still lives in Rotorua. It wasn't that hard. You used to write to Mum,' Sydney says.

'Did I? Well, I might have written to her once. It was years ago.' But immediately she finds herself remembering all her girlish outpourings in the letter she had written in reply to Doreen's, telling her about Joshua, how things had gone so wrong since their trip to Australia, and how she was trying to get her life back on track. And yes, the letter would have carried her maiden name on the back of it, the one she still uses, as does her younger sister, who never married. She and this sister see each other from time to time. They are friends now, reconciled in late middle age.

'Samson gave me some of Mum's stuff before he died, bits of paper and junk. The boys got the good stuff, her dishes and her mum's china cabinet, but that was Samson for you. Why would he give me anything?'

'Didn't you get on with him?'

Sydney's lip curls. 'You could say that.'

'So how can I help you?' Rachel says. The conversation isn't going well, she can tell from Sydney's expression, and she feels herself floundering.

'Just lately I've been thinking why am I keeping all Mum's old shit. I was going to throw it out. Then I found this letter you'd written to her and I figured perhaps you knew who my father was.'

'Oh.' It's all Rachel can think of saying. From the wide window, she sees Michael at the far end of the garden, collecting up branches from a tree that's been pruned, something he'd promised his father he would do. She still has Doreen's letter. It's sitting in a box in her wardrobe with her important documents, like her will and her passport, her birth certificate and divorce papers. She's not sure why she has kept it.

'So *do* you know?' Sydney says insistently. 'Look, I've got a kid of my own. She's ten. Her name's Gloria. I wanted her to have a real pretty name, not like mine. And do you know what she brings home from school? A flipping project about genealogy. Genealogy.' She repeats the word syllable by syllable, as if making sure that Rachel appreciates her understanding of the English language. 'Who are your parents? Well, that's a laugh, half the kids in the class can't tell you who their dad is. I keep in touch with hers.' She rolls her forearm over, so Rachel can read one of the tattoos. Rachel understands it represents a gang, although she's not sure which one and doesn't like to ask. 'So then they want to know about your grandparents. And I thought, What a load of crap. She's not dumb, she's seen the pictures of my mum and Samson, she knows we're a different colour.'

'Did Gloria ever meet Samson?'

The woman glowers, and shakes her head. 'I wouldn't have let her near him.'

'Doreen told me he accepted you when you were born, treated you as his own.'

Sydney laughs then, a disjointed unpleasant sound, as if ripped from deep down in her lungs. 'You know what Samson used to call me?'

'No.'

'Fire bug. Bloody little fire-bug baby.'

'I see.' In her agitation, Rachel stands up. 'I don't know who your father was.' She walks to the window. 'Didn't your mother have a friend called Mary Isaacs?' she asks, turning back to the room.

'Long gone. So you do know something?'

Rachel pauses again, troubled by the woman's ferocity, her strangeness.

'Samson hated me,' Sydney says, as if this will shake Rachel into some revelation. 'He never said it, because he wanted to keep her, but it was in his eyes, you could tell. And when she couldn't hear, he'd say it real mean and quiet. Fire bug.'

Rachel wishes Michael would finish his task and come inside. Sydney's eyes travel down the garden, following hers.

'Well, no secrets in his cupboard, eh? I'll bet he doesn't know what his old lady got up to once upon a time.'

Rachel feels her anger flaring. 'That's none of your business.'

'You've got a pretty nice life here.' Sydney's voice has become bitter.

'You don't know what it was like.' Rachel stops herself, incapable of explaining, and why should she? None of it matters any more. She is where she is, burnt but not destroyed. 'I don't know your father's name,' she says, 'but I think he drove a logging truck. Doreen told me he was dead.'

Sydney has jumped up, her eyes widening. 'When? When did this happen?'

'It must have been when you were little.'

'Did the bastard kill him?' She is digging in her pocket for cigarettes and a lighter.

Rachel had been about to fetch Doreen's letter but stops in her tracks. She understands that Sydney is talking about Samson.

'I've told you all I know,' she says. 'Really.'

Sydney's face is full of rage. She lights her cigarette and inhales, then blows a long stream of smoke towards Rachel. Rachel steps back and Sydney flicks the lighter on and off. Some of Elliot's drawings lie on the table beside them. Rachel has to restrain herself from snatching them away to safety. Sydney catches her glance and rolls her eyes. She drops the lighter in her pocket. 'Scared you, eh?'

'This isn't about me,' Rachel says.

'Nah. Fair enough.' Sydney's shoulders slump, the anger draining away. 'I'd just hoped, you know, there might have been something you could tell me. I guess that's a start.'

Rachel is struggling to find the right words. 'I can see it must be hard on your own. With your daughter.' There is an almost imperceptible change in Sydney's expression. Rachel takes a deep breath. 'I couldn't have managed.'

Sydney throws Rachel a look of surprise. 'Times have changed,' she says.

'Yes,' says Rachel quietly. 'Thank goodness.'

'I'm on email,' Sydney says. 'I can leave you my address. If you think of anything.' Rachel hands her a piece of desk jotter, and she scribbles on it.

And then Sydney's gone, light and fleet of foot.

Her son walks through the garden towards her. 'Everything all right?'

'Yes, it's all right.' She has a sudden urge to hold him that she resists. Instead, she gives him a playful cuff.

'What did she want? That woman?'

'Oh, I don't know,' she says. 'Information. Peace of mind, I suppose.'

He gives her an odd look. 'Did you give it to her?' He's treating her words as a joke.

'I'm not sure.'

'You mean she'll be back?'

'Perhaps.' She will keep the letter for now. You did what you could.

Heaven Freezes

Simon and his daughter Kate are on their way to the supermarket when the sky changes from its ordinary cloud-strewn breezy Wellington look to a blue of such extraordinary radiance that for a moment he feels his heart freeze with the strange icy beauty of it.

This light has all the appearance of a blue rainbow. Beneath it, the surface of the harbour has become illuminated in such a way that a band of waves seems to lift from the ocean, as if moving towards them.

When the car is parked, father and daughter stand for some minutes absorbing what — it is clear now — is some optical illusion, a phenomenon of light, one they have never seen before. Around them in the car park, others are also staring. Perfect strangers call out to one another, saying, 'D'you see that? What do you make of that?'

A woman laughs nervously. 'Perhaps it's a plane falling,' she says.

There is a nervous twitch of shoulders. The supermarket is close to the flight path of planes. But there is no sign of things falling, no wreckage, no bangs.

'I reckon a space shuttle just flushed its toilet,' says a young man who has been collecting up trolleys, and everyone laughs, breaking the tension. But Simon cannot move, riveted to the warm asphalt. Kate stands particularly close to his elbow, as if she might somehow protect him. She has a stocky build, more like that of her several aunts than her mother, who was tall and dark, rangy and loose-limbed. Kate's sister, Janet, is like her, but she lives in Canada and Simon hasn't seen her in a long time. Soon, he hopes, he will visit her and hold his grandson. He sees him in little electronic moving pictures on his computer screen almost every day, but that is not the same. He sighs. So many of his decisions now depend on Stephanie's work. It may not suit her. She may feel offended if he goes off without her, but she may be too busy to go with him.

'We should start the shopping,' Kate says gently. 'Remember, you have the boys to pick up at three, and we promised Stephanie we'd make an early dinner so she can get away to her meeting.'

'She'll probably work through and we'll end up eating without her,' he says, and immediately regrets this seeming betrayal.

'We were going to start shopping for the lunch, too,' says Kate, as if she hasn't heard.

On Sunday it will be his birthday — his sixty-second — and there is to be a lunch party. The guests will all be his friends. Although he has lived in Wellington with Stephanie for three years now, they have never had a party where the guests were not her friends. She is the director of the international section of a bank and knows a great many people with money. Because of her work, she entertains managing directors of insurance companies and property developers, investors from city and country, and she finds it very helpful that Simon is from what she terms the rural sector, because there is always someone for these out-of-towners to talk to. She knows actors, a handful of writers and several film-makers. Not all of these people are rich, but knowing them appeals to those who are.

The suggestion for the gathering had been Kate's. We should do something special, she emailed when she knew she would be visiting. She lives in Australia — not as far away as Janet, but still he doesn't see her very often. Kate is a lawyer, independent and single. She has had some relationships but does not want to be committed to anyone, she says. Not until she meets the right person.

It grieves him that what she might really be saying is that even meeting the right person does not mean that love lasts for all time, or that you are certain to live happily ever after. That you may be abandoned when you least expect it.

Kate knows too much for her own good, Simon has told himself more than once. There are things he should discuss with her, but he puts it off. He promises himself that when he and the two girls are next together he will, but he can't see when that might be.

'You should have some friends over,' Stephanie said, when the subject of the birthday came up, and he agreed that yes, it would be nice, provided his birthday was not announced. What he would have liked more than anything was to go to a good restaurant with Stephanie and Kate, and let the day unfold around them. Except that Kate and Stephanie cannot be relied on to get along, and then there are Stephanie's boys to consider, and so he let it go, falling in with the plan. Drawing up a list of friends, though, turned out more difficult than he expected. The truth is, he does not know many people well. His days stretch unpeopled before him, one after another, until he picks up his wife's children from school, and eventually she comes home to him.

When he first sees the strange blue rainbow he feels dizzy beneath the fragmented light, puts his hand on the bonnet of his silver Mercedes.

He feels as if something is passing through him — knowledge, perhaps. He hopes Kate hasn't noticed, but he believes he has not faltered, that what has taken place has not occupied more than seconds.

Inside the cool interior of New World it is still possible to see the blue blaze of light through the tall windows, causing shoppers to look up as word travels. Kate and Simon buy polystyrene containers of strong black coffee to sip as they move sturdily around the supermarket choosing good cheeses and wine. He notices how Kate smiles at the checkout attendants and addresses them by the names on their lapel badges. As if they were in the country. As Aileen would have done. So, in this way, she is like her mother.

MATAMATA SITS ON HIGHWAY 27, between the Waikato and the Bay of Plenty. There is a long main street, with trees shading the footpaths of all the usual stores, although the chain stores are edging out the little familiar shops of the past, as well as antique shops that sell very good silver. When you say Matamata these days most people think hobbits, and cameramen with rings in their ears, and girls with studs in their tongues bearing clapper boards. Peter Jackson filmed parts of *The Lord of the Rings* there. In his wake, tourists have come to view the green rolling landscape, searching for signs of magic. Simon and Aileen farmed five kilometres or so off the main highway, down a gravel road. When they were first married, everyone knew everyone, on their weekly visits to town. Much of that has changed.

Simon wasn't meant to be the farmer. His brother Eddie never wanted anything but the farm, and Simon only ever wanted to leave it. But Eddie was a cocky sort of kid. He took the tractor down to the willow paddock one day when his father had told him the slope was too muddy. When it rolled, Eddie went under and that was that.

There would be nobody, his father said, nobody to take the farm on. He said it over and over, until his wife begged him to stop. Then Simon said he would stay.

He never understood why he said this; he was due to begin an arts degree at the end of that summer. But Simon told his father that he would stay, and when he did, it seemed like the right thing. He stopped reading so much, and went to dances at the hall, and drove his Vauxhall too fast on the long straight Waikato roads, drank more than he should, and milked cows morning and night. Then Aileen arrived in town to take over as the dental nurse at the school, and he fell for her at one of the pipe band dances, which he always thought were a bit weird because some of the guys still turned up in their kilts, but they were a good place for a laugh.

Aileen had a special languid way of dancing, and ink-black hair that floated on her shoulders. Her family had a citrus orchard over near the Mount. They were plain, humorous folk, a little religious but not overly so. Simon thought he might die of happiness in her arms the first time she let him kiss her. His parents were ready to move into town by then, so the house was theirs for the taking. He knew he was Aileen's first when they got married.

YOU WOULD EXPECT STEPHANIE and Kate to get on but they don't. They have Australia in common, because that is where Stephanie comes from. When Kate stays she helps with Stephanie's boys, Terence and Jonathan. She plays Monopoly and Scrabble with them, though they are not very secretly bored by these attempts to distract them from computer games. Board games are what Kate played with her Aunt Isabel when she was a child — that is the extent of her experience with children. Still she persists with her stepbrothers (not that she ever refers to their mother as her stepmother). Terence has under-eleven cricket practice after school, and Kate picks him up and goes to watch him play. Last year when she visited she took the oranges for half-time to the Saturday morning soccer game. 'The boys' friends think I'm their grandfather,' Simon had told her. Perhaps she had seen how tired he was.

'I don't have to stay with you, you know,' she said to Simon more than once. Her visits were always connected with business, not just to see him. But on this point he was adamant. He wasn't having his daughter staying in a hotel in the same town. Country again, he knew that. This irritated Stephanie.

'Those girls rule your life,' she said during Kate's last visit, and the whole thing blew up to a shouting match before he understood what was happening. Stephanie had come in from work very late, as she often did. She had a colleague called Phil who, she had explained from the outset, was not just competent but a good friend. True, he was a needy person — a man who had never married, with emotional uncertainties about his life — but she couldn't afford to lose him. She was so busy, always so busy at work, and he really was her right-hand man, so when he crashed she had to, you know, help him work through his problems, his relationships with his fellow workers. Besides, as she kept emphasising, he was a friend.

Simon had met Phil several times, mostly at gatherings of Stephanie's work friends. He understood right away that Phil was not in any sense a threat. He was one of those neutral middle-aged men, wearing a cravat with his shirt at the weekend, and well-cut slacks, Italian loafers (although Simon himself dresses rather like that these days, now that his wife has taken his clothes in hand). Watching Phil talk to Stephanie, Simon had no sense of chemistry between them. So it wasn't that. Only, friendship can be a worry. It occurs to him now and then that people might abandon love before friendship, that one might be a substitute for the other, at least in this ambivalent political city.

On the evening his wife and daughter quarrelled, Stephanie had come in looking flushed, as if she had had a glass of wine, or perhaps two. She was wearing a brown coat like a cape and knee-high brown boots with heels. Stephanie is a small, fair woman, almost fragile in her appearance, and the way she was behaving was out of character, didn't suit her at all. Kate and Simon had made dinner and when the boys became fretful with hunger fed them and sent them off to bed.

'Phil had another crisis,' Stephanie said, as if that explained everything. 'I hurried home to see the children. Now you've sent them packing.'

'No,' Kate told her, 'their eyes were hanging out of their heads and Terence has a maths test in the morning.'

'You seem to know more about my children than I do. I like to see them in the evenings.'

'I'm sorry,' Simon said. 'They're still awake — why don't you go in while Kate and I serve the dinner?'

But that didn't suit Stephanie either. She cast off her shoes, and let her bag fall on the floor as she dropped into a chair.

'It's all work, work, work,' she said. 'You don't understand what it's like. The pressure.' She put her hands up to her face.

'What can I do?' Simon said, kneeling beside her. 'Please, let me help.'

Kate walked into the kitchen. Beyond the divider, they heard plates being pushed gently from one rack to another in the oven.

'We need to get out more. You and I.'

'Perhaps we do,' he said. 'Why don't we go out tomorrow while Kate's still here? She could stay with the boys. What would you like to do?'

Stephanie decided they should see a movie. Someone had recommended *Little Fish* at the Rialto. As she spoke the title, Kate came out of the kitchen bearing a plate in each hand and put them on the table.

'No, Dad,' she said. 'No, you don't want to see that movie.'

'Why not?'

'Never mind why not. You just don't want to see it.'

'Have you?'

Kate turned her face away. 'Just believe me.'

There was something dangerous in the air that he didn't understand, some secret hanging between them. He wanted to make her tell him but Kate's face closed and then Stephanie was shouting at them both, about how Kate ought to mind her own business.

Later, after Kate had gone, Stephanie said, 'So what was that all about?'

'I don't know,' he said. 'I truly don't.' He could see, then, how it must have looked to Stephanie — that she was being excluded from something private between him and his daughter, perhaps something about her. When she understood that it wasn't like that, Stephanie had flowers delivered to Kate in Melbourne. Please try again, Simon emailed. It will be all right.

After Aileen died, her sister Isabel came to live near Simon's farm so she could take care of the children. She was one of the plainer of Aileen's sisters, big bosomed, with a right eye that wandered slightly inwards when she stared at you. Not that that should have made a difference, but there was something about her that announced her as less likely to marry than her sisters. At first she lived in the town and drove out every morning, but then a sharemilker's house came vacant at the farm along the road, when the owners switched to beef and sheep, so she moved in there; it was almost like having her living at the house. The only thing Simon and Isabel ever disagreed on was about the girls going swimming. They were not allowed to go to the swimming hole at the river where Simon had swum with his brother and sister. Nor were they allowed to go on picnics with families who were going swimming. Isabel said it wasn't natural, he was denying them an ordinary enough pleasure. But when she saw that he was obstinate she said nothing more.

Even if she didn't seem the marrying kind, people began to expect that Isabel and Simon would marry, and for a while he thought they might too. It made perfect sense. The girls regarded her much as they would a mother, although Isabel never let the memory of Aileen disappear. But his life was changing. He had become a farmer who read, as he did when a boy at school. He joined the library committee and became involved in local affairs. Someone said he would make a good mayor — a well-known and well-liked man, even if he kept his distance. They understood that, too. Many of the people in the town had Scots ancestry. Tragedy is tragedy but a man's own business. The local farmers asked him to join him in their advocacy with the Dairy Board, which he did for some years until the big corporations moved in and changed everything. These interests took him away from the town, to Auckland and to Wellington.

In cities, he visited art galleries and saw movies and went to classical music concerts. He met women whom he could invite out to dinner and, when he had known them for a time, take them to bed. Each time it felt traitorous, although who he was betraying it was hard to say. Aileen's parents called sex 'nookie', and he and Aileen used to say that, too, when they were being playful and silly. 'Let's have nookie,' they said to each other. 'You want nookie?' It was hard to get out of the habit of calling it that in his head. Nookie: he wanted it all the time.

He invited one of the women he met home for a weekend. There was no reason why he shouldn't, he told himself, driving guiltily past Isabel's house, half hoping she wouldn't find out, knowing perfectly well that the girls would tell her first thing on Monday. In the end he couldn't bring himself to ask the woman to his bed while his children were there.

A few weeks after this, Isabel told him she had accepted a proposal of marriage from a man who did bridge-building in the district. He would live with her in the sharemilker's house, and nothing about their arrangement would change. By this time, in fact, Janet was nearly through high school, and almost everything was changing. Soon the girls would be gone. He would begin to see less and less of Aileen and Isabel's family at the Mount. Isabel and her new husband would move away, and when they did he would rent the place for help on his own farm, because he didn't want to milk cows any more.

He found himself settling into a routine of farming, reading, travelling to visit the girls wherever they happened to live, occasionally seeing women. After a time he seemed to need to do this less and less. The rituals of courting were uncertain and the publicity about STDs made him afraid; he was embarrassed to use condoms with women who were too old to have children, and frightened they wouldn't protect him with younger women who were hungrier and took it for granted that dinner meant sex. One day he was startled to realise that a quarter of a century had slipped by since Aileen died.

But just now and then he would hanker for live music and some company — something to break the dark circle of silence that enveloped the farmhouse in the dead of night. When the arts festival was on in Wellington that year, Simon found himself waiting for a concert to begin in the Michael Fowler Centre, and the appearance of the visiting conductor, a flamboyant Russian. Beside him sat a small blonde woman with a pert nose. The seat next to her was empty.

'My friend couldn't come,' she said, before the performance began, as if needing to explain why she was on her own. 'It seemed silly not to come when I already had the ticket.' She had a faint twang in her accent, so slight he couldn't immediately place it. I've been out of things for too long, he told himself. The woman's short hair curled at the nape of her neck. She was wearing a tight-fitting dark sweater with a scooped neckline and large amber beads with an antique design. When she looked up at him, her eyes seemed serious and steady.

As the musicians appeared on the stage Simon tried to find something to say before the hush for the performance began, but his voice came out cracked and raw. She leant in towards him, her fingers to her lips. 'I'm Australian,' she whispered, as if that explained everything. She had a soft hot scent on her breath.

During her first visits to the farm, Stephanie tended his garden lovingly. She found shrubs that Aileen had planted long ago covered by weeds on crumbling banks, but still going strong — misshapen camellias and rhododendrons, which she pruned and nursed, so that in the spring he saw them flowering again, and it was Stephanie he thought of, not Aileen. She planted a row of lavender along the front path, and wore big shady hats while she weeded with her slim brown fingers. Usually she flew up to Hamilton and he met her at the airport. Occasionally she brought her sons, but back in Wellington she had a housekeeper who would stay over. Once, their father, who had gone back to Australia after his and Stephanie's divorce, came from Sydney and stayed with the boys. Simon didn't know if he was aware of where she was, or whether he cared.

In the big empty red brick house he was free to do whatever pleased them both. One night she whispered in his ear, 'I could have a baby with you.'

At first he was astonished by the idea, but from the way his cock lurched back into the fray he knew the idea pleased him. 'Would you?' he found himself saying later on, even though he knew he was near enough to being an old man. Stephanie herself was past forty.

She propped herself up on her elbow and looked down at him, her big rusty-coloured nipple brushing the side of his face. 'I'd do anything for you,' she said.

This didn't, however, include coming to live in Matamata, as he soon discovered. 'I have my work in Wellington, and my friends,' she said.

There would come a time, she went on, when they would need more than each other. That was the way of marriage. And didn't he love the city? There was so much for him to do there. Was it not, she asked him directly, time to move on?

Perhaps, he thought at the time, she had seen ghosts that he believed had disappeared with her presence in the house. The crooked shrubs. The old-fashioned kitchen. The bed with the same colonial-style headboard that had stood there since his marriage.

He does go to the movie at the Rialto, to a late-morning session. He is one of only two people in the theatre. At the counter, on an impulse, he buys a glass of wine, an odd thing to do at this time of day, but the whole secretive excursion feels strange.

The movie is about a beautiful reformed drug addict who had been a champion swimmer before she got hooked. When she is persuaded to get involved in one last deal that goes terribly wrong, and people die all around her, she goes to a beach and swims out to sea. Before she leaves on this last journey, she ducks under the water and waggles her hands jauntily above the waves, then swims out strongly without a backward glance towards the open water.

The storyline is so bleak that once or twice Simon thinks about walking out. His wine stands at his elbow untouched. He is still working out why Kate had been so disturbed at the thought of him coming to the movie when the ending comes upon him unexpectedly. When it hits him, he drinks the wine straight down.

So Kate has known all along. He supposes that Janet must, too, that they have talked about it over the years. That they may well have read the coroner's report, that people have talked to them. Isabel might have mentioned their mother's illness, assuming that at least they knew this. As indeed they should have, but if he told them that, then one thing would surely have led to another. Why had he let her go swimming alone? Hadn't he cared?

Does it matter how they know? They do. They know the story of the rolling surf carrying her away is a big fat lie.

Aileen didn't even wave.

About leaving. It's about leaving and being left, Simon thinks. The gap in between is so wide that you cannot see from one side to the other. Sometimes it is hard to remember what Aileen looked like. When she first had her dizzy spells she thought it was hormones. 'I've got another of these damn headaches,' she'd say, and take an aspirin. It was the year of the Springbok tour riots and the start of the Roger Gascoigne wink on television, but she didn't watch anything — the light hurt her eyes. She decided she needed glasses. The optician in Hamilton was newly qualified and looked past the matter of her blurred vision. He thought she should see a specialist. This was how she came to learn that she had multiple sclerosis.

After the diagnosis he suggested they leave the farm. Already they were talking about ramps up to the house for when she needed a wheelchair. That was not what she wanted, Aileen said — the new pills she was taking would be sure to help. Yet she seemed to withdraw from him, as if, more often than not, she found him a stranger. This, the doctors explained, was part of the illness; mood and personality changes could be expected as parts of the brain began to close down.

But still there were times when the illness appeared to recede, and for a few days at a time she was the old Aileen, laughing, playing with the children, nuzzling him when she caught him unawares. During those times she would always suggest a visit to her parents at the Mount. The Mount was still the place she called home, even though it was built up with new houses and the drifting sandbanks had been tamed.

On one of these afternoons she said she wanted to go the beach for a little while, just her and Simon, and could her parents please mind the girls. In the car she sat quietly — not withdrawn, the way he was becoming used to, but seemingly content, as if just sitting there beside him was enough. It was a still, sunny day. She was wearing shorts and a halter-necked top, which pleased him because she wasn't disguising her body the way she mostly had since she got sick.

That was how she left him, before he understood what was happening, before he could catch up with her in the water, clothed as he was. She stumbled slightly as she got to the edge, but when she entered the water she launched herself in, her arms slicing cleanly through the waves. By the time he rushed in, helpless from the start, then back to the sand to alert the lifeguards that she was missing, she had swum beyond their reach.

Since then he has heard of other people doing it — young men and boys more often than girls. There was a boy who took off his clothes and folded them neatly in front of a waterside restaurant in Wellington, then swam past the windows, where a diner looking up from his Cajun fish and salad had seen him heading away. He had disappeared long before the man could convince anyone of what was happening. How could it be? people said. But Simon knew it was easy. None of these incidents had ever been mentioned to him by the girls. He had no reason to think they would know.

When Simon had been married to Stephanie for two years, and not long after he had seen this movie, he said to her, 'Did you mean what you said about the baby?' Around that time he felt as if he was falling in love with her in a way that was deeper, stronger than before. Life might not be perfect, not just as he had imagined it, but he was fortunate and he thought he might not have given happiness the chance that he should — he had held onto a past that should have been over. When he held her, he felt tender and virile and younger than he was. It was a silly time to ask. They were stripping paint off the beautiful wooden doors of the house they were restoring in Kelburn. 'How could they have painted over this wood?' Stephanie said, grimacing. 'Oh my God, they've had varnish on them too.'

'Well, would you?' he said, knowing she had heard him.

'Darling,' she said in a half-mocking, vaguely amused voice, 'I work.'

'But you don't have to,' he said.

'I have children already.'

'I know, and they're great,' he began enthusiastically. But he couldn't go on with this.

After a moment of silence she put the paint stripper down carefully on a cloth. Her tone was unfriendly. 'Actually, I have to work tomorrow,' she said. 'In case you'd forgotten. I need to prepare.'

ON THE DAY OF THE lunch he has managed to assemble their kitchen designer, whom he has got to know quite well, and his wife who is a painter; also the son of one of his old Matamata farming friends, who is a graphic designer, and his girlfriend, an occupational therapist. Although the man is younger than Kate at least they will know families in common, and the language of where they have come from. Then there is an older couple whom he met some years ago when fog closed the airport and they were stuck there together for hours. They are members of a chamber music society and have invited him to one or two concerts. The husband is a retired accountant and his wife teaches French. Altogether there are nine of them. He has sought to include some of Stephanie's friends but she has shrugged these suggestions aside. 'What about Phil?' he asks.

'I think he's tied up,' she says, as if Phil is a prisoner somewhere.

Stephanie has made a very large but also very light salad, and there is bread. Afterwards there will be dessert and cheeses. Simon feels that it is not enough, although this is the way well-to-do Wellington people eat at Sunday lunch. Light. He would have preferred a dinner but Stephanie thought lunch would be best. He thinks wistfully of the pot-luck dinners he and Aileen used to enjoy with their neighbours, remembers the dishes steaming in the frosty night air, the surprises inside (although everyone would have agreed in advance whether they were bringing mains or dessert). Nowadays he remembers Aileen more often, or at least their lives together. She is not the stranger to memory that she was. He tells himself this is healthy, that a sense of perspective has been achieved, that Little Fish and her wiggling fingers have freed him. Aileen would have said he'd 'stopped bottling things up'. These are private reflections but he is sure he is 'on the right track'.

The group talks in a desultory way, trying to establish links. Simon thinks the kitchen designer and the younger couple are wondering whether the salad is the first course. Stephanie attends to serving the guests, waving away offers of help, while Kate talks to everyone in turn. She draws them into talking about travel and places they have been, which takes quite a while. When that topic is exhausted, they move on — more guarded, because they don't know each other — to George Bush and the war in Iraq, and then the conversation drifts towards the weather, the odd cold summer they are experiencing, and that leads on to the blue blast of colour that lit up the sky earlier in the week. Everyone has a story about where they were and what they saw. The woman who is a painter is able to explain the phenomenon. It was, she says, a circumhorizontal arc, rare although not exceptional. The effect was created by light passing through wispy, high-altitude cirrus clouds that contain fine ice crystals. There is more to this, which the painter explains at some length. She is a middle-aged woman with heavy reddish-coloured hair that she pushes back behind her ears. Her fingernails have yellow and red paint beneath them. 'The arc is similar to a rainbow,' she says, 'but the ice crystals are shaped like thick plates with their faces parallel to the ground. When the light passes on the vertical side, it refracts from the bottom, and bends, like light through a prism.' Simon likes the warm, no-nonsense look of her, and the way she has stored up this knowledge. It is at this stage that Stephanie gets up and leaves the table.

As soon as he is able, without seeming to be concerned, Simon follows her through to the kitchen. Her car keys are in one hand, her cellphone in the other.

'Where are you going?'

'I had a text message. Didn't you hear my phone? No, I suppose you wouldn't with all that talk. Congratulations, it seems to be going well.' She glances at the phone in her hand. 'Phil is having a crisis,' she says. 'He really needs me.'

'Phil? You're not at work now. Nothing can be that bad.'

'Life and death,' she says cryptically.

He doesn't say that she has gone. Kate raises her eyebrows in enquiry and he shakes his head, in a way that only she can read.

'Kate and I will do coffee,' he says during a break in the conversation. The guests drift into the sitting room. The designer and his girlfriend say they will have to go soon. Simon can tell from their faint tobacco smell that they are in need of a cigarette. Everyone else seems content to talk and enjoy the view of the garden through the French doors. Like the garden at Matamata, it is full of lavender, and a variety of roses just finishing their spring flowering. Soon enough, the guests will discover that there is no hostess to farewell.

He knows she will come back this time. And other times, until there is a last time. She will not leave him for Phil. Or perhaps for anyone. It is more likely she will leave and come back some day and tell him to leave, and then she can get on with her work. She will be free of him wrestling with things that happened long ago, even though he has never told her exactly what they were.

He does not blame her, at least not yet, not while he is handing around Turkish sweets with the coffee. It is not as if he did not know. Just the other day, when the light passed through the sky, he knew something was up. That he had learnt to read the signs of leaving. He has seen them in himself.

Silks

When I think of love, and how things began for us, I think of a house by a lake, and us lying in bed with our skin like twin silks sliding together. I remember the Venetian blind, and the slats of light that shone through, moonlight but also sunlight, because that was the way it was, we were in that bed night and day. That was the time, too, or thereabouts, when I began a kind of worship for a writer who lived by lakes, and made love with a man in a room where the slatted blind made stripes on the soft and shining light of his back.

The writer, a Frenchwoman called Marguerite Duras, was born in Vietnam, a girl who made love with a man of another colour, a woman who lived outside the pale. That was like me, only I married the man I was in love with, when I was young. Who knew whether it would last? That was the question they all asked, the good Presbyterian men and women who were my aunts and uncles, on the day that I married. We married, my husband and I, in a church with thatched walls, while a thunderstorm broke overhead and the rain poured down, and nobody could hear the promises we made.

As I say, I was very young. My waist was twenty-two inches in circumference. I had thick dark hair. The art of love came easily to me. I worked in a library, and read French writers, and Duras was another love, a passion that went hand in hand with the discoveries of the flesh that I was making. In my lunch-hours I rushed home. My husband would be there before me. We would make love and go back to work. It was an exhausting life.

Duras led us to Hanoi, but this was many years later. Close to fifty, in fact. We could look back and say fifty years of married drama and laugh, but it held the ring of truth and remembered fires, the silky fire of sex, the fiery nights when we broke things, a couple of black ragers in our worst moments.

It was not the first time we had been to Vietnam. We were no strangers to the East, but we hadn't been to Hanoi. I had followed Duras around the world, stalked her ghost: to Saigon (which is how I think of Ho Chi Minh City, because Saigon sounds wilder, tougher, more glamorous, I suppose); to Cholon, where she had spent her afternoons in the bed of her Chinese lover when she was supposed to be at school; and along the Mekong River in a flat-bottomed barge, in search of her house (which we never found), to Neauphle-le-Château, the French town where her house stands abandoned beside the still dark pool that is another reflection of what I call my inner life. I had leant my face against her windowpane, looked at the scuff marks her feet had made on the skirting boards of her kitchen. And I had been to her plain grave in Paris, marked with the stark initials: M.D. Just that. But I had not been to Hanoi where, for a brief time, her widowed mother ran a boarding house beside a lake. My own mother had worked in a boarding house. You will see how it comes together, her life and mine, though sometimes this interest can be misunderstood. Are you an alcoholic? I was once asked by a journalist. Of course I said no, because I am a woman of good reputation, and live in a small country. I had written an account of my life and the journalist thought it incomplete. They always want to know more than you want to tell them. They want a scandal, of course. Duras was an alcoholic. She drank herself into comas. I have never done that. For a time, I drank too much. That isn't the same thing at all.

MY HUSBAND MET ME IN Bangkok airport. He had been to Phnom Penh, where he worked as a volunteer for one of the aid organisations. As he has grown older he has become more and more interested in saving the world. He does good works and changes lives. I can't be like him. I find it hard to visit slums, to work alongside the halt and lame, without assuming the zealous smile of a person offering charity. The heat gets to me, and the begging for money, and the children for whom good works will never be enough, the despairing women. And, if I'm honest, I find it hard to get along with the aid workers, who seem to me either rampantly Christian or else escapees from some other reality, jittery with cheap alcohol and casual sex, blazing-eyed and reckless. They're not all like that, but enough are to make me wary. The more time I spend with them, the more determinedly ordinary I become. Judgemental in my way, as the aunts and uncles at my shoulder, a prim elderly woman with frangipani stuck awkwardly behind my ear. My husband doesn't look out of place. He seems part of the landscape. He sits on the side of filthy streets and eats what's offered to him while he talks to the people who live there.

As soon as I saw him at the airport, I thought, He doesn't look well, something's not right. He was pale, and wandering in his speech. Although we had planned our meeting carefully, he had confused the times and gone to wait at the airport many hours before my plane from Auckland was due in Bangkok. My luggage was the last off the carousel, and by the time I came through the gates he was hysterical about my whereabouts and security guards had to restrain him from rushing through the incoming passengers to find me. But when he did see me, he didn't seem pleased, almost as if I was a stranger.

We prepared to board the plane for Hanoi, although, even as we did so, I thought it was a terrible idea. If there was something wrong, perhaps we should stay in Bangkok. We passed through check-in and relinquished our luggage and it was too late to turn back. My husband asked me to find a chair so he could take a rest on the way to the gate lounge. I said, 'Do you think you're well enough to go on this flight?'

He said that of course he was, which is what I should have expected. He doesn't give in easily. Before he left Phnom Penh some friends had taken him to a noodle shop to eat lunch. It was dirty, he said, but he didn't want to offend them. He may blend into the landscape, but he tries to be careful, particularly as he had come home to me once before with an illness that had developed in the tropics and took him close to death. Perhaps, he thought, he had eaten something at the noodle shop. Whatever it was, it would soon pass.

We arrived at night and the airport was utter chaos: hundreds jostling together, some coming, others going, taxi drivers looking for work, pushing people out of their way. Our driver found us, the board bearing our names held high above the heads of the crowd, and some time later we were being driven towards Hanoi, or so far as I knew. The roads fell quiet and a dark countryside rolled alongside us. We crossed a river and a bridge that seemed to stretch into infinity; I sensed the water beneath us.

'I think we're crossing the Red River,' I said, expecting my husband to be excited. He had wanted to see this river, which is also known as Mother River, for such a long time. 'This must be Thăng

Long Bridge.' He had done so much research, knew all the facts and figures about this extraordinary feat of engineering, and about the two villages that lay beneath its spans. He didn't answer me, and I felt irritated. I thought he could have made a little effort.

We drove on and on, and we could have been anywhere, being taken far away from our destination. There was no way of knowing or of asking the silent driver, who spoke no English. There was hardly a light to be discerned in the black landscape, and this was something I would learn, that the Vietnamese use electricity sparingly, and utter darkness is not unusual. When, at last, the glimmer of a city shone before us, my husband slid sideways onto my lap, resting his head there until we arrived at our hotel.

'I'll let you check in,' he said, handing me his passport. This was something he had never done before.

I HAD BEEN TRAVELLING FOR many hours. I gave my husband some Lomotil from our first aid supplies to cure his stomach upset, then lay down in the Sunway Hotel and slept until morning, hoping that he would do the same. The sheets were made of exquisitely fine white cotton.

He was worse in the morning, but still I thought it would pass. I went to breakfast. The dining room of the hotel was restful, like that of a French inn. The walls were covered with vivid Vietnamese artworks that, although colourful, didn't detract from the cool white and green ambience of the room. I ate some dragon fruit and melon and a little muesli. I walked along the street, a shabby crowded avenue in the Old Quarter, slung low with the great burden of electrical wires, just as when the war was on, although nearly thirty years had passed. I walked nearly to the end of the street until I came to the opera house, then became alarmed that I wouldn't be able to find my way back, and my husband would be alone and frightened and more ill. At that moment, perhaps, I understood that things could be serious and that, actually, I was trying to walk away from the situation. I went back to the hotel. He looked dreadful. He didn't want a doctor, but we agreed that if he wasn't any better by three o'clock, I would call for one. It was two o'clock when I went to the reception desk. 'Help me, please,' I said. 'My husband is sick.'

'We'll get a taxi for you, Madam, and send you to a clinic,' the woman said.

But no, I said, no, he needs a doctor to come to him, and very soon one did, a young woman, with an attendant following her, and a short time after that, an ambulance was summoned and my husband was carried on a stretcher with an oxygen mask over his face through the lobby of the Sunway Hotel, and a siren was shrieking above us, and through the window I saw the thousands of motorbikes that clog the streets of the city fanning out about us. I had dropped everything, thrown some valuables in the safe and fled.

At the clinic, he was isolated from others coming and going, though I sat beside him and laughed and made jokes. I was given a gown and mask to wear. I said things like, 'Here I am in Hanoi, looking after you, I'm pretending to be Hot Lips Houlihan', and pushed my mouth out to make it fat.

'Wrong war,' he said. 'Wrong country.' He didn't have much to say after that. Before I met him, my husband had been a pilot in the air force. I said, 'Buck up, old chap.' I sang a line or two of 'The bells of hell go ting-a-ling-a-ling'. Nothing made him laugh. I still didn't believe there was much that a quick shot of antibiotic wouldn't cure. A young French doctor came and went, his face grave. Hours passed. My husband seemed worse. 'We think he has cholera,' the French doctor said. I stopped joking.

Outside, night had fallen. The doctor said, 'You realise your husband is very ill?' Dazed, I said yes, no, yes I did, and started to cry. He looked at me wearily as if I was misbehaving. 'We're going to send your husband to a hospital where he'll be more comfortable. You'll need to check it out with your insurance company.'

But night was hours ahead of us in New Zealand, and when I tried to phone the insurance company there was nothing but a voice message giving the times that the company was open. The woman behind the desk at the clinic had an impassive Vietnamese expression. She explained that, if my insurance company could not confirm our policy, I must pay for my husband's treatment for that afternoon. Could I please hand over my credit card? The cost was five thousand dollars, or thereabouts.

In my haste to leave the hotel, I had brought only one of the two cards we carried, and it did not have enough money on it. I cried again, I may have shouted, but none of it made any difference. In the background my husband was a strange grey paste colour, and tubes and drips were poking out from all over him. I said that I would talk to my twenty-four-hour bank service and I did. In the end, the credit was authorised. As we left the clinic, we reached the street in the midst of Hanoi, its street vendors and crowds, the bright lights of open shops, the cascades of silk in front of them. An ambulance waited for us. My husband was carried by four men holding his wheelchair, but before he could be boarded he projected a wild, vile green plume of vomit that spread over everyone within reach. Green rain. Shrill cries of horror erupted from the passers-by. Those carrying my husband turned and began to carry him back into the clinic.

'Put him in the ambulance,' I screamed. 'Please get him to the hospital.'

But it seemed that first he must be made clean, so the whole process began all over again. Midnight had passed by the time the ambulance left the city. We drove, again through silence. The Vietnamese had put up their shutters, lain down to sleep. The motorbikes that had choked the streets earlier had disappeared. The lights had gone out except for the tiny flickers of fires peppering the pavements, illuminating the shadows of late workers bending over their pots. The ambulance moved very slowly. We seemed to be moving far away from the city centre. I had no idea what direction we were taking. I saw the shapes of buildings through the gloom so I knew that we must still be within the confines of the city. Days had passed since I left home, and already a day had gone since I had eaten the cloudy flesh of the dragon fruit at the hotel.

We reached the hospital, a stark building, concrete and totally without charm. A team of nurses rushed to my husband's side, and as suddenly as we had entered the fluorescent-lit space of the hospital, he had disappeared. The place appeared otherwise deserted, except for a man behind a big desk. 'You will now show me your passport,' he said.

I showed it to him.

'You will now give me your husband's passport.' He took it from me.

'Can I have it back, please?' I asked.

He shook his head, with impatience. 'Not until he leaves the hospital. They tell me your papers for the insurance are not in order. You will now give me five hundred dollars.'

'American?'

'Yes.'

'I don't have that much money on me,' I said.

'Show me how much.'

I opened my wallet and turned it out on the counter; a little over three hundred dollars fell out, perhaps another fifty in smaller notes. He picked through them. 'I have to have some money to get back to my hotel,' I said. 'I have no idea where I am.'

'Three hundred will do,' he said.

'I want to see my husband.'

'That is not possible. The doctor will come.'

I WAITED IN A VESTIBULE with couches covered in brown faux leather. While I waited, a woman I soon discovered was American came to the desk. Her husband had just been admitted with a heart problem. He, too, had gone to intensive care. 'But this is preposterous,' she said loudly to the man at the desk. 'He's had a murmur like this before, he doesn't *need* intensive care. In the morning I'll take him to Bangkok, see a proper doctor. Tell them to take him out of there.'

The man spread his hands in a gesture that said 'This is not my problem'. Our eyes met, and for a moment something like sympathy passed between us. At least I hadn't told him what to do. The woman introduced herself to me. Her name was Irene. She had just come to Hanoi with her husband, who was to work in one of the banks. I have never quite understood American women. When I travel, I find them often generous and funny and warm, but they have a brittle edge that threatens to snap if they are crossed. I've learnt never to talk about politics to an American woman. 'Hey, seems you're a bit stranded,' Irene said, when we had exchanged a few words, and gave me her card. 'If you're still on your own tomorrow night, we could go out and play a bit, what d'you think? Don't worry about your husband, he'll be fine. At least these doctors know how to fix tummy bugs.'

A Vietnamese doctor appeared and introduced himself to me. 'Your husband is now in isolation,' he said.

'Has he got cholera?'

'No. It is not cholera.'

'What is wrong with him?'

'He has rotavirus. Very infectious disease.'

A virus, I thought. 'It's not serious, then?'

'Oh yes, it is serious.'

'He won't die, will he?'

'Oh, maybe. His kidneys do not work now. He is, how do you say, dehydrated. He should have seen a doctor much more early.'

'Tonight? My husband might die tonight?'

'Prob'ly.'

'I must see him.'

'Not possible. Now he is in isolation. You go home now.'

'Where? Show me where he is.'

After a while, he relented and took me in a lift to another floor. I was led through a door that had to be unlocked from the other side by some nurses. After that, there was another locked door, and through a window, in a bare cell, I saw my husband lying naked on a stripped-down bed. He appeared barely conscious.

'I'll stay here.'

'No, you cannot stay here. You must leave now.'

A nurse took my arm. She led me back to the lift and accompanied me to the ground floor. 'You must go.'

I shouted at her. 'I'm not going anywhere. I'll sleep here.'

She shrugged and made a face at the man behind the desk. I lay down on the concrete floor. The nurse left, and I was by myself. I sobbed then, as if I would never stop. All the old fretted and worn seams of love that had stretched but never parted were laid out before me. My husband was dying, and I was alone in a city where I had never been, lying on a concrete floor. Each of us was alone.

The man at the desk came over to me. 'You may lie on a bed that is in the next room,' he said. 'It is for emergencies. If an emergency comes, you must get out of the bed.'

And this small act of kindness had its effect. My behaviour was pointless and ridiculous. I took my cellphone and worked out how to dial our children's numbers with the country code added in. But it seemed they had turned off their phones for the night. I figured that it must be about half past five in the morning. I have a friend who sleeps badly and lives alone. I called her. I said, 'Find my children. Please.'

Our daughter rang me. 'Mum,' she said. 'Mum. Don't let my father die.'

Our son rang me. 'Mum,' he said. 'Mum.' He was crying.

The man at the desk came into the room a short while later. He said, 'Your ambassador is coming.'

My daughter had rung the night desk at Foreign Affairs and explained that her father was dying in a hospital in Hanoi. The man had agreed, with a certain scepticism, to check it out. But the people from the embassy who arrived in a large Jeep at the door of the hospital were not sceptical. They were kind and practical and had brought a translator with them, and some food and bottles of mineral water and dry ginger ale. I had never been more pleased to see people from my own country. A while later, I left the hospital with them. I was told a senior doctor would see me in a few hours. They took me back to the hotel in the city, promising to fetch me when I had had time to shower and eat breakfast, talk to my insurance company and perhaps sleep a little. All of which I did, except the last. But before I did anything else, I wrote a long letter to my husband, in which I told him what had happened since we left Bangkok, because I was certain he wouldn't remember, and I thought it unlikely the nurses would have the language to tell him where he was or how he had got there or why he couldn't see me. I told him, too, how much I loved him, how he must fight to get well, because if he didn't, I wasn't sure that I could go on. Although this seemed like blackmail, it was better than saying goodbye in a letter. I needed him to help me go on with my life, I said. It was as simple as that. Once before he had nearly died, but he had got better, and he could do it again.

I SAW THE SENIOR DOCTOR, an older man, impatient with people like me who had to be spoken to about their relatives. His job was to make people better, not talk to the family. The translator from the embassy sat with me, but the doctor did command some stilted formal English. He interrogated me. 'Do you wash your hands properly?'

'Yes,' I said.

'When you go to the lavatory?'

'But of course.'

'Rotavirus comes from dirty food that is contaminated with excrement. You need to be more careful.'

'But I haven't given my husband his dinner for more than two weeks,' I said.

So then I had to explain my journey, where I had come from, how my husband and I had met in Bangkok, how I had expected him to be happy when he saw me but he wasn't. I made it into a little drama, waved my hands about, and he allowed himself a small smile before his expression closed again.

'Your husband will be here for quite some time,' he said. 'We will do what we can to make him well. Now I must see the next wife.'

The next wife was Irene, who had grown angrier since I saw her the night before, and a new wife waited behind her, a dark Portuguese woman, who was stranded and almost without language.

She was weeping in a silent persistent way, unchecked snot covering her lip. This was Maria, whose husband had fallen down some steps on a cruise ship and hit his head. Smash, she said, smash.

The translator took me to the clinic where I had been the day before. Now that the insurance company had cleared our policy I could get my money back. The clinic wanted to give me the money in dongs, Vietnamese currency. Fourteen million. In the end a deal was struck and I got the five thousand dollars, in hundred-dollar bills. 'You must make sure the safe is locked very hard,' said the translator.

SO BEGAN MY LIFE IN the Sunway Hotel. A woman who ate dinner in the Allanté Restaurant most nights of the week and came to know the waiters by their names. The food was excellent, both Vietnamese and French. It's difficult to recall what the dishes were although I would eat them over and over again, as a way of passing the time, of doing what I must in order to keep going, and yet it's hard to remember. I know that there was food cooked with nuoc mam and ginger and lemongrass, as well as boeuf bourguignon and crème brûlée. The house wine was Luis Buñuel rosé. I supposed it was named for the Spanish movie director who had taken up with Mexico and made films about violent sex and religion and ecstasy. As rosés go it was all right. The problem was how to order more than two glasses without drawing attention to myself. It was wildly expensive, but I had handfuls of hundred-dollar bills in my safe and I didn't really care. After dinner, I moved downstairs to the jazz bar and listened to a trio of musicians. I got to know their repertoire as well as I knew the menu, and have as easily forgotten it, but while I listened to them I could drink another glass of Luis Buñuel.

I was a woman who was driven across the city of Hanoi in a taxi four times each day, return journeys made once in the morning and once in the afternoon, to find out how my husband was doing, because I couldn't ring up and ask. Nobody had the language to answer me. When I arrived at the hospital I made my way to intensive care and waited for a doctor to see me, sometimes the Vietnamese doctor who got angry when he had to talk to me again, sometimes French doctors who were kinder on the whole. None of them would allow me into the room to see my husband, although I was allowed to peer through the glass. I talked to the other wives. Irene's husband had taken a turn for the worse, but then so had Maria's. The fizz had completely gone out of Irene, she was surly and tired. Maria crossed herself incessantly and cried.

'It's really a case of whose husband is going to die first, isn't it?' Irene said.

WHEN I WAS NOT BEING driven to the hospital and back, I walked the streets and lakesides of the city. There are hundreds of lakes, but when I came to Hoan Kiem I was certain I had found the one I was looking for, the lake where Duras's mother had run the boarding house, a location where Duras had suffered a great trauma as a child. I say location, because Duras was also a film-maker, so as I read her, my mind was making pictures. A red bridge led to a temple near the shore. I was constantly surprised by the redness of things in Vietnam. A pavilion that, from afar, appeared the size of a chimney, had been built in the centre of Hoan Kiem in honour of a fifteenth-century Vietnamese hero: his magical sword was said to have been eaten by a gold tortoise. Hoan Kiem means Lake of the Restored Sword. On the shoreline stood a row of French colonial villas, and I decided there and then that this was exactly where the boarding house was, or had been. I had thought there was a red bridge in Duras's story, but when I go back to her text there is no sign of one. I had begun to feel impatient with Duras, that she had led me into unimaginable danger, and I had almost had enough of her. I crossed the red bridge and came to the temple and lit some incense for my husband, then I sat and watched the surface of the lake. In the green days of love, when we were young, he and I had sat on the steps of our apartment and watched the dark light of night falling across that other lake.

ONE AFTERNOON, WHEN I ARRIVED at the hospital, a second American woman, the wife of another man who worked in the city, had set up camp at the entrance to intensive care. This woman, who was called Stacey, was very bad news, crazy and out of control, far worse than I had been. She was so thin she looked as though she might break in half. I have no idea what was really wrong with her husband, because her language was peppered with lengthy bursts of unintelligible medical terminology. From the drift of it, I supposed that, like Irene's husband, it must be something to do with his heart. Both Stacey's parents were doctors and she was on a cellphone calling them in New York, as they diagnosed her husband's condition and told her what treatment he needed. She crouched on the floor, skinny backside in the air, shouting the names of drugs as she wrote them down on a pad in front of her. 'These doctors,' she screamed, 'they have no idea what they're doing. Mommy, I can't let him die. I have to stop them doing what they're doing.' Two French doctors appeared and tried to calm her down. The Vietnamese doctor, the one I tried not to irritate, was watching, his expression implacable. He was not easy to appease. I had learnt to keep quite still in his presence, not to speak loudly or move my hands about quickly. A week of my vigil had now passed and I had been allowed in to see my husband for just one minute. I thought he had recognised me. He was surrounded by tiny Vietnamese nurses with hands like the wings of dragonflies, and it seemed that he knew them better, in that minute, than he did me. But then I was wearing a mask and gown.

Irene and Maria and I looked at one another while Stacey raved on. 'Pouf,' said Maria, and turned away. She appeared not to have changed her clothes for several days. She was still wearing the same elegant dark garments she had on when I met her, only now they were soiled and shabby and her hair was matted round the sides of her face. Irene was trying to get her husband to Bangkok but their paperwork wasn't in order, which had confounded her, and besides that, Bangkok airport was closed because of political riots.

Irene, looking at Staccy, said: 'Well, that sure as shit isn't going to get her anywhere.' We looked at one another again, for once with real recognition. The survivors. So far.

AT THE EMBASSY I HAD struck up one of those surprising spontaneous friendships that would carry on beyond the moment, past Hanoi. Anne lived by the West Lake in a tower block of diplomatic apartments. The rooms were cool and beautifully furnished, with pictures by New Zealand artists on the wall and books by New Zealand writers on the shelves. I ate with her and her husband some evenings on their balcony overlooking the lake, and near to Trúc Bac, which John McCain famously parachuted into after he'd been shot down during the Vietnam War. Anne had begun to take me in hand. She had taught me how to say *xin chao* (hullo) and *c m n* (thank you), both very useful words. *Xin chao, c m n,* I said, endlessly smiling. What else could I say? Nobody would accept my Western tips, which were not permitted in communist Vietnam. Hullo and thank you got me a long way. Anne sent me to look at cathedrals, showed me about the city, took me to restaurants I wouldn't have found on my own. I had promised the staff at the embassy that I wouldn't walk out alone at night, and I had no real wish to do so. Once night fell, I wanted to stay in the Sunway Hotel, and eat, and listen to jazz. Oh yes, and drink Luis Buñuel rosé. Anne had lent me a novel by Joan Didion, one that captured a familiar tone in her writing: a lone woman in a deserted tropical hotel, drinking bourbon and waiting for something to happen, before someone gets killed by secret agents. Often there are jacaranda petals floating on a swimming pool filled with dirty water, and riots in the distance. There was no swimming pool at the Sunway, but yes, one night, two Americans went up in the lift at the same time as I did. They were dressed in beautiful suits, wore expensive watches, sported crisp handkerchiefs in their breast pockets. The older of the two, a big man, had shining silver hair, not a strand out of place. The younger one, shorter, tubbier, said, 'So if there's nothing doing here, what happens next?' The older one said, 'We go down to Saigon and see what we can stir up there.' It was as if I was invisible. Later, in the jazz bar, I saw an Asian man, dressed with even more exquisite care — silk socks, gold-framed spectacles — sitting reading a newspaper. I thought, He's going to meet with those men from upstairs. And, after a while, the older one did come down. The Asian man produced two very large cigars and, from his pocket, a guillotine cutter that sat snugly in the palm of his hand. He squeezed his hand shut, and opened it with a look of satisfaction on what I supposed was a perfect cut before offering it to the American and repeating the ritual. They sat, with little conversation between them. After some time had passed, the second, younger American appeared, took his seat and accepted the ritual of the cigar, though he looked pale at the prospect.

Of course, I wanted to stay and hear what I could, but there are only so many glasses of Luis Buñuel one can drink, and so many times you can listen to a jazz trio when they have completed their repertoire for the third time, without being observed. The Asian man had become aware of my presence.

The younger American reminded me of someone. Not Didion, I thought, Graham Greene. *The Quiet American*. There's trouble brewing here.

TROUBLE LURKED EVERYWHERE, if you let it find you. I took a taxi to the Temple of Literature, in the heart of Hanoi. The taxi driver charged me five times the fare I knew I should pay. When I remonstrated, he pushed me out of his taxi and came round to where I stood, clutching the side of the car, demanding the money. I gave it to him, but also, wrote the number of the taxi in my notebook as it disappeared down a boulevard.

The temple I had come to visit was built in honour of literature, a university begun in the year 1076. Five courtyards lie behind thick stone walls, filled with flowers and ancient trees and white-robed monks gliding through the shadows. As I walked in the temple grounds, I thought how the concept of temples built to honour words was so different from where I came from. I have made a temple in my head for words for as long as I can remember. They have preoccupied me when I should have been doing other things. Cuckoos and crickets, spring crocuses, they have darted and bloomed in my brain. I've put them down on paper, fought them and rearranged them and regretted them. Sometimes, when we got older, my husband and I, words stood in the way of love, those wrongly chosen, spoken in haste, shouted, as if we were killing each other.

As I am drawn to words so, too, I have a passion for synchonicity, numbers and apparently random events that fall into unexpected order. A strange thing had happened at the embassy the day before. One of the women who worked there asked me what part of my city

I lived in, back home in New Zealand. When I told her, she said, 'I've got a friend who lives in that suburb. What street?'

I told her. She said, 'That's the street where my friends live. What number?'

The house turned out to be two doors away from mine. In fact, it was a house where my husband and I had once lived. Although I can see the house as I write, and could reach its gate in seconds, I haven't been back in nearly forty years. It was a house where we were unhappy, words as sour as milk on a hot day. We rescued ourselves, and our children, when we saw that the house along the street, unlike ours, had sunlight on the lawn, and we bought it.

Now, in the Temple of Literature, some other words flooded back, ones that I'd forgotten for years: I bind myself unto this day. I stood still and listened to the refrain. Not writers' words or the cruel barbs of the past. Nothing to do with Hanoi.

I bind unto myself the power

Of the great love of cherubum;

The sweet 'Well done' in judgment hour . . .

It goes on for many verses. The St Patrick's Day hymn. My father was Irish. I used to carry the words on a piece of paper in my wallet, until it grew so worn and thin it fell to pieces. Nothing and everything. What I knew was just this: I was bound each day to the hospital where my husband lay and words for the moment seemed neither here nor there.

AT THE HOTEL, I REPORTED the taxi driver. Almost as soon as I had done this, I saw the irony of informing on a man who overcharged me in a country where tipping was forbidden. What did it matter? I had my dollars. But irony, I suspected, was a Western indulgence in a life and death country. The head of the taxi company came to the hotel, gave me back my money, apologised and bowed. I said, 'I don't want him to get into serious trouble. I expect he has a family who depend on him. Don't make him lose his job.' The head of the taxi company bowed again.

I told someone at the embassy what had happened. 'He'll be all right, won't he?' I asked.

The woman looked at me and shrugged. 'He's probably been taken into the forest and shot.'

I said, 'You don't mean that.' She didn't reply.

I don't know what happened to the man. But I looked at myself in the mirror that night, Western and virtuous and deadly. Jacaranda petals on the surface of the pool.

I blame myself. That is a fact, and it doesn't go away.

In the hospital, Stacey was still crouched on the floor outside intensive care, still babbling into her phone, banging her free fist up and down on the floor. She saw me and stood up, switching off the phone. 'Do you believe it,' she screamed. 'I've told these jerks in there what to do, and they're not listening to me. My daddy knows what they should be giving him.'

'They may not have that specific drug,' I said.

'It wouldn't matter if they did, they're too stupid to know what to do.'

'Perhaps they know more than you think,' I said. I saw the Vietnamese doctor looking at me, his eyes calm and level. 'Would you like to come in and see your husband?' he said. 'You could give him a little food.'

I put on my mask and gown. 'Does this mean that he's going to get well?'

'In time,' he said. 'Soon he will go to another ward.'

I fed my husband small spoonfuls of rice porridge.

I met Anne for lunch. We went to the Green Tangerine, a restaurant in an old French building with a mysterious staircase to an upper landing. We took a table in the courtyard; for dessert we ate *citron givré*, a tangerine carefully hollowed out, and refilled with the flesh mixed with cream and liqueur. The soft substance, the tart mixture of flavours combined like shots, as if we were drinking hard liquor. I began to feel drowsy. Anne said, 'About that money you've got in your safe?'

'Yes?'

'Perhaps it's time you bought yourself some treats. How about we go down silk street this afternoon?'

So we resorted to Pho Hàng Gai, Rue de la Soie, the street lined with silk shops. I picked up handfuls of different silk, holding them to my face, and in some I thought I detected the scent of skin like warm honey on the tongue, though it may have been that of food cooking at the back of the shop or incense burning. It didn't matter. If I closed my eyes for a moment, I was overcome with a young woman's ardour, could see the golden sheen on the back of my husband, my beloved, the play of light and dark, and I thought, M.D., you haven't abandoned me. I was wrong to doubt. I ordered jackets, and skirts and pants. I went on doing this for several days, the sweet cool fabrics slithering between my fingers, like the touch of my lover, while hundred-dollar bills drifted away.

I LEFT THE THREE WIVES behind me at intensive care. No, I think Irene rescued her husband the same day my husband was moved to another room, one where I could make short visits and talk to him. Irene and her husband were returning to America. Stacey may still be in Hanoi, perhaps strapped to a chair somewhere, out in a forest. I could have spared her a backwards glance but I didn't. But I did put my arm around Maria, awkwardly, because we were strangers, only there was nobody else and she was on her own. 'He was a good man, my husband,' she said, or that's what I understood her words to mean. His body was being taken away.

ANOTHER WEEK PASSED. WE TALKED a little during my visits but not about much. My husband couldn't imagine the places I'd been visiting. I watched as the tiny beautiful hovering nurses tenderly massaged him. I saw that they liked him, and I wanted him back for myself. Early one morning, I made my forty-first taxi ride across the city. I met with a French nurse who was accompanying us back to New Zealand. Four seats were booked for our party, three at the front of the plane — one for the nurse, one for an oxygen tank, one for my husband — and a fourth for me at the rear of the plane. We boarded an ambulance, and my husband caught brief glimpses of the city as we drove through it. We passed over the long bridge I'd detected the night we arrived spanning the vast river. 'Is that the Red River?' he asked. When the nurse said yes, he turned his head and I saw he had tears in eyes.

'Well, then, I've seen it,' he said. 'The Red River.'

Tam biêt, I said under my breath. Goodbye. Goodbye Red River, red bridge, red country.

I took his hand, our two skins crumpled together. Old silks.

Part II

The Man from Tooley Street

The farm lay on the edge of the river. The river sliced through the countryside, filled with a dark swollen power. During the milking season, a launch would collect cans of cream to take to a factory. The farmers stood on their makeshift wharves and shouted at the ferryman if he was late, fearing their cream would sour as the sun rose, and hard blue heat poured across the landscape.

Les Mullens took up his land late in the 1920s. First he cleared tall slender-limbed kahikatea from the swamplands, and sold the timber for butter boxes. Then he dug trenches to drain the swamps and after that he burned the tree stumps. He could never be sure of getting the burn-off right. More than once he had had to watch helplessly when flames licked underground and ignited the peat. The fires filled the skies with smouldering light and turned sunsets into torrents of black and orange cloud that made him think the earth and sun were about to collide. Only rain would quench the underground swamp fires, so another year would pass before grass could be sown. He toiled to lay down paddocks, to build a shed for the milking, to put up fences. First he bought two cows and when they were milking well, he went to the saleyards and bought a dozen. He milked them in cold dawns, before separating the cream from the skim, in time for the launch, tooting to signal its arrival. His hands swelled with chilblains, his socks inside his gumboots smelled dank and unwashed, which they usually were, for he had only two pairs and wool took a long time to dry.

In the morning, when he returned to the shed, he scrubbed and washed down for an hour or more. There was no knowing when a man from Tooley Street might pay him a visit. They did that sometimes, turning up unannounced to check on the suppliers, wearing their London-cut suits, four buttons instead of six, sharp lapels and shoulder pads. It seemed to Les they all looked the same, with sleek cheeks and tightly clipped moustaches. Even when they wore boots they picked their way through the mud, distaste in their eyes. The job of the Tooley Street agents was to report back to their masters in London to make sure the suppliers were sending them nothing but the best butter.

When his small herd began to show a modest profit, the peat fires took hold again, driven in a tributary of flames beneath the earth's crust from a neighbouring farm. It was as much as he could do to stay put another year, and the mortgage kept falling due month after month, even though he'd dried off most of his stock and had nothing coming in. He went labouring on the roads until he could start over again the next year.

He took a couple of heifers to the saleyard the following season, where Percy George, the only man he thought of as a friend, said, 'Mate, you need a wife.'

'Christ, who'd take a second look at me,' Les said. It was years since he'd looked in a mirror, except for a quick glance when he shaved before going out on days like this. When he touched his fingers to his face he felt the skin grizzled from the weather like that of an old man.

All the same, he knew what Percy said was an answer. Married men were the ones who got ahead, acquired bigger herds and bought the new milking machines. They wore clean clothes and ate a decent meal now and then. The wives milked and turned the handle of the separator, and then when children came along they were out in the shed as soon as they could sit upright on a stool and strip a cow's teat. The more kids the better, even if it did mean mouths to feed. There were other comforts a woman would bring, although he hadn't thought of them in a long while. But now that the idea of a wife had surfaced, he was possessed with thoughts of what else she would bring to his existence.

'Reckon I'm a bit past the dance halls,' he said, the next time he met Percy. That was where men went to look for wives, only usually they started a bit earlier. 'I'm thirty-five,' he said, 'an old bastard.'

His friend leant on a railing, prodding a cow's rump, the grey felt brim of his hat pulled over his eyes to keep the sun off his face, a cigarette stuck to his lip. 'Could be you're right.' His suggestion hadn't come out of thin air in the first place. He'd talked it over with his wife, Hazel, who thought perhaps it was what Les needed, although she worried about the sort of husband he'd make, whether there was a woman strong enough to cope with him.

Les had a temper; she and Percy had both seen it in action the day he brought his cows along Hang Dog Road to put them to the bull. Hang Dog wasn't the name on the maps, but that was what the locals called it. Hang Dog Road was a straight stretch of gravel a good ten miles long. Les's farm was at the opposite end to Percy and Hazel's.

That day, when the cows were getting what Hazel called 'their little fling', Les had got in the bull's way. The beast flicked his leg with one horn, drawing blood. It was a good thing, Percy and Hazel said, that that bull had had his horns tipped or there would have been a death. Fortunately they kept a pitchfork on hand when their bull was mating because the animal got touchy if he wasn't getting his way. But it was Les who flew into such a black rage that he grabbed the pitchfork and set off on his horse. The bull raced this way and that, foaming and rearing up against the fences when Les got near him, plunging his fork into the animal's side so that there was blood and froth and screaming everywhere. Percy shouted, 'Lay off my bull, Mullens', and jumped on his own horse, pursuing Les with an axe in his hand. It was Hazel who walked out into the paddock and spoke quietly to the bull. The men, seeing her standing there, had both stopped. The bull, its eyes red and rolling, made to charge at her, then changed its mind. Hazel George didn't stand nonsense.

Later on, Hazel told Percy he should have known better than to go chasing after Les like that. A man like him. She didn't actually say what kind of man Les was, but they both knew what she meant. He got het up over little things; it wasn't as if he was hurt bad. At the time, the two men shook hands without words, and the next time they met it was put aside, except for Percy's suggestion of a woman.

'My house isn't much.' Les was speaking the truth here. His house was two rooms with a lean-to where he kept the copper and a tin bath he'd picked up second-hand. Percy's house was a big comfortable place with a dining room large enough to hold a table for eight and a dresser, a sitting room, and a row of bedrooms that led off a passage. Les wasn't sure how many bedrooms there were — it wasn't one of those things you asked — but Percy and Hazel had four children, two boys, two girls, and he supposed that most of them had bedrooms of their own. There was a dark red carpet in the sitting room with a yellow Lion of Scotland, and curtains at the windows patterned with green daisies on a cream background, and a wind-up gramophone in the corner.

'You'll step up in no time,' Percy said. 'Once you've got a wife.'

'I've got to find one first. She'd have to be desperate.'

'I'll tell you what to do,' Percy said, looking over his shoulder to see that nobody was listening to their conversation.

KATHLEEN KEATS WAITED FOR THE phone call from Auckland. She had hardly ventured out of the house for a week. For months she had kept her own solitary company, walking downtown only now and then to buy necessities, and some days to have a cup of tea in H & J Smith, where she sat in the corner of the tearoom and watched passers-by in the wide Invercargill street. She liked the wild red roses that scrambled down the sides of a raised garden, first as they came into bud, small bright sparks of colour, as tantalising as happiness, unfolding into bloom, and beginning to fade as the season ended. It seemed odd to her that a town would plant wild roses at its heart. In England, where she and her sister Dorothy had spent their childhoods, she was used to town gardens that grew neat ordered rows of flowers. Now and then a car would pass by, as she sat with her eyes turned towards the window. She didn't know anyone who owned a car, although her late husband had driven one, an Oldsmobile that belonged to the company. The country was hardly out of the sugarbag years, when people looked for handouts at best, or cigarette ends in the gutter. She saw herself as fortunate that she had her own little house, paid for before all her family's trouble began, and there were the four of them, her and her husband, and their daughter Joy and son Ben. Ben was now God knows where, although the last she'd heard it was one of the mining towns in Australia — Kalgoorlie, she thought — and shuddered at the thought (Invercargill was a temperance town). Her daughter — her pride and Joy, she often said, and now for six months she had said, in the same breath, pride comes before a fall.

Now the time was nearly upon her and the worst would soon be over. But was it upon her, or was it on Joy? As she sat in the department store and licked sweet crumbs from her lips, and wiped them for good measure with a napkin, she tried to convince herself, as she had all these past months, that she had nothing to reproach herself for, that the awfulness of what had happened couldn't be laid at her door. But the wickedness of her daughter still scorched her with shame. And she, Joy's mother, had told so many lies that no prayers said morning or night would take them away.

'Where's that lovely clever girl of yours?' asked the woman behind the tearoom counter.

'She's gone north,' she said. 'Up to stay with my sister Dorothy in the North Island.'

'Oh really? I'd like to go to the North Island,' the woman said. 'I'm hoping to get to Christchurch some day, but that would be a big step.'

'It would,' said Kathleen, willing the conversation over.

'So where does your sister live? Will young Joy be able to get a job there?'

'They're travelling around together, exploring the countryside,' said Kathleen. 'It's nice for my sister. She never married so it's nice for her to have the company of a young person.' Her hands shook so much when she sat down that her tea was tipping into her saucer. She sat up as straight as she could, a woman above average height, but neat in her bones, her faded floral dress ironed to perfection. Her husband had insurance when he died. He was a herd tester who had been kicked in the head by a cow, although the doctor who performed the autopsy said it was actually his heart that had given out. There was a little company payout all the same.

'No,' she told a neighbour who enquired, 'Joy hasn't decided whether it'll be teaching or nursing at this stage.' She thought she saw the neighbour's sideways smile when she told her about Joy going up north. The neighbour was a younger woman with children at school. It was hard to know what the woman thought. She wasn't to know that the neighbour told others that Kathleen seemed a bit touched in the head, but it was probably the change.

Kathleen knew, in fact, that it wouldn't be nursing, because Joy wrote piteous letters to say how afraid she was of the nurses, how the girls really disliked them, and how they threatened them with a good slap if they didn't behave themselves when they went into labour and told them they could look ahead to their feet in stirrups for a few hours, and it served them right. Before Kathleen collected her bread and milk deliveries from the box, she had taken to checking that her neighbour was inside, so she wouldn't have to speak to her. She should have been working in the garden — soon it would be time to plant out the bulbs — but she walked past the rows of red and pink phlox that she so enjoyed every summer, now smothered in weeds. Some days she would simply make breakfast, then sit with her cat in her lap and the newspaper in front of her until it would be eleven o'clock and she had no idea where the time had gone. Other days, she cleaned and rearranged the furniture, or picked up things that had belonged to Joy and Ben when they were children. Ben's wooden trucks that his father had made him, Joy's teddy bear that sat on the quilt of her bed, her clothes hanging in the wardrobe, dresses she had worn only the summer before. Or she inhaled deeply the cracked end of the apple soap that Joy used to wash her hair, now dried out on the bathroom ledge.

Kathleen had rehearsed her response when the call came. She would stay calm, ask the necessary questions, make sure that her daughter was recovering well. She would be short and to the point:

after all a toll call from Auckland was a great expense and the charges would be reversed. A collect call, Madam. Will you take it?

And then. And then, she didn't know. She saw herself replacing the telephone in its cradle and sitting down to make more tea. To work out what happened next. To wait for Joy to return. Joy, with the neat wavy bob of brown hair and serious blue eyes, the firm pointed little chin that Kathleen would cup in her hand when the child was small, the forehead she kissed. Goodnight princess, sweet dreams. She had let go of her anger. Joy would come back unchanged, as if nothing had happened. What she wanted more than anything was to hold her daughter and whisper to her, It will be all right. It's over now. You don't have to think of it again. She should never have let her go to the dances, but they were, after all, run by the Bible class, and it wasn't what you expected when the church was involved. Nor, at seventeen, was Joy a child. The boy's father had thrashed him for doing what he did and let it go at that. Kathleen hadn't set foot in the church since Joy went away, although sometimes she dropped to her knees and prayed, because that is what she had done all her life. She prayed that Joy and Ben would come back soon, that the house would be full of their voices again. Bring back Joy, she prayed, and none of the old guilt about praying for her own ends entered her thoughts.

But until the phone call came, she knew the pain for Joy still lay ahead, and in the night, she woke sweating, dreaming of pain, the way it had been for her, and she took rapid panting breaths. After these dreams, she was sure the phone would ring at dawn, but days passed beyond the expected time without a word from the matron of the home.

In the end, Kathleen rang. She put it off as long as she could. A letter a week will be quite enough, the matron had said firmly when Joy first went to the home; please don't unsettle her. You must understand, Mrs Keats, that we are very busy here. We have all the new mothers and fathers coming to get their babies, and the children to feed and care for. We simply haven't got time to talk about how these girls are on a daily basis. We'll let you know when the time comes.

She rang the handle of the phone and gave the number to the operator. She didn't know the woman but it was said she listened in to calls. You could hear her breathing sometimes.

When the call was answered in Auckland, it took a long time for the matron to come to the phone. Kathleen had almost given up hope when she heard the other woman's brisk voice.

'Yes, Mrs Keats? Is the girl home?'

'Home? You must be thinking of someone else. I'm *Joy's* mother.'

'I sent you a letter. I'd have thought you'd have got it by now. And the girl should be arriving any time now.'

A letter. It hadn't occurred to her that the matron wouldn't have contacted her straight away. 'I don't understand,' she stammered.

'Mrs Keats, listen. Joy had a girl, a nice little baby with a good weight. She had no trouble with the delivery, but she certainly made plenty for everybody afterwards. She knew she couldn't see her baby but she kept on screaming and crying. She was upsetting all the girls. Really, I didn't have time to make a telephone call — we had our hands full with that naughty girl of yours. We told her and told her that the child has gone to a good home but she wouldn't listen.'

'When was this? The birth.'

'All of six days ago now.'

'Perhaps if I could talk to Joy.'

'But Mrs Keats, this is what I'm trying to tell you. Joy isn't here. She was in good health. When she said she wanted to go home I deemed her fit to travel. She caught the train south yesterday. Well, she should be home tomorrow, I expect. I know it's a long journey. Now go out to your letterbox, I'm sure you'll find my letter there. The postal service is very efficient.'

The letter was delivered that day, but Joy didn't arrive. After another three days of waiting, Kathleen rang the matron again. 'I'll call the police,' she said.

The matron's voice hardened. 'That doesn't sound wise, Mrs Keats. What would you tell them?'

'That my daughter was sent to your care and is now a missing person. How do I know my daughter's even alive? What are you trying to cover up? Yes, that's what I'll tell them, that you're hiding something from me.'

'I'll get someone to look into it,' the matron said, after a difficult silence. Kathleen thought she heard breathing on the line, but she supposed it was the matron's, and anyway, she didn't care who knew her business any more. She felt a terrible rising panic beneath her breastbone.

When she put the phone down, she sat for a moment before making a second call, this time to her sister Dorothy, who really did live in Auckland, and telling her what had happened, about Joy's disgrace, about her missing child. Her missing children. Her missing granddaughter. For now she had begun to comprehend the whole story, the one she had refused to acknowledge until now. She was a grandmother without a grandchild.

Dorothy clicked her tongue behind her teeth. 'What do you want me to do?'

'I'm not sure, but I'll let you know.'

Kathleen packed a small suitcase in preparation for a journey, although as yet she had no idea where it would take her. What she knew for certain was that she had to travel north to find Joy. During that evening the phone did ring. It was Joy.

Her daughter's voice had a bruised husky quality to it, not like the girl's voice she knew. She remembered that the matron had mentioned a great deal of yelling and screaming.

'I'm in a hotel in Ngaruawahia,' Joy said. She repeated the name slowly for her mother. 'It's by a river, to the south of Auckland. There are farms all around here. I've met a farmer who's asked me to marry him.'

'Where did you meet a farmer?' she whispered, clinging to the back of a chair.

'At the train station in Auckland.'

'You talked to a man in the train station?'

'He arrived just after I did. He said he'd seen me with the nurse from the home. Oh, he didn't know where I'd been, at least I don't think so. His name's Les Mullens, Mum.'

'You can't marry a stranger. Come home this instant, Joy.'

'I have to have your permission to get married. It seems the best thing. He's got land near here. What else can I do?'

'I'm not angry any more,' Kathleen said. 'Dear.'

'It's for the best,' Joy said.

'I'm leaving in the morning. You're to stay where you are. Do you hear me, Joy? I'll see you in Ngaruawahia.' She edged out the strange vowels of the place name, a town she couldn't imagine.

This was the first time that Joy disappeared.

JOY KEATS, WHO WAS SHORTLY to become Joy Mullens, sat in the dining room of the old hotel and waited for her mother. She sat by a window picking cracked varnish from a sill with her fingernail. The smell of cigars and brandy was heavy on the air, from gentlemen taking their leisure the night before. She watched the huge river that flowed through the town, beneath the railway bridge. From where she sat, the water looked green and as thick as sauce. The day was hot for the time of year, and very humid. 'It's the Waikato climate,' the woman at reception told her, when she asked for a fan. She was a woman of perhaps fifty, with tightly permed hair and bright lipstick. 'It's either very hot or so cold the clothes will freeze in the tub if you leave them overnight. Just you wait,' she said. 'Black frosts. Well, you might get to see them.'

She looked at Joy with undisguised curiosity, as if she had seen it all. As if she knew that Joy was here for a reason, that she was thinking of staying but might not. Since she had agreed to Les's proposal, Joy had changed her mind several times. The thought of fleeing crossed her mind often. Only it was difficult to go far, because her Aunt Dorothy had arrived on a Road Services bus the morning after she rang her mother. She liked her aunt and it was suddenly comforting to have someone she knew close by. Dorothy, understatedly elegant in dusky pink linen and pearls, was older than her sister. And Kathleen hadn't been young when Joy was born. Yet, although Dorothy seemed elderly to Joy, she had been surprisingly kind. When she saw her niece she embraced her. Over afternoon tea, she leant forward and placed her thin veined hand on her knee. 'I was young once,' she said in a conspiratorial way. So that Joy wondered what secret her aunt harboured and whether her mother knew, and guessed that she probably didn't.

As soon as she had placed her suitcase in her room and removed her coat, Dorothy went to the hotel desk and placed a call, holding out a piece of paper with a number written on it for the receptionist. She spoke in a curt voice to the matron of the home, advising her that Joy was safe, and of their whereabouts, and giving her home number in Auckland as well. She banged the receiver down unnecessarily hard, and said something under her breath that Joy didn't quite catch. She had been taught that swearing was wicked.

'My mother told people I was travelling around the north with you,' Joy remarked. 'Perhaps we could do that.'

'Not just at present,' her aunt replied. 'I think you're still very tired.' They had been for a walk through the small town, past a row of graceful old houses, built for military men and their families, housed at the time of the wars seventy years or so before. 'The natives, you know,' Dorothy murmered. They saw children clustered near the river, diving into the water and surfacing, their white teeth flashing against their dark complexions. Joy, from Invercargill, could not remember seeing Maori before. Her aunt told her that she would see plenty more of them if she was going to live in the Waikato, although they kept to themselves in their own pas. When they came close to the railway bridge, Joy looked at the languid river and shivered in the bright hot air.

'You're not feverish?' Dorothy asked anxiously.

'I don't think so. It looks so far down, doesn't it? Such deep water.'

'You're tired,' her aunt repeated.

'I am tired,' Joy admitted, when they reached the hotel again. While she slept she didn't think of her baby for whole hours at a time. A girl. She was told it was a girl, and she had heard her cry, a few tiny whimpers as she was whisked out of the delivery room. As if the baby was calling out to her: never leave me, never abandon me. And she had.

'Do you have much bleeding?'

'Not as much as I expected.'

'Does Mr Mullens know your circumstances?'

Joy reddened. 'I think so.'

'He'll have to respect you for a time,' Dorothy said in a tactful voice. 'It might be better if you came and stayed with me for a while before the marriage takes place.'

But Joy's mother was already on her way north. Her train was due that evening. In the morning the three of them, Joy, her aunt and her mother, would meet Les Mullens.

A YEAR HAD PASSED SINCE Percy George had suggested that Les find himself a wife. At first, Les had considered hastening to Auckland the very next week to wait outside the home as the unmarried mothers were discharged in the mornings. You could tell them by their suitcases, as they came out the gates, Percy said, or so he'd been told.

Percy persuaded him to wait a while. 'You need to fix yourself up a little bit. Even girls as hard up as that lot might take fright at a scarecrow like you.'

Les listened. The past year, 1932, had been a good one for him. The herd was doing well, there had been steady rain, new grass, the peat fires appeared to have burnt themselves out, at least up Hang Dog Road. In winter, when the cows were dry, he spent time on the house. He added two more rooms, replaced the flat roof with a pitched gable. It looked like a proper home now, square and plain, but solid enough, and free of leaks. In the summer he put white paint on the walls, and red on the new roof. At the auction rooms in town he found two fireside chairs, covered in red velvet. He also bought a double bed and a chest of drawers.

Another season was drawing to a close. Les shaved every morning, and his skin had acquired a smooth mahogany tan. The man who presented himself to the three women in Ngaruawahia was dressed in grey flannels, baggy at the knees to be sure, but clean, a checked cotton shirt, a red tie knotted beneath a black jersey. His thinning black hair was slicked above his ears with grease he'd bought from the Rawleigh's man. When he asked for Joy at the desk, she hurried towards him from out of the lounge, where she had been waiting. The receptionist smiled and glanced down at her oval fingernails.

Kathleen's and Dorothy's eyes met. Kathleen shook her head, her eyes filling with sudden tears. 'I never did trust a man with a cleft chin,' she would confide to Dorothy that night. But Joy was walking towards them with a resolute air, the man at her side, and he was extending his hand to shake theirs.

They sat, the four of them, in an awkward circle on the cracked leather couches in the hotel lounge.

'As you know, I've asked Joy to do me the honour of becoming my wife,' Les began. He reached out in a possessive way for Joy's small hand. Her nails were short, and the skin reddened. She had scrubbed a good many corridors in the home. But Les's hand looked huge, engulfing hers, a forest of black hairs covering its back. Kathleen noted the rime of filth beneath each nail. There were still things he had to learn.

'I have a house,' Les was saying, 'and a hundred and twenty acres in grass, eighteen milking cows that will be added to as soon as I get machines. You'll know what I mean, I'm sure, Mrs Keats, coming as you do from Southland. I understand it's dairy country, too.'

Kathleen said that yes, she did know, and it sounded as if he was very secure, and she admired a man for that.

'I run Friesians. Holstein-Friesian cows,' he added by way of explanation. 'I put them to a Hereford bull. I prefer them to Jerseys because you can run them for beef as well as for milking.'

'I see,' said Kathleen. 'Yes, I do see.'

'Hard work, I tell you,' Les said. 'It's bloody hard work. Oh, I beg your pardon. I've lived alone for a long time.'

Once they had sat down, he carefully placed Joy's hand back in her lap. As if reading Kathleen's thoughts, he said, 'I'll take care of your daughter. I can see she's a girl from a good family.'

Kathleen closed her eyes. 'And what of your own family, Mr Mullens?'

'My parents? Dead now. I was one of twelve, up Dargaville way. One of the younger boys, so the family farm was passed on above me. Well, that's the way it goes.'

'But you have family who'd come to the wedding?' The words were out before Kathleen could stop them. They sounded as if she had already agreed to this marriage taking place. Yet there was still so much for her and Joy to talk about, an alternative future that could work. She saw Joy going off to Dunedin Teachers' College, and herself with a job in H & J Smith, for which she had long hankered. Now that times were looking up, she thought it possible. From a conversation overheard in the tearoom, she happened to know that there would be a vacancy in haberdashery. In the weekends, Joy would come home to her, and she would fuss over her, and they would both save money, perhaps take a trip to see Ben in Australia. Oh, there was still so much they could do.

The man sitting before her shrugged his shoulders. 'There're none of them I'd want to see,' he answered. 'I thought the wedding could take place as soon as the licence can be arranged. While you're here, Mrs Keats. Perhaps at your sister's house.' And here, he nodded towards Dorothy. He has this all planned out, Kathleen thought. He is ahead of me by far.

'Your teaching, Joy,' Kathleen whispered. 'What of that?'

'What of it?' Joy said shortly. Her eyes were weary, almost colourless. 'Sooner or later I'd go to some country school and meet a nice man, just like Les, and get married. Why not now?'

Kathleen wasn't certain that Les was nice. He was not what she would have chosen. An old saying clanged in her memory: beggars can't be choosers.

As if he had not paid much attention to what had just been said, Les added, 'I've got a friend, a neighbour of mine, who will stand up for me, name of Percy George.'

In this way, Joy came to be married to Les, in Dorothy's crowded little sitting room, full of fat cushions and crocheted doilies on the side tables. The sisters had made a tray of sandwiches and a cake with lemon frosting. Joy wore a grey voile dress that Dorothy insisted on buying at Smith & Caughey's, one that made her look more shapely. Kathleen said, 'She's sure to get her figure back, you shouldn't waste the money, Dorothy.' To which Dorothy had retorted, through tight lips, that she expected there would be more occasions when Joy would lose her shape. Dorothy wasn't struck by Les Mullens either, but, as she said, all things considered, they could make the best of things.

A minister came to hear the couple's vows, and Percy was there in his suit, and wiry old Hazel, who wore a hat, the two of them acting as the witnesses. Kathleen promised herself not to give way to tears. Inside, she felt as if Joy was dying in front of her eyes, but she couldn't show that. Joy herself looked bewildered, somehow apart from the proceedings. She held out her hand for Les to put the wedding ring on her finger. When the ring was in place she looked down at it with curiosity, seeming to wonder how it had got there.

While Kathleen and Dorothy were clearing away the last crumbs of cake, the phone rang. Percy and Hazel had already left, and Joy and Les were preparing to go to the station to catch the train.

The call was from the matron of the home. The people who had taken Joy's baby had brought her back. The child had birthmarks down one side of her neck and it had to be agreed that she was a little unsightly, although pretty enough in other ways. The couple hadn't been bothered by the marks at first, but now they were home, their friends had commented, and they'd had a change of heart. The matron thought they ought to know. They were not to worry; she had no doubt someone would take the child.

'How can they pick and choose like that?' Dorothy cried, her face flaming with rage.

'Les.' Joy was looking at her new husband with startled excitement, her eyes alight at last. 'We can have her. The baby.'

Les looked at her with barely disguised disgust. 'I'm not taking someone else's bastard,' he said.

Everyone stopped whatever they were doing. The silence in the room was palpable. Joy, possessed by sudden anguish, looked at her left hand. She pulled at the ring, but it was stuck firmly on her finger.

'That won't be necessary,' said Kathleen, stepping forward and placing her hand on Joy's arm. 'Now stop. I'm going to collect the baby.'

'You, Mum?'

'Yes, me. I'm going straight to the home. I'm going to take the little girl with me. You can come and see her whenever you like.' She looked fairly and squarely at her new son-in-law. 'If you will allow it, Mr Mullens.'

LATER THAT NIGHT, LES TOOK his new wife to the house he had prepared for her. He had left his old Chevy flatbed parked at the railway station. They were both silent as she climbed into the cab. There had, actually, been nothing to say on the train south. Les had made a tentative peace offering. 'I'm sorry about the kid,' he said. 'You can see how it would be, can't you?'

Joy shook her head and looked out the window.

'We need to start with a clean slate, you and me. That's what you'd decided, hadn't you?'

She nodded and hunched her shoulders, refusing to look at him.

'Well, say something,' he said. When she wouldn't, he muttered under his breath and kicked the seat in front of him. 'Frig it,' he said.

As they drove down Hang Dog Road, he sniffed the wind. 'Jesus, no,' he groaned. 'The fires are back.'

Joy smelled them, too. Smoke, laden with a spicy aromatic scent, like good pipe tobacco, swirled towards them. She saw the tongues of fire in the paddocks, leaping and licking, flames hopscotching between sods of earth, along the edges of deep trenches carved in the soil. In the dying light of day it looked like a scene from hell, the rushes in the swampland turned to tips of fire, ash melting away in the breeze. Later, when she had been there for a matter of years, she would learn the names of the plants that grew between the rushes: flax, wild orchids, sundew and bladderwort that consumed insects, and the frothy feather-duster heads of sedge. That night, she heard only the screams of dying frogs, thin wails of despair.

At the house, Les showed her to a room, furnished by a lone camp stretcher, a blanket thrown over it. 'You'd best sleep here for the time being,' he said. Through the thin plywood wall she heard him moving about in the next room, his shoes dropping to the floor, the rattle of a coathanger, the creak of a mattress that she supposed she would share in time.

In the morning he was up and gone from the house before Joy woke. Outside lay a thick cloud of smoke, or was it fog? Fog was something else the receptionist had mentioned, and although she was no stranger to fog down south, the way the woman described it — the damp rising up from the swamplands, wrapping its clinging embrace around you, heat and water mixed in the atmosphere — had made her skin crawl. When she was dressed, she walked outside. Fingers of clammy fog reached into her hair and when she breathed she felt her nostrils fill with it. A trumpet of sound bellowed beside her, making her shriek with terror. Through the mist she made out the side of an animal pressing against a fence, and recognised the outline of a cow.

She retreated inside. When she had recovered herself, she examined her surroundings. Tin dishes stood in a sink half full of scummy water. She looked at what had to be done. After an hour or two, he came back to the house, his face covered with black soot, his baggy trousers held up by braces, soaked at the hems.

'I've lit the copper,' she said. 'Give me your clothes.' He turned away from her, and let his trousers go. She saw his lean buttocks, gleaming like tallow, the way he covered his nakedness at the front with his free hand. She leant over and touched his backside and he flinched.

This was to be the way of it: the fires, the heat, the darkness, the blackened man, her entrance into torment.

RUTH MULLENS REMEMBERED A TIME when her name was Ruth Keats, but that was when she was a very small child. She recalled a town, far in the south, with pretty frilly-faced Victorian buildings and a water tower. The house where she lived shone with waxed furniture and a polished kitchen floor, and there was always hot water for baths. She wore new clothes and patent leather shoes. Her mother, whose name was Kathleen, called her her precious little jewel, and tucked her in bed with a big teddy bear that was the only thing that didn't smell new. The smell was familiar and comforting, though, and at night she whispered to it as if it was a living friend. Her mother said that it had belonged to her Auntie Joy who had lived here when she was a little girl, just like Ruth did. Some day she would meet her aunt, but not for a while. It would be wonderful when Auntie Joy came; they would have such fun together.

Ruth asked, 'Is she your sister, Mum?'

Kathleen hesitated. 'Sort of,' she said. 'Yes, I suppose you could call her that. My very little sister.'

'When will she come?'

'Soon, I hope. She works hard on her farm.' Ruth knew about farms because she and her mother travelled through the countryside from time to time on buses, and Kathleen pointed out paddocks and cows. 'Joy lives in a place that looks like this,' she said, although she didn't know for sure. 'When you're a big girl and go to school you can write her a letter and tell her what you've seen. And perhaps she'll write back to you.'

'Has she got children too?'

'Not yet.'

Not yet. Joy had written more than once to say that another baby had gone. Les wasn't happy. *I think,* Joy once wrote to her mother, *that it's the work in the shed. Hazel George has told me I shouldn't carry cream cans, but it's part of my job. The cream truck comes along the road now, and Les has built a cream stand. We put the cans out every morning. The herd is getting bigger and bigger. We have machines now, but Les has his hands full. I'm hoping I'll get down south in the winter, though Les gets in a mood when I talk about it. Well, that's life. I think a bit of rest and a change of scene might help matters. I know he's dead keen on kids. Kiss Ruthie goodnight from me.*

And then late in May of 1938 another letter came. *Thanks for the money, Mum. I'll use it for a ticket, as you suggested. Looks as if it won't be long now. I talked to Les this morning. He said well go when you like. He's not happy, but he knows I need a visit home. Five years, it's been a long time. I'm being as nice as I can to Les, mind you, because I need him to take me to the train. Is Ruthie enjoying school? I can't believe she's started already. Oh, I want to see her with her schoolbag. Perhaps I can walk her to school and meet the teacher.*

At the end of June, Kathleen wrote to ask if a date had been set. She received no reply to her letter. An odd sense of foreboding had overtaken her. It felt, in some unaccountable and indiscernible way, as it had when Joy had been in the home years before. As if somehow she had mislaid her daughter. After another week passed, she phoned the home of her daughter and her husband. The operator put the call through: 3 M, two long Morse code signals, like a frog's dying croak. Les Mullens answered.

'Can I speak to Joy?' she asked, when it was clear no conversation was forthcoming.

'Well, that's over to you, isn't it,' he said. 'She's your visitor.'

'Don't be silly. Where is she, Les?'

'Staying with you as far as I know.'

'When did she leave?'

'I left her at the railway station a month ago.'

'She never came here.'

'Then don't ask me.'

'Did you see her get on the train?' Kathleen felt her voice rising as she tried to contain her panic.

'I had work to do. This is a farm, Mrs Keats. I need a spare pair of hands round here.' He had never called her Mum or Mother, as a son-in-law might be expected to do, but then they had met each other only briefly, years before when he married her daughter. 'I left her at the station.'

'Something must have happened to her,' Kathleen said. 'She's not here, I swear to God.' Her hands were shaking so badly she could hardly hold the phone.

'Oh well, who knows what Joy did. Joy does what Joy wants, if you ask me. Perhaps she's gone off with the man from Tooley Street.'

'The man from Tooley Street?'

'She was making out pretty friendly with him the last time he called, if you ask me,' Les said, warming to his subject. 'Scones and tea, she had it all laid on for him.'

'We'll have to call the police,' Kathleen said, and the words sounded unpleasantly familiar.

'Well, you call the police if you like. You'll look a right fool, I reckon, when it turns out she's gone off with some man.'

Kathleen rang Dorothy, but her sister hadn't seen or heard from Joy in a long time. She rang Percy George, who had become vague and had trouble stringing words together. He'd lost Hazel to pleurisy the winter before, and she recalled now that Joy had mentioned that in one of her letters. He couldn't remember when he last saw Joy. A good girl, he said, she's a good one. Les got a gem there, even if she is on the quiet side. He took himself along the road for dinner now and then and she always had a good stew on the hob, did Joy. The last time? Oh, he was sorry, he'd have to think about that. Kathleen saw him in her mind's eye, scratching the back of his head, a habit she'd noticed at the wedding. Be a couple of months back now, he thought. She was talking about going south.

'She didn't mention the man from Tooley Street?'

Not that he could recall. Fact of the matter was, he hadn't seen a man from Tooley Street round here in a long while. They mostly paid attention to the factories these days, which was really their job.

'Les says he was at the farm. He says Joy made him scones and tea.'

'Well, I dunno about that,' Percy said. 'That's a bit of a surprise, to tell you the truth. There was one here a couple of years back. Very natty he was, too.'

'You wouldn't have forgotten?'

'No, I wouldn't forget something like that. Not the man from Tooley Street. You don't forget them. A queer bunch of jokers. They don't stand round having cups of tea, not them. Not unless they took a great fancy to the lady of the house.' And here he chuckled, an old man's grubby laughter.

Kathleen did go to the police in Invercargill. She sat in an interview room, a little box-like room with initials scratched on the table, permeated with the stale smell of urine as if someone had peed in the corner. Because of the war, the police force was down in numbers. The sergeant who interviewed her was older, courteous, kind enough. When he asked if Joy had ever gone missing before, and she had to admit that yes, once she had gone off on her own for a bit, he bit the end of his pencil and made a note.

Was it a happy marriage? Kathleen said there may have been some problems, but she didn't know much about that. It was a long time since she'd seen her daughter. He made another note.

Could she have gone off with a man? That was what her son-in-law had suggested, Kathleen said carefully, but Joy wouldn't do a thing like that. Please listen to me, she said to him, all sorts of things happen up in that place. There was a man who'd fed his wife to the pigs not that long ago. Besides, Joy wouldn't go away for all that time without letting her know. Not with her having the little girl and all. The little girl? So then she had to explain about Ruth. The policeman sighed and shut his notebook. They would make some inquiries up north, he said, but he couldn't promise anything.

'You don't understand,' Kathleen cried. 'Joy was desperate to come and see her. She's a very good girl, my daughter.'

WOMAN DISAPPEARS IN THE WAIKATO

A woman has disappeared from the railway station at Ngaruawahia. The woman, Mrs Joy Mullens, aged 25, is a farmer's wife, last seen in early May. The police have ruled out foul play, but anyone with information regarding her whereabouts is requested to report the matter to their nearest police station. Mrs Mullens has short brown hair and blue eyes, with a fair complexion. She was last seen wearing a green blouse, red cardigan, and black pleated skirt. She was believed to be carrying a small suitcase. It is possible that she embarked on a ship bound for England, under an assumed name.

This piece of paper is one of the items that Ruth will discover among the possessions of Mamie Mullens, but this will happen far in the future.

There was another clipping from *Truth* newspaper with a headline that said:

WIFE KNOWN TO HAVE HAD A PAST

MRS MULLENS, VANISHED WIFE OF WAIKATO FARMER, HAD A SECRET LOVE CHILD. MR LESLIE MULLENS SAYS IT WAS NOT THE FIRST TIME SHE HAD DISAPPEARED, OR THE FIRST FANCY MAN SHE HAD HAD, AND IT COULD HAVE HAPPENED AGAIN FOR

ALL HE KNEW. MR MULLENS SAID HIS WIFE HAD ENTERTAINED A
GENTLEMAN FROM LONDON IN THEIR FARMHOUSE. 'I'M BLOWED
IF I KNOW WHAT SHE GOT UP TO,' HE TOLD OUR REPORTER.

Underneath this was a blurred photograph of Joy, and it was on this
yellowed page that Ruth first deciphered the outline of her mother's
face. Whatever other images of her there may have been, none existed
any longer. And whatever story might have been the truth, she never
learnt more, when she went to live up north where, soon after, she
became Ruth Mullens. Her stepmother, Mamie, wasn't really her
stepmother because she and Les couldn't get married until Joy
had been gone without trace for seven years and could be properly
pronounced dead. But Mamie, who was a widow, said it didn't really
matter, and to hell with what people thought because she wasn't a
conventional kind of woman, no sirree, she was the woman to turn
things around on this farm. She had arrived on the farm as a land
girl, during the war. Mamie was a tall powerful woman with bulging
grey-green eyes and a mane of wavy reddish hair that swirled around
her shoulders. Her first husband, she said, had died of tuberculosis
during the depression. Galloping consumption, she called it. She had
a daughter called Patricia, who was strong and tall, too, for her age,
and already worked in the shed alongside Mamie and Les. Her eyes
weren't as prominent as her mother's but still large and overly bright,
and her hair sprang from a centre parting in the same startled way.

'You can get your hands dirty, too,' Mamie told Ruth, the first
night she was there. 'You're old enough to do some jobs around
the place. Just do what your big sister tells you.' This was how she
referred to Patricia. Her daughter had taken the name of Mullens,
too. It took years for Ruth to figure out that Patricia wasn't Les's
daughter, any more than she was. When Ruth was ten, Mamie had

a child with Les, who was called Blanche Mullens, and all three of them, she and Patricia and Blanche, were described as sisters.

'Make sure you keep your mind on your work, too,' Mamie told Ruth. 'From what I've heard, your mother never did a tap around the place. What could you expect? She had her mind on a man as it turns out. I hope you're not going to be like her. You're a milk and no cream girl, if I may say so. You need colour in your cheeks. And mind you stay put at school. We'll have no running away tricks from you. You're here to stay.'

At first Ruth was frightened of the cows, the big ruminative animals with their patchwork flanks and pansy-like eyes, but she grew used to them. 'I suppose that's something to be thankful for,' Les grumbled. He never spoke to her if he could help it.

Some weekends, Mamie's sisters would come down from Auckland to visit. The sisters would sit in the front room that now had prints on the wall, and a tea trolley covered with china cups and an organdie throw in the corner, and talk loudly and laugh. They talked about 'our boys overseas' and knitted socks as they chatted. Or they discussed the war effort and the threat of the wharfies and the commies and how it was important to be vigilant, and never let a Catholic cross your door or you're doomed. 'Her mother wasn't a Catholic, was she?' one of the sisters asked, nodding in Ruth's direction one afternoon. Mamie said no, she didn't think so, a Pressbutton like them, but from what she'd heard she was such a drink of tap water she could have been anything, couldn't she. Drip, drip.

Perhaps they thought Ruth couldn't hear, or perhaps they thought that with luck she would. She and Patricia had been sent out to 'play'. 'Playing' with Patricia meant she had to do some menial task for the older girl, like making daisy chains for Patricia to wear as crowns.

Other times she walked on her hands while Patricia held onto her feet, to make a wheelbarrow. 'You're ugly, you know,' Patricia said, in a matter-of-fact way. Sometimes Patricia simply ignored her, and took herself off to the cream stand, where she sat on its deck, staring into space with a strange avid concentration, at odds with her usual liveliness, until a mouse scurried past. She would leap on it, catch it in her hands in one lightning motion, then calmly break its neck

'Got one,' she would shout to Les, whirling it by its tail, and he would wave and grin in acknowledgement. Patricia was always the child he liked best. As likely as not, he would be pottering in the vegetable gardens these Sunday afternoons, until afternoon tea was called, or watering the hydrangeas Mamie had planted. He seemed happier than in the past, although Ruth didn't know what he had been like before, but that was what people said. In middle age, he was a thick-waisted barrel-chested man. He took his boots off at the door before going in to join the women.

Ruth would long remember the sluggish Sunday afternoons, the weatherboard house surrounded by acrylic blue hydrangeas. Once, Patricia said, 'You know your mother ran away.'

'She died,' Ruth said.

Patricia snorted and laughed.

HOW HAD ALL OF THIS come about? When Ruth thinks back, she remembers a time when Kathleen lay in bed for days at a time. 'I've got a sick headache today,' she would say. 'Just move around quietly until it goes away, and I'll get some dinner later.' There were mornings when it was all she could do to get up and make Ruth's school lunch for her, but she managed somehow, because it meant silence in the house. She couldn't stand noise any more. Ruth stayed home from school once because her cold was so bad that Kathleen had no choice. A district nurse came in to change Kathleen's sheets and give her an injection of morphine. The woman stood with her hands on her hips and looked at Ruth. 'Kathleen Keats, you have to do something about that child. It's time you went into the hospital.'

'I've written to my sister and asked her to come. I worry, because she's getting old.'

'But not too old to make arrangements for the child?'

'Oh, I'm sure she will be able to take care of her, for now.'

'What about that son of yours?'

Kathleen turned her face to the wall. 'I haven't heard from him in a year. I doubt he'd be much help. He was working in a mine last I heard from him.'

'But he'll inherit this property, won't he?'

'I've made it over to the child,' Kathleen said.

'Well, she can't live in it by herself.'

'Dorothy will take care of it,' Kathleen said, her voice stubborn.

Kathleen's cancer had started with a melanoma which, by the time she saw a doctor, had spread to a dozen different places. Just so tired, she told him, so tired I can't lift a finger. Surely not all this from a small spot of sun, she said when the doctor explained. I think it's from my broken heart, perhaps.

And the doctor thought that, yes, this might have had something to do with it, although he didn't say so. Anyone as sick as Kathleen would surely have come to him sooner if she wasn't so stricken with grief. My heart, my poor heart, she said then, holding her hands to her chest. I can't leave the little girl. There is nobody at all, now that man up north has gone and killed her mother.

This is what she believed, although the police had gone to see Les Mullens several times. They had looked on the riverbanks, searched the milking shed and other outhouses and found nothing at all. A detective was assigned briefly to the disappearance of Mrs Joy Mullens, married woman of Hang Dog Road. His name was Dave Rogers. He wore a hairy brown jacket, tweed pants and brogues. His heavy black-framed spectacles looked as if he had dipped them in his breakfast. First he made inquiries at the local dairy factories, to see if there had been a man from Tooley Street in the area at the time, but the managers shook their heads. The information had also been checked out in London, and the same answer came back.

'That just goes to show what a liar that man is,' Kathleen said. 'He knows as well as I do there was no man round her who shouldn't have been.'

The detective went around the farms and asked questions of the neighbours. If anything, they seemed ill-disposed towards Mrs Mullens, who kept herself to herself. She was said to keep a good house, but she never lifted a finger to help Les in the shed, even though she didn't have children to see to. As if she was better than the rest of us, some said, although now they knew she'd had a kid before she married poor Les, you'd have to wonder.

Percy George, at the end of the road, scratched his head and shrugged. His eyes were rheumy, and the lower lids drooped so that you saw his flaming red eyeballs. These days he didn't shave. 'I told her mother all I knew when she rang me up that time. Joy was a nice enough girl,' he said. 'My Hazel liked the look of her, first time she set eyes on her. Reckon she'd have run off sooner if it hadn't been for Hazel.'

'You think she's run off then?'

'Well, she must have, mustn't she? I mean what else could have happened to her?'

'That's what we'd like to know.'

'I blame myself, you know,' Percy said, his voice quavering.

'Why's that, Mr George?'

'Oh nothing. Nothing. I'm sorry, I don't know much about it. My Hazel up and died, you know. Perhaps that's why she left. Nobody much to talk to. You'd see Joy out there talking to the pukekos in the swamp half the time. Just so long as the cows didn't come after her. Folk round here, they thought she was a bit queer in the head. But anyone who tells you Joy didn't keep the house good is a liar. She was a good cook, I know that for a fact.'

'So tell me, man to man,' said Dave Rogers, 'did Mr Mullens mind his wife talking to the birds?'

'Not that I noticed. Well, he would tell her to shut up, now and then.'

'He did?'

'Men do that. Some men. Hazel didn't like the way he talked to Joy. He'd say, "Just shut up, for Christ's sake will you, woman." Well, women can talk all right.'

'But you said she was quiet.'

'Ah, come on now, you're just trying to tie me up in knots. It's what you say, isn't it? I grant you, Joy never seemed to utter a damn word that pleased Les Mullens. It's a good thing Les has a woman who pleases him these days. It's not as if he's a young joker any more.'

'So why did he tell her to shut up? Exactly? Was it about the birds?'

'I tell you, it was my wife who overheard that, and as I've told you, she's gone to her rest.' He clenched and unclenched his fist, although his thumb barely closed over the tops of fingers that had once held strainer posts in place. His shoulders shook. 'Ah Hazel,' he said.

'Take your time,' the detective said.

'Nothing. Nothing to say. Les let little things get to him. In the past. That's how he used to be, but I'd say he's all right now. That's all there is to it.'

To Kathleen's sister, Dorothy, Dave Rogers said, 'Do you think Joy is alive?'

'No,' said Dorothy, 'I don't think she is.'

'Do you think Mr Mullens killed her?'

'No, I'm sure he didn't,' said Dorothy. 'I think there's been far too much loose talk.'

'How do you think she might have died then?'

'Drowned. I believe my niece went to the river and drowned. Not that I'd tell my poor sister that.'

'But Mr Mullens said he took her to the station that morning.'

'That river is everywhere,' Dorothy said. 'It's a very big river.'

'You think the police looked in the wrong place?'

'Swept out to sea long ago. Long before anyone went looking for her.'

'It's an interesting theory.'

'I knew my niece,' Dorothy said. She was sure she did.

'And what did you know about her?' the detective persisted.

'That she was an innocent.'

Dave Rogers took a handkerchief out of his pocket and used it to clean his glasses, taking his time. 'Innocent? That's a strange thing to say. Given all the circumstances.'

'Innocent of the world,' Dorothy said, with impatience. 'Don't you understand plain language?'

DOROTHY ARRIVED IN TIME TO take care of Ruth in the last weeks of Kathleen's life. But it was as Kathleen said: Dorothy was old now, her hands too frail to whisk an egg beater, her arms not strong enough to lift a heavy load of washing. After the funeral, she and

Ruth travelled back up to Auckland. In time, Invercargill would become some other place Ruth had known, a place that returned only in dreams. She would not forget Kathleen, although, eventually, the presence of Mamie would fill her life so completely, the need to be obedient to her, and to please her when she could, that she came to think of her as a mother of sorts. Not the sort she would have wanted, and not the one who had given birth to her, as she would discover, but a mother who at least provided for her welfare. Her last memory of Kathleen was seeing her lying in a white satin bed with deep wooden sides, and touching her cold face. Kathleen wore an expression of grief that she was taking to eternity. 'She has gone to Joy,' said Dorothy. Ruth dimly understood that she wouldn't see Kathleen again.

The train going north was full of soldiers. It was the second year of the war and excited young men were still leaving for overseas. Dorothy sat up, never taking her eyes off the child for all of the three days it took to get to Auckland. Ruth woke in a hazy fuddle now and then to hear laughter and strange voices, and to see her aunt weeping. She remembered that.

When the child was put to bed in her stuffy little house, Dorothy took up a pen and wrote to Les: *Dear Mr Mullens. You married my niece, Joy Keats, at my home. I write to inform you that Joy's mother died last week. I have heard the story of Joy's disappearance. It is hard for me to know what to believe. I suppose anything is possible.*

I have Joy's daughter Ruth with me, now a child of seven, quiet and obedient, but then her mother was too. I have made some enquiries and I understand you have a very good housekeeper, with a child of her own. I would consider it a great service if you would take Ruth in. I know this is not a request that will rest easily with you, but all I can do for this child is to place her somewhere that she will get care and, if her mother ever did come back, she might yet be reunited with her. I hasten to say that Ruth is a child with means. Her grandmother left her a house of considerable value, as well as money in the bank. True, much of the estate will be left in a trust with her lawyer, and a small portion of it is for her son, should he ever turn up. But there is money available now that can be used for all Ruth's requirements.

I will leave my own modest estate for the care of the child. Who knows the hour of their death, but I do not think I have long to live. I will make arrangements for the money to be available for the child's education.

'Money,' said Mamie, her eyes gleaming. Les had thrown the letter down in disgust when he opened it, but Mamie snatched it back from the table. 'Money, Les. We can go up to Auckland after the milking and be back in time for the evening shift.'

Dorothy wrote another letter, for Ruth to open when she was older. This, too, Ruth found in Mamie's possessions, along with the newspaper clippings. *My dear great-niece,* Dorothy had written, *much trouble has visited your life at an early age. I want you to know that Joy, your true mother, did love you even though she only heard your cry without ever laying eyes upon you. There are many stories about where she was going when she went to catch that train, but it seems she was taken by a stranger, or met with some accident, on her way to see you. She wanted to see you so much. She had a way with words when she was a girl and wrote a good letter. You must try your hardest at whatever you do.*

WHEN BLANCHE WAS BORN, RUTH watched over her. She had taken an instant liking to the baby when Mamie brought her home. Patricia had no time for the infant. A baby, she said in a tone of scorn. Our mother should be ashamed of herself. Bang bang bang, you can hear Les at it all night with her, and now look what she's got. Noise, bloody noise. Patricia was twelve and had learnt to swear. Mamie didn't seem to care. She was bigger and bossier than ever and proud of having delivered a late baby. Nothing to it, she said, although that wasn't wholly true. After the birth she had stayed in hospital for three weeks, 'getting her strength back'. Patricia and Ruth ran the house for Les, as well as mucking out in the cowshed.

Blanche was a tiny child, just over five pounds at birth, and smooth all over, not like Ruth with her neck stained with the strawberry mark. 'As if someone had strangled her,' Mamie once remarked.

'You shouldn't talk like that,' Les said, asserting himself for once in her presence.

'Oh, shut it, Les,' she said, and swiped the side of his head, not hard enough to damage him, but enough to hurt.

Blanche was like her name, pale as a little lily. When she was older, she and Ruth hunted for ferns in the swamp, their gumboots squelching through the mud, Ruth all the time keeping close to the child, holding her hand when they came to a ditch.

'Just make sure you keep her away from the river,' Mamie said to Ruth when the two of them set out on their expeditions. 'And don't go near the pa. No messing around with those Maori kids.'

'And no mucking round near the drains,' Les said. The winter had been particularly wet, and the ditches he had dug long before, when he first came to the farm, had filled up higher than in years. 'In fact, I'll have your guts for garters if I see you round them,' he added.

Apart from that, neither he nor Mamie appeared to notice much what the girls did. Now and then the fires flared up in the area, but didn't return to Les Mullens's farm. A prosperous farm. Percy

George died, the property was sold, the farms along the road changed hands or were taken over by sons and their wives. Some called Mamie 'mad Mamie' because she was loud and bold and her husband never had much to say for himself. She went to the local dance hall on Saturday nights, bearing plates of apple shortbread for supper, and sat with the older women who didn't dance, merely gossiped and kept time to the music by tapping their toes. Les went to the saleyards, a cigarette stuck to his lip like Percy used to when he first knew him. After the war finished and the men were back on the land, he and Mamie were married in the registry office in Auckland, without telling a soul.

'I suppose you'll be off before long,' Les said to Ruth. 'Like your mother.' But it was Patricia who left first to become a dental nurse. She boarded the bus that went past the end of Hang Dog Road these days, with a toss of her curls, and without a backward glance.

The child Blanche remained Ruth's friend, the one member of the family who never referred to the mysteries of the past. One day Ruth and Blanche discovered a fernbird's nest in the swamp, a deep hollow in some cutty grass, four spotted eggs lying in its cradle. They decided not to tell anyone. Ruth believed for a long time that she was bound to stay, not to abandon Blanche. As the two of them fossicked through the shrinking swamplands, they sometimes glimpsed tendrils of fire in the distance, wisps of smoke. But the days of summer were long, and as the grass flourished across the broad paddocks, the landscape was covered with gold mysterious light.

Some Other Man

The boy is falling and falling and Colin believes that their eyes lock for an instant and that the boy is trying to climb back through the air. But it is too late. Once begun, the step into the void is irretrievable. When he thinks about it, it is always in the present, it is always now. Colin knows in his heart that he hadn't seen the boy's eyes. What Colin heard was a different matter. He heard him land on the bonnet of his car, the sickening thud, before he bounced and rolled onto the tarmac.

When he stepped out of his car, he saw what he saw, and never expected or wanted to see in his life. The boy on the road and, up above, the unbroken night air beneath the bridge. By the blue-yellow arc of light from a street lamp, he saw that the boy's eyes were open but unseeing. Behind his car, the traffic had begun to pile up, drivers at the rear of the queue honking angrily for him to shift, drivers at the front jumping out of their cars and rushing towards him. A man said, 'Stand aside, I'm a doctor', just as it happened in stories. Someone helped him to the side of the road where he collapsed with his head in his arms, and vomited. The man said, 'Not your fault, mate.' A woman screamed hysterically. Soon sirens began to wail, and the night was full of flashing lights and rain began to fall, as fast and as unstoppable as the boy wheeling through space.

At the coroner's inquest, the boy was described as the victim of a tragedy, the kind that 'happens too often', the kind that is reported as a tragic accident until it is simply not mentioned at all. They did a terrible thing, these children who fell from the sky, who took pills, who hung suspended in their bedrooms, who slashed their wrists, who sat in cars filled with toxic gases, and nobody talked about it. But Colin wanted to talk. He felt as if he was a victim, too, an unwilling conspirator. Yet for all its horror, it didn't seem like the worst thing that had happened to him, and this filled him with unreasonable guilt. The worst thing that had happened to him was the day his wife left him, and the thud he heard on the crumpling bonnet of his Ford saloon was like the thud he felt when he had come home and found her gone. As if, this time, the echoing pain from that night had a sound all its own.

WHEN THE BOY FELL TO his death, Patricia was the person Colin wanted to see. He wanted her to hold him, and stroke the back of his head, and tell him that it was all right, not his fault. He had been in the wrong place at the wrong time. He knew, of course, that this wouldn't have happened, because Patricia wasn't like that. And yet, surely, this once, it might have. It was what he had longed for when he was still married to her.

Instead he went to visit the family of the boy who had died. They lived on a road that snaked between the hills above Aro Valley. Although it was evening when he knocked at the door, he could tell it was a house that didn't get much sunlight. The ground was damp underfoot, last season's sodden leaves on the path. He had waited until after the funeral, for he didn't want to appear to be taking advantage of their grief. In his hand he carried flowers, a bunch of yellow tulips. His parents owned a shoe shop in a small town south of Auckland. Trade. Never upset the customers, his mother would say, a phrase he would use to his friends, and, later, his wife, by way of explanation for his own reserve, a humility that could irritate some. When he thought of his mother, he saw her tender hands, the way she eased the feet of strangers into new shoes.

He rang the bell twice, and waited. The door was opened by a sad dark young woman, who introduced herself as Eleanor. From the death notice, which he had memorised by heart, he understood that this was the sister of Roy, the boy who had died. A narrow passage opened into a small sitting room. On one wall hung pictures in heavy frames, but on another, he was immediately struck by a group of tiny pictures, not more than five centimetres by perhaps three, delicately framed in threadlike gold on pale backgrounds.

'Aquarelles,' she said, as he moved forward to look at them. She had taken his coat, accepted the flowers, apologised because her parents weren't there. They had not, she said, been able to face meeting him. Already they knew more than they wished to. She knew that he, too, would be suffering, that it wouldn't make it easier if there was nobody there to receive him. She hoped he understood. Her air of resigned sorrow came as a relief. He had feared her anger, for people at work had told him that families who had experienced a suicide often raged at each other, or outsiders.

The watercolour miniatures on the wall showed scenes of Wellington, and of the countryside. There were some portraits, too. She pointed to a picture of a young man. 'That was Roy.'

He had to look closely to see the youth's shock of bright hair, the green eyes that he had seen in death, the full mouth. Yet in this minute space, he saw his face more acutely than in more conventional pictures she would show him later.

'I'm so sorry,' he said. He felt futile, not knowing where to stand, given that she hadn't invited him to sit down, but he was fascinated by the pictures, and in a way it didn't matter.

'You did these?'

She nodded.

'My wife does portraits. Photography,'

'I know. She's Pattie Mullens, isn't she?'

So she had done her homework. 'Was. Did. I mean, she was my wife. She's gone back to her maiden name. She doesn't do many portraits now, I believe.'

'Well, I guess she's very busy,' said Eleanor. 'Running all those galleries. She's an important person in the art world these days.'

'She still takes some photographs,' he said, as if apologising for Patricia.

'Of course,' said Eleanor quietly. 'I know how famous she is.'

ALL THOSE YEARS AGO, WHEN his marriage to Patricia began, Colin loved her with a fieriness that astonished even him. At school, he was a sandy-haired youth, in the top stream. The yearbook entry, in his final year, described his career ambition as 'airline pilot' (which it was), his likely career as 'pen pusher'. His eyesight let him down. He needed glasses when he was sixteen and he wore them still. The astigmatism, once it was diagnosed, meant he didn't get into the air force. Instead, he went south, took a masters degree in geography, and went into the public service as a cadet. First he worked for the housing department in Wellington, although what relevance that had to his degree he couldn't fathom. But, before long, he was marked out as a career public servant and moved to a department that managed conservation programmes, which suited him very well. He found the work rewarding. This was around the time he met Seymour, the same age and, like him, apparently in a job for life. Seymour was working in a department that dealt in overseas trade. Only he had grown up in Wellington and came from a family that 'knew people'. His family held weekend parties and had friends around who worked in music and theatre. Seymour got given tickets to plays and took Colin along to the St James and the Opera House. They hung out in the Espresso Bar drinking coffee and nipped along the road to risqué films at the Roxy. To Colin, Seymour was a revelation, coming from what seemed an urbane way of life. He was handsome, Colin supposed, in a clean-cut smooth-shaven way, though he wasn't good at evaluating the looks of other men. Girls liked to talk to Seymour but, to Colin's delight, he preferred his company to that of the young women who interrupted their conversations. Seymour would smile absently, say a round of hellos and continue his conversation with Colin as if he had hardly noticed their presence. They were girls from 'good' families round Kelburn way, where Seymour had lived: it was an expensive suburb filled with rimu-panelled villas and leadlight windows and rooms spacious enough to hold cocktail parties. He had to be polite to these girls, or it would get back to his mother. Colin supposed Seymour must be a good catch, for all the good it did the girls. Every now and then he would sigh and say that his mother had persuaded him to do his duty and escort one of them to a ball. Sometimes Colin wondered whether Seymour really liked girls at all. Once he asked Colin to come along and make up a foursome.

This meant Colin had to learn to dance. It was while he was taking lessons at the Majestic Cabaret in Willis Street that he met Patricia. She seemed a wild girl to him, all flying curly hair and rhythmic feet. He couldn't see why she needed lessons, but she said she'd left home before she was allowed to go to dances and she had some catching up to do. The age of enlightenment, as they would laugh and call it later, was fast approaching.

'I've found a girl,' he told Seymour. For some reason, he had to summon courage to tell his friend this.

'What girl?' Seymour said, his face blank.

'Someone to take to the dance.'

'But you've got a partner. The girl I'm taking has a friend, don't you remember? It's all arranged.'

Colin stammered, said he seemed to have made a mistake.

'I think so. What am I going to tell Mama? She was counting on you.'

'I can put her off. This girl. Her name's Pat.' Inside, though, he was panicking. If he did this, he was sure he would never see her again.

'Well,' Seymour said, relenting, 'if you've made an arrangement, I suppose it's all right. I've got a friend from school who can take this other girl. We can have six in the party.'

On the night of the ball, Colin could see Patricia didn't really fit in.

'So what do you do for a crust?' Seymour asked her, and Colin knew instinctively that he was being rude. People like Seymour didn't ask questions like this.

She told him she worked for a photographer, taking family portraits.

'You always done that?' he asked. For Patricia was a couple of years older than Colin and Seymour, and she looked experienced about life.

'I was a dental nurse after I left school,' she said in a cheerful even voice.

'Country girl, eh?'

'You could say that.'

'Well, one wouldn't want to do that for long, I suppose,' Seymour said, sounding sympathetic.

'Brats,' she said. 'I used to tie the screaming monsters to the chair with my cardigan. The department didn't supply chains.'

The other girls in the party shuddered in mock horror, and raised their eyebrows at each other behind Patricia's back.

'Anyway,' she continued, 'that's in the past. I'm studying photography at night school. I don't plan to take portraits forever.'

'I remember you now,' one of the girls said. 'You took some snaps at Government House when Daddy got his medal.'

'Probably,' said Patricia, brisk and no nonsense now. 'But you don't remember those grandstanders, when they're lined up against a wall. Or wait, were you the girl I shot in the conservatory?'

'Shot,' said Seymour laughing. 'Oh, that's very good. Shot in the conservatory.'

'I want to dance, Colin,' Patricia said. And they were off again, waltzing in the Majestic Cabaret, moving like well-oiled machines. Colin discovered, all of a sudden, that if he listened to the music and let his feet move in time, he would stop tripping over himself. Once or twice Patricia seemed to be gazing over his shoulder and smiling, but he thought she was simply happy.

When they stopped to fan themselves, Seymour said, in a voice that Colin would later remember as cool, that perhaps it was time they were all getting along. His goodwill seemed to have dissipated.

All the same, he agreed to be best man when Colin and Patricia were married. He had been transferred to Foreign Affairs and was off on his first posting, in Washington. They would see him perhaps once a year over the next decade or so. Each time he returned, he would look much the same, perhaps smoother still, more sharply dressed if that were possible, his figure lean, thick hair crisply styled. Colin and Patricia, or Pattie as their friends called her now, grew their hair longer. Patricia's had been long to begin with, but now it

fell in an untrammelled mane to her waist; Colin, out of deference
for his job, didn't let his grow past his shoulders, but he did have
long ginger sideburns and a droopy moustache. He pretended that
the bald patch inching its way round the top of his head wasn't there.
Patricia's ears were so laden with hoops and studs that her lobes
were stretched. They built a house surrounded by native bush in
Ngaio. Patricia had a studio for her photography built at the end of
the garden. By this time, she was working on her own and holding
exhibitions. Some of her work sold for fabulous sums. She hardly
ever took portrait photographs now. Their children, a boy and girl,
played in a paddling pool wearing only sunhats, even when friends
came for a party, and everyone was drinking wine. Sometimes
Patricia lazily aimed her camera in their direction. Stunning pictures,
as the catalogues said.

Patricia held parties every few weeks. She loved organising events.
At some point, Colin realised that several of the women who came
to their house didn't particularly like her. The couples came because
Colin was now the head of his section at work, and the husbands
didn't want to offend him. They came with their children who were
put to bed when the party grew late, altogether in one bedroom,
draped with odd blankets and their parents' coats. 'Time for a
smoke,' Patricia would cry, and a joint would begin to make its way
around the room.

Some of the women didn't want to smoke, or they were pregnant
and thought they shouldn't. 'Oh, for goodness' sake,' Patricia would
cry. 'What are you? This is a party, for goodness' sake.' Colin sensed
their anxiety.

After they had all gone home one night, he said, 'Perhaps we
should be careful, Pattie. You can't necessarily trust those women.
Perhaps you need to let them make up their own minds.'

'Careful,' Patricia said, in a slow stoned voice. 'What does being careful do for you? I've been careful all my life, and where has it got me?'

'Here,' said Colin, 'here with me.'

'Well, that's better than where I came from, I suppose.'

WHERE SHE CAME FROM. HE had been there only once or twice. Where she came from was a Waikato farm on a wide rolling plain, with a river running beside it. When they married, she had agreed with reluctance to a wedding at a church near the farm. Her mother, Mamie, a big untidy woman who rattled on about nothing much, had wanted it.

Before the wedding, Colin had to visit and meet Patricia's family. The ramshackle farmhouse looked as if it had had bits added on over the years. It stood at the end of a very long road dotted with letterboxes standing in front of houses surrounded by roses on trellises. There were no roses around Patricia's old family home: it felt neglected rather than poor. The pasture beyond looked lush and green, but inside the house there was an atmosphere, not exactly of squalor, but of a deep-seated untidiness that felt incurable. Newspapers had been pushed into the corners of rooms, as if some effort had been made to tidy up. A slightly rancid smell pervaded the rooms. Mamie said she was glad there was going to be a wedding, because there could be a bit of dancing in the hall, which she liked to watch. She displayed little interest in Colin or his family. Patricia's sister Ruth had arrived and would stay for the wedding that was to take place a few days later. She had short brown wavy hair and a large birthmark on the side of her neck and face. Throughout most of the meal she sat with a book held straight up in front of her face, except when she stopped to eat. The effect was disturbing. Colin supposed it must be because of her birthmark.

'Ruth is a librarian, can't you tell?' Patricia said. 'She drives a truck.'

'It's a Country Library Service van,' Ruth said, from behind the book.

'I suppose we should be grateful she's come,' Mamie said. 'She hasn't been here in years.'

'She can't keep away from a wedding,' Patricia said, something taunting in her voice.

Ruth put down her book. 'I came to see Blanche,' she said.

Beside her, Blanche, who was still a schoolgirl at the time, looked down and smiled. She had grey eyes, and although Patricia had described her as 'the albino', Colin saw that she was nothing of the sort, just a girl with a very pale complexion and her straight hair tied in a braid. Later in the afternoon, he saw Ruth and Blanche walking together across a paddock. Blanche was wearing one of her father's old hats pulled down to shade her face from the sun, so he thought that she must like the way she looked, the fairness of her complexion, when all the other girls he knew were trying to get suntans.

When the meal was over, Patricia's father Les, who had had little to say, signalled for Colin to follow him outside. Colin supposed that this was for the talk, the one that must take place between a father and his prospective son-in-law. Les was a heavy man with deep-set eyes and a cleft chin, his features thickened and coarsened with years of work on the farm. Once, he'd milked cows but these days he ran beef cattle. Les had pulled out a cigarette and was leaning against a verandah post. 'So I've got a son at last,' he said.

'Yes,' Colin said, 'it seems like it.'

'She's a pretty good girl. Taken her a while to find the right man. You better look after her.'

'I'll do my best.'

Les looked suddenly wistful. 'Don't suppose you're a fella who'd have a game of bowls now and then?'

Colin said he hadn't thought about it, but of course he'd be interested to learn. On the clothesline he saw a pair of cream trousers, and a cream shirt ballooning like a cloud before rain.

Les spat on the ground. His mouth had settled back into a grim line; his voice had become hectoring. 'Ah, never mind. I reckon you're a city slicker. Kind of joker who'd try and milk a bull's tit. I know the sort when I see them.'

Colin told himself, as he drove away that afternoon, that he wasn't marrying Patricia's family, only her.

On the day, his parents drove down for the service, not more than an hour's run south. Seymour had arrived from Wellington in the morning, and he and Colin went straight to the church. The two men stood awkwardly in the plain little country chapel, feeling out of place in their dark city suits, as they waited for Patricia to arrive. Mamie bustled in, wearing a long burgundy-coloured dress. She came up and stood beside Seymour. 'You are the bridegroom, aren't you?' she said.

When Seymour said no, it was Colin, she looked at him, disappointed. 'Oh goodness, yes, of course I remember, she's marrying some other man, isn't she?' As if Colin wasn't there. This odd turn of phrase would come back to haunt him. Mamie's memory was already leaving her, would eventually abandon her altogether. This was no more than a lapse, but it would come to seem like a portent, with an inevitability that he should have foreseen.

Patricia's sisters were bridesmaids, and as the day wore on, Colin thought that neither girl was as odd as he had first thought, and he was comforted by this. He and Seymour danced with both Ruth and Blanche, and Seymour danced with Patricia several times. 'The handsome one,' Mamie said, in passing. He didn't learn for years that Ruth wasn't really his sister-in-law. 'Why didn't you tell me?' he asked, when Patricia let it slip one night that Ruth had been fostered by the family.

'Oh, I don't know,' she said. 'She was one of the family's dark secrets, I suppose.'

'What other dark secrets have they got?' He asked it as a joke, but she didn't take it that way.

'Oh, we know you're perfect, Colin baby. Just a perfect man from a perfect family.'

'Don't,' he said, putting up his hand as if to shield himself. Patricia had always talked in an outrageous way; it was part of her excitement. But these days he often felt slow beside her, and overly methodical. Confrontation wasn't his style. At work, he led his team by demonstrating what he wanted done, what he expected of them. Yet, he told himself, they had a happy life. Their children were healthy and apparently well balanced, even if their parents' lives were erratic. His wife, despite her wildness, was no longer a country girl. She had developed a taste for the theatre, and for politics; she knew how to work a room, had learned to make a soufflé. It was as if she had acquired some private knowledge about how the world worked that she wasn't willing to share with him. She was successful in a way that other women envied. He supposed that that was why some of them were aloof in her presence. They were all in the process of liberating themselves, but it was Patricia who shone, a woman who already had it made.

Secrets came up once more while he was still married to her. Mamie, her memory lost, had gone into a rest home in Hamilton. 'Oh, where did I put it,' she would say. 'The memory thingie. If I could find it they'd let me out of here, wouldn't they? Patricia, did I put it in a box? Is it in a cupboard?'

'It's not a thing, Mum,' Patricia said. She and Colin had driven up one weekend to visit her. Their children were older now, the boy already a teenager, able to stay with friends while they went away. The word was that Mamie didn't have very long to go.

Ruth and her husband, Neil, who was a surveyor, had gone to Hamilton, too. They lived in Hawke's Bay where Ruth was apparently content. She had a garden, she said, when pressed to speak of her life. And yes, of course, she still read books. As if none of it was really their business. Les was visiting, too, leaning heavily on a stick. Colin thought he shouldn't be driving the car. He'd had a whisky or two by the smell of him. His mood was mean.

'Well, what is it then?' Mamie asked. 'If it's not a thing.'

'It's a concept, Mum. An abstract. It's not something you can find, just like that.'

Les said, 'You're better off without it.'

Mamie looked dispirited and sighed. 'Never mind. Perhaps tomorrow.' Patricia shrugged and wandered off, aiming her camera at some of the other gnarled residents, until a nurse came up and said that she didn't think that was very nice.

Ruth hadn't got married at the farm, and Neil was someone Les barely knew. He was a broad-shouldered man with a Dagwood haircut, wearing walk shorts and long socks.

'So what did you say you did for a living?'

'I'm a surveyor.'

'What's that in plain language, boy?'

Neil reddened. 'I measure land.'

'Maps and drawings?'

'Something like that.'

'You needn't come measuring up my land.'

'Oh, leave it, Les,' said Ruth. 'Just let it go.'

'Don't you tell me what to do, young lady. You want to remember who gave you a roof over your head.'

'I won't forget that, Les.'

'Les. Les. I used to be Dad.'

When they had all left Mamie's room and were standing around in the car park, Les put his arm around Patricia's shoulder, leaning against her. 'Don't want anyone sniffing round our farm, do we, girl?'

'Best not, Dad,' Patricia said.

'We've got our little secrets, you and me, eh girl?' He squeezed her shoulder hard, and Colin saw that for once in her life Patricia flinched.

'Sure have, Dad,' Patricia said, and patted his hand before removing it from her shoulder.

'And tell that no-good sister of yours to come and see her mother some time.' He was talking about Blanche, who had gone teaching, but didn't stay in any job long. She liked to travel, and stayed at a school just long enough to earn the airfare to go off to some unusual destination. Mexico. India. Egypt. Patricia said she was so colourless she gave indigenous people something to notice.

On the drive home, Patricia asked Colin to stop along the Desert Road so that she could take some more pictures. She got out of the car and wandered over to a bench in the picnic area where he had pulled in. The mountains reared up through mist; the air was ink blue in the shadow of the clouds above. Beyond them lay the tussock land and overhead the electricity pylons sighed and sang in the wind. Patricia shivered and pulled her coat around her. 'God, I love this place, Colin,' she said. 'I love the space. I love the colour.'

He looked towards her, thinking of her as she was when he first met her, a reckless dangerous girl who threw herself at him as if she wanted to be rescued. This hadn't occurred to him at the time. But now that he saw her like this, wan and slightly drawn after a day with her odd disconnected family, he felt a tenderness he hadn't experienced in years. There was something he wanted to ask her, but as she raised the camera, he couldn't bring himself to do it. It would ruin this absolute peace that lay between them.

SEVERAL WEEKS PASSED BEFORE THERE was another party. It was wilder than any they had held before. At one point, Patricia disappeared. She had been drinking gin and tonic, but Colin saw she wasn't pouring much tonic. Some of the children wanted to have a barbecue. He went to look for her, to see if she'd got sausages, because he couldn't find any in the fridge. He opened the door of the bedroom, and his wife was lying on their bed among the coats, having her breasts kissed by a woman, a colleague's wife. The woman's hand was between Patricia's legs.

They jumped, startled at his entrance. Patricia pulled her dress up over her shoulders, covering her small breasts with their large dark nipples.

'Just fooling about,' they both said at once. Patricia rushed out of the room, although her gait was unsteady. Her dress was still slipping from her shoulder as she went down the stairs towards the lounge. One of the men laughed and grabbed her naked breast. She stood stock-still on the stairs and let him suckle her, laughing out loud, holding his head against her body. One of the men called out, 'Can anyone have a go?' Colin, standing above her on the stairs, put his hand up for silence.

'I reckon we'll leave it there for tonight.'

When the house was clear of guests, she turned on him. 'We were having fun,' she said. 'Where's your sense of humour?'

'Patricia. Pattie,' he said, 'were you abused when you were a child?'

'What are you *talking* about?'

'Your secrets,' he said. 'Did Les do things to you?'

She looked at him as if he was mad, or as drunk as she was, but he was completely sober.

'Oh. You've been stewing on that? I might have known.'

'So were you?'

'No.'

'So what was the secret?'

'I saw a body on the farm once. That was all.'

'A body?'

'Just some old bones really.'

'I don't believe you.'

She hesitated, and in that moment Colin decided that whatever she said was just some drunken lie. 'Les thought they would have been Maori bones. He didn't want people all over his land upsetting the cows. They were just coming into their milk.'

'That's bullshit.'

'Okay. You asked. Make up your own story.'

He thought she was lying. He was sure he knew the truth and she was hiding it. When they went to bed he wanted sex.

ON MONDAY, WHEN COLIN ARRIVED home from work, the house was very quiet. The door was unlocked. He called out but nobody answered. Not even the cat came to greet him. Before going inside, he checked down the path, to see if Patricia was in her studio. A huge purple rhododendron was shedding spent flowers across the lawn. He pushed the liver-coloured branches out of his way, thinking he would have to cut the tree back. Patricia wasn't in her studio. If she was using her dark room she put a sign up that said 'Work in Progress'.

In the house, the cheerful clutter of their lives had been tidied away: the kitchen table was bare, the dishes put away. He went upstairs to check that neither of the children was in their rooms. They often had sports, or stayed over at friends' houses these days. The bedrooms had an odd deserted atmosphere. There were no clothes on the floor. The beds were made up. On an impulse he opened the door of his son's wardrobe. It was empty. He went into his daughter's room, and found the same thing.

When he got to the door of his and Patricia's room, he felt paralysed with fear. This can't be so, he said to himself. The room was like the others.

He went out to the landing and sat down. In his mind he replayed the events of Saturday night. Things had all gone too far. At work, his colleagues had dropped their eyes when he looked at them. In a meeting that afternoon he had snapped at someone. Nothing was resolved about the business on hand, and it occurred to him, as his afternoon tea was being wheeled in, that perhaps it was time to think about a change, a job in another department. He'd been here long enough.

As he stayed sitting on the landing, he tried to work out what specifically had caused Patricia to react in this way. Was she ashamed of the way she had behaved? Had he forced her hand about the secrets of her past? Or perhaps she felt he had violated her, taken advantage of her when she'd been drinking. Surely not, he hadn't forced her; he never had. He was flooded by a rising tide of anger. The children shouldn't be drawn into this mess. She couldn't just drive them away: they had school the next day.

Only he knew that they hadn't just gone for an outing. He guessed that, if he went back down the garden and opened the door to her studio, it would be as emptied as the house. That would be final.

He wasn't ready to do that. Not yet.

The phone rang. He rose stiffly to his feet. It was her.

Her voice was calm and natural, as if she was delivering news about dinner. In fact, she said, 'There's steak left over from Saturday night. I took it out of the freezer.'

'Where are you?'

'I'm at Seymour's.'

Relief flooded through him. 'Is he back? Son of a gun. Where's he staying?'

'At his mother's house.'

'Of course, yes, I forgot.' Seymour's mother had died recently. At the time, Seymour was in an important meeting at the UN. Colin had been to the funeral, as a mark of respect for his friend, and had written to Seymour afterwards. 'I know how hard it must be for you not making it back. We had great times at your mother's place.'

'He'll have things to settle up,' Colin said. He was thinking, at the same time, it will be all right, Seymour will calm things down. Patricia will be talking to him, and soon she'll be home, and we'll pick up the pieces and carry on.

'He has,' Patricia said, still in her same matter-of-fact tone. 'We're going to keep this house on. It's very comfortable, and has everything we need. Silly to shift from it.'

'Pattie?"

'We've been going to tell you. But then when Sey's mother died, it seemed best just to wait. He's finished in the diplomatic service, by the way.'

Sey? When had they ever called Seymour that?

'We're together,' Patricia said, as if her patience was wearing thin. 'You must have guessed, surely.'

'I didn't. When?' Meaning when had it begun.

'At the wedding.'

'Our wedding?' And from her silence, he knew that the answer was yes. She had gone off with some other man all right, the best friend he'd ever had.

Later, he found the steak in the fridge, fresh eggs, a bottle of his favourite wine, newly bought bread in the bin. He tried to eat a little. This was the beginning of the worst time in his life.

THEY WOULD MEET, OF COURSE. There were papers to be signed, the first steps towards a divorce. Later he would sell the house. At first, he thought the children would want to come back and spend weekends with him, that he should keep things as close to normal for them as he could, but soon he realised that their lives at Patricia and Seymour's were more interesting. The suburb where they had mixed with the neighbours for all those years had become an empty wasteland to him that he didn't want to face alone. This didn't mean that he wasn't expected at school prizegivings and at the children's birthday parties, at least until they were older and had parties that didn't include adults. Seymour was present at these gatherings, behaving as if the situation was perfectly normal. He never commented on the end of the marriage, or treated Colin as other than a guest. The children called him Seymour, and he played fisticuffs and made jokes with them, as Colin would have done had he still been their father. Now, in their presence, he fell silent, beyond the usual standard enquiries about grades and exams. More like an uncle.

IT WAS AFTER THE YOUNG man had fallen to his death in front of him that Colin finally made the decision to move. Each weekend that he spent in the house had become a form of torture. When he drifted off into fitful bursts of sleep, he had lurid vivid dreams of bodies. He woke with dreadful starts, often realising that the body he had just seen was not that of the boy, but of some faceless person on the farm where Patricia had grown up. He knew, now that he had a body to haunt him, that it could appear from anywhere. Surely she had lied to him that night. And yet he had begun to ask himself questions about what she might have seen. Where was the body positioned on that benighted farm? Was it a man or a woman? The recently dead or, as she had said, as she had turned away, the skeletal remains of long ago? He supposed he would never know. He visualised the tumbledown home where his wife had spent much of her childhood, and thought that they had somehow exchanged places. He wasn't much interested in housekeeping. Since the children had stopped coming to see him, he had closed their bedrooms for good. After Roy's death, and a long time after his visit to Eleanor, he had called Patricia and asked if she would come round and have a coffee with him. Just to talk — he needed someone to talk to. She listened in silence. 'Someone said you'd been in a nasty accident. I'm sorry that happened to you.'

'So can you come around?'

She sighed on the other end of the line. 'I think you need a counsellor, Colin.'

Many nights now, he lay awake in the dark and imagined Roy's eyes following him. What he did know was that he needed to get away from the house, to find another place where he could sleep at nights.

He arrived early at the lawyer's office on the day that the sale of his and what was still Patricia's house was to be signed. Patricia was there already, for once unaccompanied by Seymour.

They sat on opposite couches, thumbing through magazines. By then, he had changed his job, taken a sideways shift to another department. His appearance was different. The day he had decided to sell the house, he had looked in the mirror and judged his appearance shabby and middle-aged, and saw that that his moustache didn't suit him. At the barber's, he instructed the attendant to shave him and cut his lank greying hair very short; as the hair fell away he was left with ginger stubble around the shiny dome of his head. His new image took him aback, the loose flesh under his chin revealed, the grey pouches beneath his eyes more noticeable. But he felt tidy and changed.

If Patricia noticed, she didn't say so and he wasn't inclined to make conversation. But, in the end, the silence unnerved him. 'So how is it?' he said. 'With you and Seymour?' The words just slipped out.

She raised her head, putting her finger in the magazine to mark her place. She was reading *Vanity Fair*. After a silence, she smiled. 'Much the same as it was with you. Without the sex.' He read her expression as one of relief.

He nearly said, 'Well, why bother being married at all?' but stopped himself in time. The answer, he supposed, would be that their marriage had failed because it was all about sex, and he should know there was more to it than that. This would be neither true nor fair, but it would keep him in the wrong.

Colin thought, instead, that marriage was what kept them safe, Patricia and Seymour. Besides, power was a pretty strong aphrodisiac.

HIS NEW HOME WAS AN apartment in an art deco building on Oriental Parade. The façade had curved corners, and so did his sitting room, although the rest of the rooms were regular and square. He liked its plainness, its proximity to the sea. Most of all, he liked that in these rooms, which he had decorated and furnished with simplicity, he could shut the door on his days at work, and on the past. Some evenings he sat in total silence while the sun slid over the waters of the bay, and the moon rose. On other nights he played classical music, about which he knew very little, although he was learning. He listened often to Sibelius's soaring turbulent notes, before they sank into peacefulness. In the music he felt his own life passing by, reliving its roller-coaster ride.

He had been living alone for some years when Eleanor tracked him down. It was 1985. Already, he was a grandfather. His children did visit occasionally, to present their offspring to his not unwilling arms. His grief, if not over, was in abeyance, a shadow that crouched in the corners some nights, ready to spring, but he believed he had discovered the strength to quell it.

'You said to me once that if there was anything you could do, you'd help me,' Eleanor said, when she rang. 'I never thought I'd ask, but something's come up, and, I thought, Well, I can but try.'

They met in a café near the waterfront. Eleanor was wearing a plain dress made from a silky pink and grey fabric that gave her dark hair and fair skin a soft look. She was still curvaceous, in the way that he remembered from their first meeting. It all seemed such a long time ago. He guessed that she was still quite young, perhaps thirty-five. She still wore an air of slight melancholy, and he wondered if this was her natural disposition. After Roy's death, of course, her sadness was to be expected, but by now he would have hoped her to be recovered.

When they had ordered coffee, a flat white for him and a long black for her, he said, 'So are you still doing those exquisite miniatures?'

'That's what I wanted to talk to you about. I'd like to have an exhibition, but I can't find any gallery space in town.'

'Really? But that's ridiculous. There must be plenty of galleries.'

She explained to him then that the galleries were very tightly held.

There were privately owned ones, of course, but the public spaces were controlled by a group of people who decided what would be seen. 'Really, it's a case of who you know,' she said.

'Closed shop?' he said.

She shifted uncomfortably. 'I don't like to say this, but the committee exhibits their friends' work. Watercolours, miniatures like mine, aren't held in very high regard. I don't fit in the image, whatever the medium. I'm not *modern*. If you know what I mean.'

He did know. Politics was like that now. The new economic era. Who was in and who wasn't. He was feeling it, too. All the same he was puzzled. 'I don't see where I come into this,' he said.

'The committee. Patricia's on it. I wondered if you and she . . . well, I'm sorry.' Her face was crimson. 'I thought you might be able to talk to her. I think I've made a mistake.'

'I could probably talk to her,' he said. 'It's not impossible.' He wasn't sure if what Eleanor said was strictly true. He could think of a number of places where exhibitions were held, and he was sure Eleanor's work wouldn't take up much space. For a fleeting moment, he wondered if she had simply wanted to see him again, but dismissed it just as quickly. If that were true, she would have been in touch long ago. More likely, she really did lack the confidence to approach the right people. Patricia would be hard for someone like Eleanor to deal with. Nowadays she ran all sorts of things, and sat on arts committees. She had her name in the papers not just as a photographer, but also as an administrator. Privately, Colin thought the quality of her work had diminished. Seymour was never far away in these reports, for he had become a philanthropist, giving away money. As a couple, they looked rich and formidable. In her last newspaper picture, Patricia was imposing, her shoulder-length hair swept to one side; wearing a slim black dress, she was talking to an artist. She held a wine glass in one hand, and gestured with the other. She had power, no doubt about that.

'I do see her now and then,' he said slowly, although this was increasingly rare. There had been a baptism ceremony for one of the grandchildren the previous year, which he found odd, given that marriage had been dismissed by his children as too old hat for words. 'Would you like me to arrange a meeting?' He knew this was impulsive, even rash.

'I'M REALLY PLEASED COLIN'S MET someone at last,' was the first thing Patricia said. She was wearing a loose T-shirt, tight jeans and high heels. At fifty-five, she looked much younger. She twirled the ends of her hair in her fingers while they ordered, at the same café on the Parade.

Eleanor blushed again. 'I've known Colin for a long time.'

'Really,' Patricia said to him. 'You old dark horse.' For a moment she looked offended.

And then Eleanor rushed to explain, her eyes filling with tears, stumbling over her words, about the way her brother had died, and how Colin had come to see her.

'Pretty awful,' Patricia said crisply. Her fingers drummed on the tabletop. 'I'm sorry, I should be getting along.' Even though their orders hadn't arrived.

'I'll walk you to your car,' said Colin, signalling to Eleanor to wait for him. Already Patricia had picked the car keys out of her handbag and was standing up.

'It wouldn't have hurt you to talk to her,' he said, when they had walked a little way.

'I don't know that she's right for you,' Patricia said.

'That's really none of your business. I wouldn't have picked Seymour for you, as a matter of fact.'

'Payback time?'

'No, Pattie. What's really eating you?'

'Nothing's eating me, Colin. Stop following me, I don't like it.'

And then he remembered. 'Was it about the body?'

They were nearly at her car: he could see the smart open-topped MG sparkling in the sun. He knew he couldn't lay hands on her, physically restrain her, yet his words had some effect that halted her. She stood shaking beside the car, holding onto the door.

'It must have been horrible,' she said. 'The boy dying. The worst thing. I wasn't very kind to you then.'

'It wasn't the worst thing. It should have been, but it wasn't.'

'I'm sorry I couldn't stay and talk to your friend. I just couldn't.'

'So there was a body on the farm?'

Patricia pulled her sunglasses out of her bag. 'A skeleton. I told you, it was just old bones.'

'But they were a secret?'

'I was afraid of my stepfather. Les. He had a nasty streak in him. He belted the hell out of Mamie. I'd have got the same.'

'Do you know whose bones they were?'

'No.'

'Did he?'

'A woman disappeared on that farm.' She was still shaking. 'It was before my time there.'

'My God. Who was she?'

'I don't know.' She had begun pulling herself together. 'Why don't you ask him? I know where you can find him.'

'Pattie?'

'He's in hell, where he belongs. Of course I don't know. I'm glad Les is dead. I told you, hon, you'd have kept it secret too if you were me. It kept me out of trouble. Now I do have to go.'

THERE WERE GALLERIES TO BE had, of course. What Eleanor really meant was that she wanted an exhibition space where there would be an opening night and champagne, and critics, and a crowd full of people like Patricia, with their quick talk and sharp lines. When he offered to help, she settled for something more modest. It was a beginning, as he said. The critics stayed away, but the pictures sold. When the last of them had gone, she said she wished she had kept them, in a way, because part of her life had disappeared with them. So he knew it was true: she was melancholic, and it would be his cause, his task in life, to keep her demons at bay, as far as possible.

After they had been married for a time, she wondered if they might have children. Colin thought not. He encouraged her to keep on with her painting. Some nights he lay awake and listened to her weep for her brother, and tried not to complain.

Under Water

That summer, the temperatures soared day after day, and even the Norfolk pines along the esplanade seemed ready to wilt. The sky was golden, but that was to be expected in this town; it was what the tourist brochures promised. Yellow light spilled across the beach, through the pretty town with its glamorous art deco buildings in the main street, over the tall trees, the giant spreading palms; the scent of flowers was abundant and people sat under umbrellas drinking wine beside the sea. Like a mini-Riviera, idyllic really, if you looked at it like this, but what was the sum of it? Jemima was trying to work out the meaning of poetry that summer, but it wouldn't come to her. She had read a lot recently about the aesthetics of poetry, delving back to the centuries before Christ, the time of Gilgamesh. She tried different forms in her own work, and struggled over villanelles and sestets because her online poetry instructor said that if she mastered different forms then her open form would develop a more poetic sense.

What Jemima was really looking for, she supposed, was the meaning of life. A life. Her mother's life and her own. The fact that she was a poet, or someone who aspired to be one, was merely incidental. She thought she had come close to understanding some important truth when she and her mother had taken a trip to the gannet colony a year or so earlier, near her hometown of Napier. It was one of many trips, but her mother said it would be her last. When Jemima was a child, it was an annual family ritual, insisted upon by her father.

JEMIMA HAD BEEN MARRIED TO a playwright called Nick, who was a celebrity because of his hard dark theatre and also because he had grown up in the wild Chatham Islands and was expected to be a fisherman, not a writer. (And there was the matter of his looks. It was regarded as tactless to mention them, as if talent were not enough, but there was no doubt that they helped.) Nick had trained first as an actor and sometimes performed in his own works. They had met some years before when she was given tickets to the first night for one of his shows. She had written the advertising copy for the play and, somehow, because the theatre was short staffed at the time, she had finished up doing the programme notes as a favour. The play, 'a stark metaphor for the lives of men who lived by the force of water', was about fishermen who had drowned in the Chathams, and there were many. At the end of the play someone suggested she go on to the opening night party, and she had found herself face to face with Nick. She hadn't been to much theatre and found herself at a loss for words. My programme, she had said, offering it to him, perhaps you could sign it? There couldn't be a more gauche opening gambit, she knew, but there it was. She explained that she had written the notes. His eyes travelled over her swiftly as he took her pen and wrote: Roses are red, violets are blue, my heart pants 4 U. Beside this silly message, he had written his phone number and a question mark.

'Touché,' she said, wishing she could flee. 'I really loved the play.'

'Your notes are very good,' he said, 'especially as you hadn't been to rehearsal to know what was in it.'

'I did read it,' she said.

'Go on,' he said, tapping the programme where he had written his phone number. 'Swap.'

So she wrote her number on the other side of the leaflet and he tore it in half, folding his piece carefully before placing it in the inside pocket of his brown suede jacket.

Six years after this encounter, he left her for a blonde Canadian girl with a ponytail who was working in a Dunedin bar he met her in while on tour.

Jemima's father, Neil Hutchings, wanted to break his neck, but then he thought Jemima was foolish to have made such a reckless mistake in the beginning. She knew the reproach in his voice wasn't intentional. He and her mother, Ruth, had been steadfast. That was the word he used. Steadfast. Whether the weather be wet or whether the weather be cold, he would say, we weather the weather together, whatever the weather may be.

JEMIMA AND HER OLDER BROTHERS knew all her father's family. Neil was a surveyor who had grown up in town, but his working life had been spent in the countryside, making charts of landscape, measuring the surface of the earth point to point, determining its boundaries. There were eight children in his family, people who stayed close to one another and remained with their partners in these shifting times.

His children knew their grandparents, and all their aunts and uncles, and their first cousins numbered nearly forty. Because there were so many of them, Jemima never really stopped to ask her mother much about her family or why they didn't visit their other grandmother, whose name was Mamie. By the time she had given the matter more than a passing thought, Mamie had died, and so, too, her husband, Les Mullens. Jemima did understand that he was Ruth's stepfather, but the only father Ruth had known. Now that she was older, there were things she did want to know, but her mother brushed her questions aside.

Because of his job, Neil owned a Land Rover, and had access to the long Cape Kidnappers peninsula that had to be travelled in order to see the gannets. Sometimes the cousins would accompany them, although the journey was one of such special quality, so important, that he didn't like the chatter that erupted when there were several children together. He didn't care to be there when tourists arrived on trailers pulled by tractors. Jemima supposed that this, for Neil, was a kind of spirituality. He never entered a church. But she knew how he loved the big white gannets with their gold and ebony crown, thousands upon thousands of them, living side by side, nesting on the bare pale sandstone rock. Just sit and watch, he would say, and you'll learn all you need to know about love. They would watch the birds diving into the sea from a great height, sudden bolts of white-feathered light flashing through the sky. As the birds hit the water, they emerged with silver fish in their mouths. Then came an ungainly walk to the nest, delivering the fish to the family, followed by the twining of necks that went on between couples.

He believed that before you married, it was important to get to know another person, to court them, the way he had courted her mother, Ruth Mullens, as she was then.

IT WAS HARD TO TELL whether Ruth's marriage was perfect, however Neil saw it, because Ruth was such a very quiet person. Yet Jemima believed it was enough. Ruth loved her children with an intensity that sometimes seemed fierce, and plants and books and birds, in roughly that order. These were the elements of her life. The house where Ruth and Neil lived from the time when they were married, and where Jemima and her brothers had grown up, was on a rise overlooking the sea. It was an ample open house, with French doors opening onto wide verandahs, and a garden like an artist's palette that Ruth had created. My Giverny, she called it, even though she had never been to France, but it did have water features and a small lake. There wasn't really a time before this house, Ruth used to say, when asked about her early life. She had gone to library school, and started driving the Country Library Service van early on, and that was that. On the whole, she liked the people in the country who invited her for meals. Some places were strange, as she later described them, but then she knew about strange places. That was as much as she said, really, about where she had come from. When pressed, she said vaguely that she had sisters, Patricia and Blanche, but they had drifted apart. Once Jemima's Aunt Blanche had come to visit. She was still a small child at the time, and she remembered that Blanche had a bagful of sweets, and spoke with a slight stammer, as if afflicted by a shyness even greater than Ruth's. The sisters had embraced when they parted and promised to keep in touch.

It was while delivering books to the town library that Ruth met Neil. Every three months, new books would be brought to the library and exchanged for the last lot. Neil enjoyed reading, particularly travel and adventure. He would go to meet the van, and it came to be expected that he would be at the library on the appointed day, four times a year. After a time, Ruth had taken to choosing special books for him, and putting them aside so he could read them first. This was against the rules, but she did it anyway. This went on for five years before he proposed to the quiet girl, with her strong broad hands on the wheel of the big van, and the strawberry birthmark on her neck that flared up when she was shy, which was often. She referred to it sometimes as her 'disfigurement' but nobody in the family seemed to notice it. It was part of who she was.

Despite his love of other people's adventures, Neil didn't like to stray far from home. Ruth was sometimes wistful about this, because when she had chosen his books for him, long ago, she had begun to dream of travel, too. As she drove the van around the remote countryside, she had imagined the places she would visit. Where she and Neil would go. But if Neil was part of the dream, he was the part that was realised. He liked to stay at home. He could be stubborn.

When they were already in their sixties, and Ruth had been diagnosed with Parkinson's disease, they did go for a trip to Europe. Jemima and her brothers had urged them to take a chance, take a risk and go. They went to Italy because Ruth said she would die happy if she saw the Sistine Chapel and Venice and the Duomo. They never did make it to Paris because her medication wasn't suiting her and it seemed best to come home. But she said she was content.

AND THEN NEIL DIED. HIS heart gave out. He did everything for me, Ruth told Jemima, in a subdued voice. She told her daughter this on that last visit to the gannet colony.

As they sat watching the entwined necks of the gannets, Ruth said, 'You might think I'm a sentimental old fool, dear, but that's how I think of my life with your father. We were good to each other.'

'Yeah, okay, Ma,' Jemima said, embarrassed.

But Ruth had pressed on, determination in her voice. 'I need to hold onto it. I grew up without love.'

'Mum,' Jemima said, 'what do you mean?'

'Well,' Ruth said, 'perhaps that's not quite true. I experienced love when I was a very small child. I lived with my grandmother down south in Invercargill. I thought of her as my mother. Her name was Kathleen Keats. But then she died and I went to live with my birth mother's husband and his family on their farm. It wasn't what my grandmother wanted, but it's the way it worked out.' Her fingers moved to her neck. 'I used to think that this was a punishment for something I did wrong. That I'd been sent away from Kathleen, and had to wear the mark forever. '

'I didn't know,' Jemima said. 'I never thought of you as different.'

'You get used to hiding things. Patricia called me Strawbs. Short for strawberry,' Ruth said, as if it needed explaining.

'That's horrible,' Jemima squeezed her mother's hand.

'I went to her wedding, but I've seer her only once since then, when Mamie was dying. Seeing her acting like the queen of the May, when she was no better than the rest of us. She was a cruel bitch.'

Jemima was shocked. Her mother never used language like that. 'That was Auntie Pat? The *famous* photographer?' Her inflection was sarcastic. Although she didn't mention it, she had had a passing encounter with her aunt, Patricia Mullens, or Pattie Mullens, as she was known professionally. But Ruth was focused on her own train of thought and Jemima, aware of how fragile this had become, knew better than to interrupt it.

'It wasn't just that,' Ruth said. 'When I went north, I had my identity taken away from me. I was called Ruth Mullens, but that wasn't my real name, I was born Ruth Keats. My mother's name was Joy. Mine was changed by deed poll by Mamie, who I was supposed to think of as my mother.'

'So you were adopted?'

'No, I just had my name changed. I still think of myself as Ruth Keats. I remember a town with a water tower, long summer twilights and my grandmother teaching me how to write my name.'

'Was Mamie awful? We never used to visit them.'

'I wouldn't have taken you there,' Ruth said sharply. 'That farm had the smell of death.'

'Mum, I don't understand.' Her mother was shaking again. Jemima covered Ruth's hand, and suggested that perhaps it was time they went home.

Ruth was recovering her composure. 'Mamie wasn't so bad, she was just dippy, I suppose. I hope I don't get like her. She had Alzheimers, you know.'

'You haven't, Mum. Your illness is different.'

'Patricia is no relation of mine at all,' Ruth said with what sounded like satisfaction bordering on delight.

'Really? So was Les her father?'

'No.'

'And he wasn't yours either?'

'Not as far as I know. He didn't act like a father.' And here Ruth flinched, and held her trembling sick hands tightly together.

'What about Auntie Blanche?'

'She and I aren't related either,' said Ruth. Her voice was quivering with exhaustion. 'But she was my friend. We would go out together and search for frogs and wild ferns in the swamps together. We found a bird's nest once, with eggs in it. They were beautiful. Blanche was Les and Mamie's daughter, the one they had together, but there was no love lost between her and her dad. Les wanted a boy for the farm, someone he could leave it to. I felt bad when I left Blanche on the farm. She was still a little kid. I've heard she's living in an ashram in India. She always was different.'

'What happened to your mother? This Joy?'

'That's a very good question, dear. I don't know. Nobody does.'

PATRICIA MULLENS WAS AN OLD woman when she phoned Jemima, looking for Nick. Her voice was husky but honeyed and, yes, powerful. That was what came to mind. She was older than Ruth, and newspaper pictures showed her as a broad heavy woman with a short grey bob which revealed her strong features. Jemima had read that Patricia was a widow, but still a philanthropist to the arts, like her late husband. They had set up trusts to deliver funding to several projects before his death.

Nick and Jemima were still married then. Patricia wanted a photograph of him. A special favour. She didn't take many photographs these days, but she'd been talked into a series of artists' portraits and Nick seemed like a perfect subject. She wondered whether Jemima could give him a message.

Jemima said, 'I think we're related. Aren't you my Aunt Patricia?'

There was a pause on the other the end of the line.

'I think there must be some mistake,' said Patricia.

'I'm Jemima, your sister Ruth's daughter.'

'I don't have a sister called Ruth,' Patricia had said. Jemima wondered if this was the confusion of age, in spite of Patricia's profile and reputation. It was, too, the moment when she began to take an interest in her mother's past.

Nick had agreed to the picture, of course. He was honoured to be noticed by Patricia. His career hadn't been holding up so well just of late.

Patricia came up to Auckland and spent a day with Nick, taking pictures of him around the city. She didn't want to photograph him at home, she said; domestic interiors were not really her thing. Nick said she was a fantastic vibrant woman, with an earthy turn of phrase.

'Did you talk to her about being my aunt?' Jemima asked.

'Oh sweetheart, we didn't have time to get onto things like that.'

'But you said you would.'

He shifted uneasily. 'I just don't think she was that interested,' he said finally.

The image of him, as it turned out, was magnificent, showing a delicate dark face, tragic eyes beneath a thatch of straight black hair, a deceptive smile. But by the time it appeared in a gallery, Nick had already gone. Jemima didn't get an invitation to opening night.

RUTH WAS DYING. FIRST SHE had pneumonia, then another adverse reaction to her medication. The doctors were 'working on it' but Ruth wasn't responding. She was very thin, and Jemima, remembering the day they had gone to see the gannets, had a suspicion that Ruth didn't plan to get better. That she had simply had enough. Jemima took six months off from her job in Auckland to care for her mother. There would be a plus to this: she could use the time to think about poetry. Being back in her hometown, but apart from it now, would give her a fresh sense of perspective of her life up until now. She was thirty-five, had been married to a celebrity, who didn't think she had talent, though of course (he said) he wished she did (she had had a handful of poems published in small magazine), divorced and ready to start again. In a way her mother's illness was a gift, she decided, as she packed up her desk.

It was all much harder than she expected. Her mother's speech was mostly unintelligible, and she became irritable at the smallest thing. The heat was oppressive, soaring close to forty degrees in the shade some days, and they had only fans to keep the air moving. Her father hadn't believed in air conditioning. The district nurses were rushed off their feet, with cutbacks to the public health system, and sometimes they didn't make it until after lunch, by which time Ruth was fretful and unresponsive, and Jemima's back was aching from trying to settle her comfortably. At least her father's relatives brought meals. They sat with Ruth and told Jemima to go out and get some fresh air. It wasn't all bad. But poetry seemed increasingly elusive.

In the interval between her mother's revelations at the gannet colony and moving home to stay with her, Jemima had had the opportunity to make some enquiries about her missing grandmother, Joy Mullens. Ruth had two newspaper clippings, yellow and crumbling with age, that she had given Jemima. Let that be an end to it, she had said. It was all she knew. Joy's appearance was described, and what she was wearing when she was last seen by her husband.

So that was Joy and that was Ruth. One of the clippings, from *Truth*, showed a grainy indistinct picture of an ordinary-looking young woman with a pleasant smile. Her grandmother. 'Wife Known to Have Had a Past', said the headline.

There were many questions she wanted to ask her mother, but the time for that was over. What she did find, among her mother's papers, which she had begun to sort, were three letters from Blanche Mullens, written over a period of years, from India. They asked about Ruth's children, and contained vivid accounts of life in the ashram. There was nothing about their childhood. She could be any friend keeping in touch by mail. The address, in an area called Rishikesh, remained consistent. Jemima, chewing on the end of her ballpoint one day while her mother slept, wrote a letter to Blanche, instead of a poem.

A LETTER CAME FOR JEMIMA, forwarded from her Auckland address. By now her leave had passed and she had let her job go. Summer had been and gone. The decision to stay had been easy, even though caring for Ruth was so exhausting. The thought of leaving her mother in a hospital or a hospice seemed out of the question. Ruth would not be abandoned again.

The letter was an invitation to be a guest poet at a reading at Te Papa, in Wellington, the following week. The event would take the form of a panel for 'emerging poets'. Her fares would be met and there was a modest fee, which was welcome. Her funds were running low. Jemima rang the organiser and explained the delay in receiving the invitation. She was in Napier, she said, and probably couldn't get away because her mother was so ill. There was a sigh of relief. 'Well, we'd have to scratch for fares,' the organiser said. 'It's dearer to fly people from the provinces than down from Auckland. Silly, isn't it?'

Jemima mentioned this to her aunt, one of Neil's sisters, a woman with a shining white halo of hair, when she brought over a casserole that evening. She told it in an anecdotal way, as something that had simply happened during her day.

Her aunt said, 'You have to go. I insist. I'll pay your fare if you like. It'll do you good.'

When Jemima remonstrated, her aunt said gently that she wouldn't be any help to Ruth if she didn't look after herself, and not to worry, that she would be by Ruth's side every minute that she was away.

In the end, the organisers said that it was all right, and if she didn't mind waiving the fee, they could probably afford her. It seemed magnanimous: she wondered if a certain notoriety surrounded her now, as the ex-wife of the noted playwright. She'd heard that Nick had shifted to Wellington since going off with his latest, a married woman.

THE READING WAS TO BE held in the Te Papa theatre, where Jemima was taken to meet the others on the panel. She had been met by the organiser of the event, an older woman dressed in black. A group of five poets was taking turns to test the microphone. The atmosphere in the room seemed chilly, the lights cool. Most of the other poets, four women and a man, were younger than her. She wondered if she might already be too old to be an emerging poet. In Auckland, she held her own, but after months in the provinces, she felt suddenly down at heel, as if she had slightly lost the plot, was not properly groomed. She was wearing dark trousers, one of last season's jackets, flat shoes, a casual look that she associated with poetry readings. She'd worn her fair hair loose, a style left over from her days with Nick. Beautiful hair, he'd said, the night he met her, his fingers holding a handful of it, his mouth nuzzling her throat. She knew now that all his women were blonde, as if to offset his own appearance. One of the others, a petite smart woman with a cap of yellow hair, and dressed in an orange designer dress and blue Minnie Cooper shoes, sidled up to her. Her name was Gail, and she wanted to know all about Jemima and the work she was doing. She said she'd seen a very significant poem of hers that made her cry.

'Which one was that?' asked Jemima.

'Oh goodness, I should have written the title down,' Gail said. 'Something about loss.' Jemima supposed that they had all written poems about loss, but didn't say so. Something about Gail made her cringe.

'I'm going to read a series of linked poems about looking at birds,' Gail said.

'Blackbirds?' said Jemima, without meaning to be unkind. That had slipped out.

'I don't do the Wallace Stevens thing,' said Gail, her voice sharp with anger. 'Besides, my poems are sonnets.'

'I'm sorry, I haven't read your poems yet. But I'm looking forward to them,' Jemima said, wishing she had kept quiet.

'Of course I may not have time to read them all,' Gail said. 'Timing's important, don't you think?'

'I've timed mine,' Jemima said. 'I promise I won't go over.'

'Who's for a coffee?' Gail cried, in an over-enthusiastic way, intended, Jemima thought, to convey what great friends they were, or were about to become. Everyone agreed that that was what they needed, but it was Jemima Gail wanted to walk with on their way to the museum café.

'Friands,' Gail cried, when they arrived at the counter. 'We must all have friands, give us some creative energy.'

And Jemima was agreeing that yes, she would like a friand, but could she have peppermint tea rather than coffee.

'Just like my boyfriend,' Gail said, a half-hidden glee in her voice.

Jemima had a sudden queasy feeling in her stomach.

The woman was giving her a sly look. 'His name's Nick,' she said. 'He's a writer too.'

JEMIMA WALKED QUICKLY ALONG CABLE Street and turned left at the next set of lights. She wasn't exactly sure where she was going, but if she kept turning left she would, she thought, end up in Cuba Street. It was a while since she had been to Wellington. At first she had thought of walking along the waterfront, but a stiff late autumn wind was scuttling leaves and bits of rubbish across the street, and hard spots of rain were spitting tacks in her face. She felt shabby and disorientated. Around Cuba Street, as she recalled it, she could disappear into the crowd, find a tearoom (did such things exist in Wellington now?) — somewhere to sit down and stop the trembling in her knees. She walked up past the bucket fountain, tipping and swaying, past second-hand clothing shops, the entrance to an art gallery, a pub or two, crowds of youths playing with a hacky sack — a game of 'chills', Jemima thought, as one of them demonstrated a foot-stall. Her nephews played this game, and there she went again, her heart aching as if it would break. How she had loved Nick.

Wanted children. How she still did. On second thoughts, perhaps she hated him. Nick had children, two born before they were married, with two different mothers. It kept them poor. The real reason he had gone off with the Canadian was because he was sick of her counting out maintenance money from his royalties, and from her wages as well, and her complaining about going on working and not having children of her own. If it hadn't been the Canadian it would have been someone else. And now it was Gail.

The poetry reading would be in progress. It was unlikely they had waited for her. She saw the likely scenario in her head. Gail would have told the organiser that Jemima, the 'one from Napier', hadn't looked too good, just got up and walked out, without saying a word, didn't even pay for her order. They would have looked at each other with knowing smiles, all in on the secret that wasn't a secret. They would be on stage, their cadences poised, voices under control, the young man clearing his throat, the way he had when he was introduced to her. She had read some of his poems. They were dense and torrid. There would be hushed moments at the end of each reading before the round of applause. At least Gail would have longer to read her sonnets.

Jemima stopped to draw breath. Beside her was a shop with wispy curtains on either side of the battered doorway. A board outside offered psychic readings: $35 for half an hour. And somehow, suddenly, she found herself inside, where crystals dangled from the shelves, asking if it was possible that she might get a reading done now. She had never been to a medium before, but she liked the idea that secret knowledge lay close at hand.

The woman behind the counter shouted out to someone called Magda that she had a client.

Magda appeared in a doorway leading from a backroom and

invited Jemima into a recess at the side of the shop. She was a large woman with long thin bleached hair sprouting in several directions, a tasselled scarf at her throat and many rings on her fingers. The rings were grimy, as if she wore them in the garden, and several of them were engraved with coiled snakes. Bangles clanked on her wrists. She invited Jemima to sit opposite her at a small plastic table .

The room was constructed of white concrete blocks, as if it had been tacked onto the older part of the building; a net curtain drifted across the open doorway. There were so many crystals hanging in this room that they tinkled against each other when one moved quickly. Jemima sat very still.

Magda leant forward and peered at her. 'You've had a shock,' she said, and Jemima agreed that yes she had.

'You've run away from it, though. An impulsive gesture, but then you're a Piscean. That's what Pisceans do, off at the first sign of trouble.'

'How do you know I'm a Piscean?'

'You're impressed. You think it's a trick. Well, my dear, you're wearing an amethyst ring. Someone might have passed it on to you, but I don't think so. From the way you turn it on your finger, I believe it means something special to you, that it was chosen for you personally.'

'Yes,' said Jemima, 'that's true.' The ring was for her engagement to Nick, although she wore it on her right hand now. She hadn't been able to put it away for good. When they agreed to marry, he wanted to give her her birthstone. She was special, she was the one, he'd never given a girl a ring before. She was impressed by Magda's quick eye, by the fact that she'd told her how she'd worked out her birth sign, rather than pretending it was some psychic knowledge.

'You need to slow down,' Magda said. 'You're carrying too many burdens.'

When Jemima nodded, Magda said, 'I think you're a giving person. But sometimes it's necessary to put down your burden and let others carry it.'

'I can't,' said Jemima, and began to cry.

'Soon the burden will be gone. It will be taken from you. You must know how to let go when the time comes.'

'How did you know?' Jemima whispered, and then felt stupid. She had no idea what she was doing here. If she could leave the poetry reading, she could leave this place just as easily. But when she shifted suddenly, the crystals touched her hair.

'My mother is very ill,' she said.

'Oh yes, of course, she's been ill for a long time. But you've done everything for her. You've been loved and given love in return. It's the best anyone can do. There's a man in your life, too.'

'No. Not really.'

'A dark man.' Magda waved a small fan in front of her face, and just for a moment Jemima thought she saw a little grin tucked behind the fan, which was black with Japanese women in kimonos strolling across it.

'He's gone.'

'He was draining your powers. I think you're creative, but as long as you let him steal your energy, he'll stop you in your tracks.'

'You sound like Gail,' Jemima said, and suddenly laughed. 'Creative energy. I think I need a friand.'

Magda looked offended. 'Well, perhaps you'd like to leave it at that.'

'I'd like to leave the dark man out of it. You're right, he gets in the way.'

Magda nodded in a wise and knowing manner, and waited.

Jemima started again. 'My mother, there's more.'

The woman leant forward. 'Go on.'

'This sounds ridiculous. But my mother's mother, my grandmother, that is, disappeared many years ago. I want to know what happened to her.'

The psychic looked flustered and blushed. Now, Jemima thought, now is the time to leave. We both know that she's not going to take a chance on this, that she might get herself mixed up in something public, or with the police. And perhaps this was a betrayal of her mother, the story she had entrusted her with, laying it out to this woman, this phony. If Magda were to say that she, Jemima, was a little crazy right now, that would be right, and she wouldn't have had to feed her too many clues. Probably people who came to her were always like her, despairing and powerless at some given moment. Yet the impulse to continue was overwhelming. She said: 'My grandmother was a woman named Joy Mullens who vanished from a farm near a river a year or so before the last war.' She related the story then, of how her grandmother had set off for Invercargill, how her husband had left her at a railway station and gone home to feed out hay to the cows, it being wintertime.

'The police went looking for her,' Magda said, as if this was a fact.

'Yes, for a while, but she was never found.'

Magda closed her eyes. 'I see green grass.'

'Well, yes, there was a lot of grass. It was a farm.'

'I don't see a train.'

'So you think she might not have gone to the railway station?'

'Foul play, I suspect foul play.'

'My mother thought that, too.'

'I think she was under water.'

'In the river?'

Magda closed her eyes. Her eyelids were waxy and blue and there were deep pouches beneath her eyes. Jemima felt sorry for her, this large elderly woman, making up tales for money. She looked tired and poor.

When she opened her eyes, Magda said, 'No, I don't think she's in the river. I see long straight lines.'

'The railway line?'

'No, I told you. Under water. Straight lines. We need to do the cards. We're running out of time.' Magda handed her a pack of tarot cards, her movements agitated. 'Go on shuffle them. Think of a question.'

Jemima shook her head. 'I don't think I can do that. About the straight lines?'

'Well, that's all for today.' Magda stood up; the crystals swayed and clinked. 'Your half hour's up. I need to go home for a rest now.'

RUTH DIED ON A SUNDAY morning, towards sunrise. Jemima and her father's sisters and two of his brothers, and Jemima's own two brothers were there through the night, making cups of tea, taking it in turns to sit by Ruth's bedside. The doctor had been at seven in the evening to administer morphine. He didn't believe Ruth was in pain, but it would ease her restlessness, the occasional moments when she woke and looked at them with startled eyes, sudden bewilderment, even anguish.

Jemima looked out across the sea and saw that dawn was about to break. Ruth opened her eyes, with a look of lucidity, of happiness. 'Is it spring?'

'Soon,' Jemima said. 'In a little while.'

'The gannets,' Ruth said. 'The little chicks.' And in a moment it was over, her breathing shallow against the oxygen mask propped over her face, and then it stopped and the mask was clear.

WHEN JEMIMA AND HER OLDER brother Kirk saw Blanche step off the small aeroplane at Napier airport, Kirk said, 'Just all we need.'

And Blanche's appearance did seem incongruous. She had a curiously pale face, although her hands were ravaged by the sun. In some ways, she looked like the psychic Jemima had visited in Wellington — her hair thin and ragged, her patterned cotton skirt trailing above her sandals, a shawl around her shoulders. But she wasn't decorated with hoops and bangles, the way Magda had been, and her light eyes were hooded and piercing. On one arm, she carried an enormous patchwork bag with wooden handles, dusty with red earth in its folds.

'Your luggage shouldn't be long,' Kirk said, taking charge.

'This is my luggage,' Blanche said, indicating the colourful bag.

She had arrived in time for the funeral. 'I'd hoped to see Ruth once more,' she said wistfully. She had flown through time zones for twenty hours.

'But you've come, Auntie Blanche,' said Jemima, and hugged her, this strange woman who wasn't her aunt, although for the moment this didn't matter.

'Did you let Patricia know?' Blanche asked, almost straight away.

'No,' said Jemima and Kirk, almost in one voice.

'Thank goodness,' Blanche said.

'There's no reason for her to know,' Jemima said, taking charge.

'Perhaps not,' Blanche said, and bent her head slightly.

There was standing room only in the cathedral. For every member of Neil's large family, there were twenty more who had known him and Ruth. And her mother had more friends of her own than Jemima realised — people who had visited her garden on tours, gardening circles, bookclub members. Jemima's brothers read the psalms. They had suggested that Jemima read a poem, but in the end she didn't.

It seemed pretentious to read one of her own, and nothing else she could find seemed to fit. Instead she spoke for a few minutes about the last visit to the gannets, about how she and her brothers were so loved as children, and how that was their parents' legacy. She spoke of how the gannets entwined their necks, and stayed together for life, and then she left it at that, because her voice broke. Afterwards, people came up and said that that was the part of the service they liked best. Jemima didn't tell them that she had had to stop because she was thinking that she had failed the test.

At the last moment, Jemima asked Blanche if there was anything she would like to say, and was relieved when Blanche said no. Jemima had looked up Hindu customs on the internet, and realised that funeral services were conducted in a different way. Blanche simply said that the soul was indestructible, and that Ruth was released from worldly needs. She was now immortal. This was how she saw things, and it gave her comfort that her sister had reached this place. She had no need to say it in public.

After everyone left, and the dishes were stowed and the living room vacuumed, Blanche and Jemima were left alone in the house. Jemima had no idea what Blanche might want to do next. She hoped she would go to bed soon.

'Let's open some wine,' Blanche said. Jemima wanted to cheer. She thought that perhaps Blanche wouldn't drink.

After they had each drunk three glasses of pinot gris, Blanche seemed perfectly normal to Jemima. All the same, she couldn't help saying, 'You chose an unusual life. Like a saint.'

Blanche shrugged. 'I'm no saint. There're a lot of us in India, doing what we can. I've tried to model my life on that of a woman I know who runs an orphanage. A writer, as it happens.'

'Jean Watson?'

'That's the one. Now she is a saint. Are you going back to Auckland?' she asked as if wanting to change the subject.

'Not for the moment. The boys don't want me to sell just now. They want to see the garden kept up. Perhaps later on. I don't know really.'

'What about that no-good husband of yours?'

Jemima felt herself bristling. 'Nick and I just didn't get along too well.'

'When was his last play?'

'A couple of years ago. About the time we split.'

'Hmm. Still living on his looks, eh?'

'I don't really want to talk about Nick,' Jemima said.

'No, perhaps you don't. You know, I keep up with things here. I expect you think I'm eccentric. People have thought that all my life. I just don't want to see you ending up like me.'

'I thought you were very happy. With enlightenment, I mean.'

'I'd have liked children. It's not too late for you. There'll be someone, you're very pretty.'

'That's not really the point, is it? I'm sure you could have had someone if you'd really wanted.'

'I thought not.'

'But why? Was it Patricia? My mother told me about her. Cruel, she said she was cruel.'

'She had her own problems, I think.'

'Oh, that's too full of karma for me, Blanche, sorry, but really it is. Do you keep in touch with her?'

'I haven't seen her in a long time. She was at my father's funeral. There were only five of us there. Me and her, and her boyfriend Seymour, who I heard she'd married, and a neighbour doing his duty, and a lawyer. People didn't think too well of my father. Patricia inherited the farm, you know. Well, that was a long time back.'

'Why didn't people like your father?' said Jemima, pouring them the last of the wine. But Blanche just sighed. Jemima felt tipsy and tired, and knew she was on dangerous ground. She hadn't slept properly for three nights. She walked through to the kitchen and unwrapped a plate of asparagus rolls from under a dampened cloth, and found a camembert in the fridge, and a loaf of bread. When she put the food on the table in front of the older woman, she noticed the way her hand shot out to take a roll, the hungry way she ate.

Jemima felt better, her head clearing. 'Do you know about my grandmother? About Joy who went missing?'

Blanche gave a barking laugh. 'I heard about it on my first day at school when I was five years old. My father wasn't trusted. Well, why would he be? Who knows, he might have killed your grandmother. Nobody knew for sure.'

'So, is *that* the point?' Jemima said.

Blanche's eyes were raking Jemima's face, as if appraising her. Still she said nothing.

'I'd like to find out,' Jemima said. 'My mother only spoke of it the once.' As Blanche didn't demur, she went on, telling her about the newspaper cuttings, and the visit to the psychic. 'You'll think I'm stupid,' she finished, trailing off.

But Blanche was leaning forward, her eyes intent. 'Straight lines, well, yes, of course. That woman sounds as if she was quite good.' She was shuffling through the objects in her bag, pulling out a bottle of vitamin pills, some tissues, a notebook, a thin wallet, a spare pair of voluminous pants, all of which she placed in a heap on the table. 'Now here we are,' she said. In her hand she held a small plastic bag that, on opening, revealed a worn piece of fabric. It might have been green once, more like lichen now, or the colour of mildew. She held it out to Jemima.

'What is it?' Jemima reached out gingerly; the cloth was so weathered and thin that the threads seemed to be falling apart.

'I brought it because I thought Ruth might want it at the end. But of course I see now it was truly in the past for her. She was in a state of detachment from the moment she left the farm. Perhaps she reached a state I've never been able to achieve.' Jemima gazed at her blankly.

'You see, after Ruth left,' Blanche continued, 'I went on hunting the swamps, walking in the paddocks, searching for wetland ferns, the little wild orchids and the birds' nests. I was on my own, not a child that anyone wanted to play with. And I came upon this, sticking out from the side of one of the drains my father had dug. The ground had been dug over and over again, but by then I think it had been compacted down several layers. The water was very low that year — usually it would have been full. My father didn't mind that I walked in the swamps, but he said I must never go near the drains. I supposed it was because he wanted to keep me safe, although later I learnt that nothing was safe when my father was in a rage. I found this ordinary piece of cloth. I pulled and pulled at it but it was stuck in the earth. It tore away in my hands. I see pictures of mass graves in countries like Cambodia and Kosovo, where bodies have been left, and the tatters of their clothes are visible in the dirt, and I think of this discovery of mine. At the time, of course, I knew none of that, and those horrors were still to come. All the same, something made me hide it. At first, I wanted to keep it because it seemed so mysterious. I thought that the next time I saw Ruth I would tell her that I'd found something quite different in the paddocks. But then . . .' and she seemed ready to stop again. 'But then,' she resumed, 'as I grew older and began to truly understand, I thought it best not.'

'Did you ever tell anyone?'

'Never. You asked me the point. Well, that's it, of course. You grow up thinking you've got bad blood in your veins. The murderer's daughter.'

Jemima stood up unsteadily. 'No,' she said. 'No.' She pushed the cloth away. Outside the dark closed around the house. Someone had left a window open to air the place. Cold air and the scent of wintersweet and early daphne filled her nostrils. She thought she could hear the sea against the distant shore but perhaps it was the sound in her ears, some terrible knowledge that was being laid out before her. She picked up the cloth again, stood holding it.

'The next summer,' Blanche said, 'the peat fires flared up again. The peat used to burn underground. They were especially bad that year, smoke and fire billowing across the landscape. But the smell was lovely, rich and aromatic. I've smelt that smoke in India sometimes. Smoke that reminds me of it. In the winter the rains came again. When I went back to the drain, there was nothing to be seen. It was under water.'

WHEN SOME WEEKS HAD PASSED, Blanche went back to India. Jemima asked her to stay on as long as she wanted, and her brothers seemed to have taken a liking to her too. She hadn't told them of the conversation she had had with Blanche on the night of the funeral; she didn't know whether she ever would. There was so much to think of: the garden to plan for the coming year, her mother's affairs to put in order, lawyers to see. She thought about burying Nick's ring in the garden, but that didn't seem final enough, as if she was leaving a place where she could find it. Instead, she put it in a bubble wrap bag and sent it to him, with a note suggesting he might want to use it again.

She also bundled up some poems and sent them to a publisher of slim books of verse, and hoped for the best.

'I love it here,' Blanche had said longingly. 'It would be easy to stay and make myself useful in the garden. I'd like that. But I have to go back.' The ashram took in poor people who were sick and injured and had nowhere to go. When she was a teacher in her youth, she had learnt first-aid skills. She knew how to bandage wounds, to clean out infections. She wished she had been a doctor. It was time to go back and see how everyone was.

Jemima drove her up to Auckland to catch the plane. On the way, they detoured across the plains to the Waikato farmland where Blanche had grown up. Hang Dog Road had been renamed, but she knew the way. You never forget, she said. The countryside of your childhood is like the palm of your hand, an indelible imprint to carry into eternity.

The old farmhouse had been stripped of lean-tos, tidied up and painted, and given a new roof. Nearby stood a brand-new house with Mediterranean-style arches, painted terracotta. 'Now there's a statement,' Blanche said. 'Wow, goodness me. I bet the old place is the sharemilker's or some such.'

This turned out to be correct. A young man, tousled with sleep, came to the door. He was having forty winks he said, before the second milking of the day.

'How early the cows come into season these days,' Blanche said, and he looked at her as if she was an apparition on his doorstep.

'Just go ahead, help yourselves, don't go near the bull paddock, that's all,' he said, waving his arm, when they asked if they could look around. A child cried in the background, and a cross-looking young woman appeared behind the man.

'She was probably just getting the baby off to sleep,' said Blanche. They walked across several paddocks, Blanche reminding

Jemima to shut the heavy gates behind them.

'The paddock. Do you remember where the drain was?' Jemima asked, trying to hide her impatience.

They stopped, while Blanche stood staring in a puzzled way across the paddocks, dappled beneath passing clouds. 'That stand of trees wasn't there,' she said.

The trees were tall and shapely, soft with spring's new colour, shelter for stock. Soon it would be summer. The river flowed dark and insistent between the stopbanks. 'I never thought I'd come back here,' Blanche said.

After a few moments, she shook her head. 'I'm sorry, Jemima. I've brought you on a wild goose chase. I've no idea where that drain went. There's no sign of it now.'

Jemima stood silent. The thought had crossed her mind, more than once, since Blanche's extraordinary disclosure, that she would lead people (the police perhaps, that seemed the obvious thing) to uncover a body. That it might still be preserved in the peat of the Waikato farm at the end of Hang Dog Road. The mystery solved.

Blanche stood beside her, muttering to herself. She was saying something that sounded like a prayer, an incantation, about being led from untruth to truth. 'Lead us from darkness to light,' she said in a firm clear voice. She opened the bag. Jemima knew she was going to offer her the piece of cloth and shook her head, although she reached out and touched it once more.

It was nothing, no proof of anything at all. She stood quite still. This was a place where her mother had stood. And, it seemed, her mother before her.

Part III

Fragrance Rising

SWIMMING

THE PRIME MINISTER'S TOWEL IS green with a narrow pink stripe at either end, a towel chosen by a woman. It lies where he's tossed it aside before stepping into the swimming bath. In his woollen bathing suit, straps taut over his shoulders, he is a black seal slicing through the water, powerful arms plunging, shoulders rearing up and down and up again in a perfect butterfly stroke. Despite all the speed and energy, this is his time for reflecting, a place where there are no secretaries, or bells calling him to the chamber, or papers that can be pushed beneath his nose. This is the place where, in his head at least, he cannot be joined by others.

Not that he is without his spectators. There are people who enjoy the sense of being close to power, who can say that they have seen Mr Gordon Coates himself in his swimming trunks. So near I could almost have touched him, they will say, when they return home, for most of them are from the country come to town to take in the sights. And they love him, because he is one of them, a country boy who made good. Not an educated man, they will continue, someone like us who didn't stay long at school, but look at the way we get by — like him, we don't need fancy letters after our names, and he has risen right to the top. He has worn a braided jacket and white breeches and shoes with buckles when he went to meet the king. These viewers, who have come to watch the prime minister take his daily constitutional, huddle on the lower path near the water, rather than the sheltered gallery, so that when he has done with his swim he must pass them. The Thorndon Baths have a square tower above the dressing rooms and two domed ornamental roofs. Winter is close; there is menace in the wind. You would think that would deter the prime minister but it seems he swims wet or fine or even when Wellington's southerly is whipping the harbour into a frenzy. The watching men wear trousers that are a little baggy and shiny at the knees, their Sunday best, and high collars beneath their jackets, scarves billowing about them. The women clutch their wraps, legs quivering with cold beneath the new short skirts of the day, woollen cloche hats pulled round their ears.

He lifts his head from the water, and on this fresh morning in late May, he smells a whiff of wood smoke curling from the houses nearby. All of a sudden there is an ache at the back of his throat, and he sees not the blue floor of the swimming pool but the heavy green light that glances through the ebb and flow of the Arapaoa, the slow salt tide between mangrove banks. He catches the fragrance rising from log fires in open paddocks, a fallen macrocarpa perhaps, or old apple trees from the orchards. Beyond the sky-high flames stands a house built close to the ground with low-slung verandahs and creepers winding around the pillars. Across the green lay of the land, there is laughter and song on the quiet still air of the Kaipara, telling him his Maori neighbours have risen to begin their day. He stops to listen.

In that moment when he lifts his head, he sees the child, a little girl with eyes as dark as a zoo panther's hide, although her complexion is pale sepia. She is perhaps five or six years of age, shivering in a ragged yellow cotton frock. She doesn't appear to know where she is. The prime minister is aware that poor children live in this area but as a rule they stay close to their homes along Sydney and Ascot streets, where the workers' cottages huddle side by side, close enough for the children to hold hands with each other if they reach out the windows. This child looks as if she is lost.

There is something wrong here. For a moment he thinks, It can't be, it isn't her, one of them. How could she have found him? And then he thinks, Of course not, the child is too young. He pulls himself up on the edge of the pool, his taste for swimming over, and stands, abruptly shaking water from himself, his moustache showering tiny arcs of dew over his chest as he grabs the towel to wipe his eyes clear. A man steps out, pointing his Box Brownie at the prime minister's large frame.

'No,' he says, holding the towel up and shielding his face. 'Not today.' He recognises the man's peaked cap, worn back to front with a journalist's flamboyance. He has seen the fellow more often than he likes, and it wouldn't surprise him if he was a plant for the Liberals. The pictures he takes of the prime minister have been snapped at the oddest moments, such as when he is dancing in the most gentlemanly fashion with the wife of one his cabinet ministers, the kind of duty he undertakes out of the goodness of his heart, or when he is dining in a restaurant and stops for a cigar between his meat and potatoes and the arrival of dessert. There is a suspicion in his mind that the man wants to make something of a clown of him at least, or a womaniser at worst.

'Mr Coates,' calls out an admirer, holding out a scrap of paper and a pen, 'your autograph, sir.' He brushes past without a second glance. 'Brusque, a man who can be a bit short,' they will say later on. 'He has much on his mind. The economy, it's not in good shape. It's us he will have been thinking of. He just didn't see us that day.'

In the dressing room he breathes deeply and evenly, trying to recover his composure. He dries himself with care, lifting his balls above his groin as delicately as a girl's dress, dusting the folds with talcum powder. When he is fully dressed he stands in front of a mirror, adjusting his spotted tie, buttoning his waistcoat, checking the white handkerchief in his pocket, then flicks a tailor-made from the packet in his inside pocket and inhales.

Outside, a sleety rain has begun to fall. The crowd has dispersed. Only the child is standing there, looking at him. Or perhaps just at the space before her, as if trying to discover where she is supposed to be.

'What is it, child?' he asks her. He has daughters of his own.

Still she does not speak. On an impulse, he kneels before her. 'You've just come here to live, eh?'

She nods.

'How many days?' He holds up one hand, the fingers splayed, counting them aloud, curling his thumb in his palm then the others, one by one. When he comes to two, the child puts out a hand and clasps them in his.

'Two days, eh? Just two days. Where are you from?'

She shakes her head dumbly.

'What is your name?'

'Janie,' she whispers.

'Janie who?'

'Janie McCaw.' He catches the slight burr in her voice.

'Do you know where you live now, Miss Janie McCaw?'

Again she shakes her head, but he has decided. The name has told him as much as he probably needs to know. There are few Maori here nowadays, although once they had pa sites all over the town. The child will live in one of the workers' cottages, probably along Ascot Street. There will be a Maori mother, a Scotsman for a father. If her father was Maori he wouldn't have been given a place to rent. I have a wife and a child, the man will have said, and nobody the wiser about the wife until he had moved in. Janie will have set off for school, on this her second day, and now she has lost her way. Mr Coates has worked all this out as he stands and takes Janie firmly by the hand. There is a cabinet meeting in half an hour but if he moves quickly, he will just have time to return Janie McCaw to her mother. His towel is damp, not soaking, and he wraps it around the child to protect her from the wind. In truth, his curiosity is sparked. He wants to see this mother of whom he already has a picture in his head.

Hand in hand now, the two of them walk briskly, or rather Janie trots as she tries to keep up with her protector, back along Tinakori Road. He picks up his pace as he passes his own house, preferring not to be seen. They pass shops and the Shepherd's Arms, where a few men are taking the first drop of the day, a refreshment after work, possibly on the night-cart, which collects the buckets of human faeces. Or perhaps they are bakers who have made the morning's first batch of bread, or railway men. You can't tell one from the other when they are tired and unwashed, and banging their fists for a pint, except for the bakers, dusty white with drifting flour. In response to a shouted greeting, Mr Coates touches his hat without a further glance, intent on the task he has set himself. The pair make a sharp left turn, and then again, and they have entered Ascot Street.

'Is it here, Janie? D'you think you live in this street?'

The child nods and points. The houses are small and shabby, paint peeling and bubbling in Wellington's salt-laden air, but there is an atmosphere of respectability here as well, lines of washing flapping in the damp air, rows of winter vegetables, cabbages and carrots, the soil dark with recent tilling. Only the house that Janie is pulling the prime minister towards is forlorn and neglected, a blind hanging askew in the window, weeds flourishing in the wasteland of what was once a garden. The family has just arrived, Mr Coates thinks to himself. Soon they will have this place shipshape.

The little girl releases herself from his grip and darts along the path. Before he knows it, she has disappeared into a lean-to washing shed to one side of the building, and next thing a door bangs, and she is gone.

This is not good enough. He gives a peremptory knock on what passes for a front door.

Over the fence a woman's head appears. 'Why, Prime Minister, to what do we owe the honour of this visit?'

'I found the child wandering,' he says stiffly, feeling as caught out as if his own wife had appeared out of Premier House, these few minutes past. 'Where is the mother?'

'Ah,' says the woman, 'there's no mother there. Just a man called Jock turned up with the kid last week. Dead, he reckons the mother is, taken with flu in the epidemic.'

'I thought the child younger than that.'

'Oh who can tell, that's his story. She looks after herself. Which way did you walk, your honour? Past the Shepherd's Arms? I'm surprised you didn't see her old man, or perhaps he's passed out already. Someone will bring him home round dinnertime.'

The prime minister fumbles in his trouser pocket. 'I'd be obliged if you'd keep an eye on her for me.' He presses a pound note into her hand.

He hesitates before stooping to pick up the green and pink-striped towel where it has fallen from Janie McCaw's shoulders onto the path.

GOVERNING

HULLO, THE GANG'S ALL HERE,' the prime minister shouts as he rushes through the cabinet room door, as if he is exactly on time and waiting for his ministers, not they upon him. He waves a sheaf of papers over his head.

The men gathered at the table look up from their study of the day's order papers, and it's hard for them to suppress smiles behind the wreaths of smoke. This is the way it is: just when things seem gloomy and the books don't balance, Coates bounds in and the serious business of governing the country seems lightened. But this morning he is not in a mood to dally with jokes.

'I have a new idea,' he announces. 'I'm going to introduce a bill that will provide more educational opportunities for young Maoris.'

'That's not scheduled on the order paper,' says Albert Davy, an adviser to the party who, of late, Gordon Coates has begun to look upon with suspicion. He has appeared a stalwart friend in the past, but these days he has a sly air about him, as if he is not quite open. At times he is aggressive in his manner. The night before, he and Coates dined together at Bellamy's. Over pork chops and a whisky or several, Mr Davy had said, in a tone tinged with dislike, that the Right Honourable Prime Minister was playing to the Maori vote to the detriment of the wider population. 'Do you not think,' he had said, 'that if the banks run out of money, your European constituents might have grounds to complain that not enough of the vanishing funds have been spent on them?' This is the very same man who devised the brilliant advertising slogan, 'Coats off with Coates', which helped sweep him to victory in the last election.

'I have the support of Sir Maui Pomare,' the prime minister had said then, 'and on the other side of the house, Sir Apirana Ngata will support me to the utmost, no matter that we are in opposition to each other.'

'That is the trouble,' Davy had replied. 'You have friends in all the wrong places. You're a farmer but you run with Maoris and Red Feds. You've lost your sense of the rest of this country.'

'I'll thank you to keep a civil tongue in your head, Mr Davy,' Coates had said. He had lit a cigar and blown some smoke over Davy's roast potatoes. Now he wished he had not.

'I suppose Sir Maui already knows of this,' Davy says evenly, turning to the Minister for Internal Affairs alongside him. 'But the honourable member is Minister for Health, not of education.'

Maui Pomare turns his large handsome head towards the adviser with an expression of contempt. A doctor once, he had spent many years in America. He speaks with a faint twang. 'Health, education, they go hand in hand. Ask any fool that, and he will tell you the obvious: it's not enough for Maori children to be sound in body, though that is surely a beginning, but they'll go nowhere in the Pakeha world without knowledge of its ways.'

'Perhaps Sir Maui has known what is in your head a lot longer than the rest of us, Prime Minister.'

Coates returns Davy's stare. 'This idea of mine is one I thought of on my way to work,' he says. 'It's to do with the responsibility of parents to ensure that all children attend school on a regular basis, whether they be native schools or otherwise.'

'Then if you have only thought of it this morning, we can't put it through on today's order paper. The bill has to be written.'

Coates shrugs. 'The matter will be raised, the public made aware.'

He laughs, runs his hand through his auburn hair. The debating chamber awaits, with its ornate furnishings, lush carpet and green leather chairs. He prepares himself for a performance to the visitors' gallery, where the public watch. The ladies sit in a separate compartment and, even though they have to queue for a ticket in the way that the gentlemen do not, there are always several there, many of them dressed to kill, a fur stole draped casually around shoulders, hats with tilted brims, mouths red bows. He looks up now and then, aware when one tries to catch his eye.

He will keep his cabinet guessing. He knows the rules as well as they do; whether he will try to break them or not is entirely his business.

HOMING IN

THE GREEN SWEEP OF THE trees beside the driveway is what he loves best about Premier House. They are true trees of New Zealand, glossy-leaved, dark and dense and, on a night like this, dripping with fog-strewn cobwebs, shining in the light spilling from the house. When he walks up the drive he remembers a particular section of land up north that stands apart from the burnt-over earth, with its stumps of scrub where grass has been sown. He owns this piece of land; it's best not to remember that, but it keeps coming back to him, as if in a dream. It's an area of bush so thick that a man could lose himself in a minute if he didn't keep his wits about him. He has planted a kauri tree here in the grounds of his official residence, and one day, a thousand years on, someone will look at it in wonder, marvelling at how it came to grow here in the city.

Premier House, 260 Tinakori Road — the two-storeyed wooden house also known as Ariki Toa, home of the chief — is set above the road. A huge glassed-in verandah on the right shelters the entrance-way; beyond is a reception area, bay windows with handsome stained glass and leadlights, twinkling chandeliers. Its grandeur encompasses him. He always knew he had a place in the world. Like destiny.

The children's voices rise to meet him, and then they are throwing themselves at him, one grabbing a hand, another throwing herself at his knees, a flurry of arms and legs. Irirangi, the one on whom he has been allowed to bestow a Maori name, although her skin is as pale as buttermilk, her hair with a hint of auburn gold like his own; and Patricia and Josephine. 'Father, Father,' they cry. 'Where have you been?'

And he's telling them that it's been a busy day at work, and the nanny is saying, 'Quietly girls, quietly, now mind your father', and in the background one of the older girls, Sheila, he thinks, is at the piano playing something sweet and dreamy — 'Für Elise', perhaps, which is what young girls love to play when they are just getting the hang of music and their fingers are spreading across the keys beyond scales and nursery rhymes. A house full of women: five daughters, the sweet scent of their creamy freshly washed bodies and the nanny, who is still young herself, with dark hair and eyes, and a flair for fashionable clothes, even if her ankles are not her strong point. He has thought, in passing, of slapping her bottom, just to see what she would do. And, somewhere, somewhere in here beyond the noise and bustle of welcome there is Marge, his pretty English wife with her big blue adoring eyes.

'Where is she?' he asks the nanny. She looks at him and scowls and his spirits sink a little. He had forgotten that the nanny is given to moods. Marge has told him that she has been unlucky in love and that they should be kind to her when she is down. But sometimes he fears she is showing the disapproval Marge would never express, on his wife's behalf. What has he done now?

'Lying down,' says the nanny.

'Is she unwell?'

'It's the Irish in you,' responds the woman, 'all mad. You never stop to think, do you?' The nanny is Scots Presbyterian. She had to think twice about taking on a job in this house, even if they were Protestants. Not the same kind of Protestants as her; the Irish never could be, she said at the time, which had made the prime minister laugh. Now it looks as if nobody is amused.

Marge is coming towards him, her hair dishevelled, her cheeks flushed and damp, as if she has indeed been lying in bed, and crying at that. In her hands she clutches the *Evening Post*.

'Gordon,' she says, 'how could you?'

There pictured on the front page, him walking, hand in hand with Janie McCaw, out of the Thorndon Baths.

COURTING

PERFUME. IT WAS MARJORIE COLE'S scent that had attracted him from the beginning. She had been piteous on the first occasion he met her, a young woman from England who, against all her father's advice and at only sixteen, had come to join her sister and brother-in-law in New Zealand. Her father was a doctor, a man of the world. The thought of this child going to the colonies seemed absurd when she could have a life of comfort at home. But her brother-in-law was sick and, as Marjorie had said to her father, 'Whatever will Babs do among all those Maoris if poor Otter becomes worse?' Her sister had written that they were going to take a small cottage near the sea at a place known as the Kaipara. The weather was good, orchards had been planted, the water teemed with fish. Somewhere Marjorie had read that the first settlers heard the sound of snapper fish crunching the shellfish on the shores of the harbour, and this information she read aloud to her father. The living would be easy.

'What of these Maoris?' her father asked.

'Not many of them,' Marjorie had replied, undaunted. 'On the Kaipara they have mostly killed each other off.'

Babs and Otter were waiting when her ship sailed into Auckland. The three of them set off with little delay for the Kaipara, travelling by train and ferry, to their home near the sea. Marjorie had become uncertain about their venture. On the voyage out, some people who came from the north had told her of the dangers of the Kaipara Harbour entrance, the people who had died. When the ferry rolled and pitched on the last stage of the trip, she thought she might die too.

The small cottage proved to be nothing like an English cottage, more like a shed where a gardener might keep his tools, except a little larger, with a curtain dividing off what passed for a bedroom, a double bed on one side and a single bed for her on the other. The travellers had brought a leg of mutton in their provisions and, on that first night, Marjorie put it in the cold oven of the stove and tried to light a fire. Otter had retired to bed, while Babs mopped him down from a fever that had overtaken him on the journey.

Outside, in the failing light, a man approached on horseback. Gordon Coates had ridden over from Ruatuna, the family home, when his sister had remarked on the newcomers arriving with their bags and a cabin trunk, heading for the cottage next door.

'Everything all right?' he called out to the girl standing distractedly in the doorway, running a hand through the waves of her hair.

It was so clear that nothing was right that he dismounted and walked over to her. She put her face down so he couldn't see the tears. He put his finger under her chin. She had the bluest eyes of any girl he had ever met. Even though she was in such a dishevelled state, he detected rose water, mixed with the girl's own fresh scent. He had waited for this moment all his life.

Only she was little more than a child. He could see it wouldn't do.

Later, when Otter had died, and Babs remarried and gone to Australia, he found Marjorie working behind the perfume counter at Kirkcaldie & Stains, the big department store in Wellington. No, that isn't quite how it happened. Babs had written him a note to say her sister had gone to the capital. She didn't want to impose on him, and she knew he had affairs of state to attend, but Marjorie was still a young girl. Perhaps he could look in on her at work. This was before he became prime minister, although such was the force of his delivery in the House, and the changes he had brought about for the poor, that everyone knew of him. He was just about to go to war. When he entered the shop, the doorman tipped his hat to him. The graceful notes of a piano being played on the second floor floated down the stairs. Ladies were making their way to the tearooms where he knew, from past visits, there would be tiered stands of cakes and scones and tiny cucumber sandwiches.

The perfume gathered from many gardens now assailed him. Marjorie was absorbed in her task of dabbing scent on the wrist of a customer. When she looked up, she smiled with her pretty rosy mouth, as if she already knew he was there. An elegantly draped dress fell from her bustline. The hands that worked their way over the elderly wrist she supported were soft and white, with small shell-shaped nails. He wanted to hold her in his arms. He wanted her to lie in his bed with him. He thought, This is love. Although he had taken women in his arms many times and they had told him they loved him, he had yet to tell a woman he loved her. He thought his heart a cold stone, but now it was not. For a moment he had to steady himself, so dizzy did he feel with emotion, not to mention the persistent drift of jasmine and lavender that suffused the air.

Because he was who he was — Mr Coates — the supervisor of the counter agreed, without even raising her eyebrow, that Miss Cole might take an early lunch with her gentleman caller.

'We're apart in years,' Marjorie said, when he blurted out his confession of love. They were not even properly seated.

'Not enough to matter, surely,' he said. 'A dozen or so years. It's neither here nor there.' He had spoken to an attendant as they entered the tearoom and now, as if by magic, the woman appeared bearing tea and one of the laden silver stands.

'You hardly know me,' she said, as she bit into a cucumber sandwich, shunning the scones with their jam and cream.

'Of course I do,' he said. 'You think I didn't watch out for you up north?'

'I heard you had others to watch out for.'

His face flushed then. 'There's always idle gossip in small towns.'

'Is it not true then?'

'It's in the past,' he said, after a pause. 'Whatever it was, it's long ago gone. I would have married by now, were it not the case.'

'You're certain of that?'

'I'm bound to the Maori cause in politics,' he said gruffly.

'But not in your heart?'

'Of course it's in my heart. One cannot stand by and watch injustice. I owe an allegiance.'

'To whom, Mr Coates? Who do you owe?'

'The people,' he replied. 'You've seen the Kaipara. I owe the people of the Kaipara.'

Her fingers pleated the sharp edges of the linen cloth in her lap. 'Our home will be there?'

'Eventually,' he said. He spread his hand over hers, sensing her capitulation. 'But for now you will stay here, and, God willing that I should return from this war, one day, I promise you, you'll live in the prime minister's house.'

For her wedding gift, the following week, he bought a dressing-table set of amberina perfume bottles, the glass full of reflected yellowish fire. He would have her, and have her, before he sailed. He would leave her with a daughter, but then Gordon Coates often did that to a woman. He would come back to her, a hero, and the daughters would keep arriving.

LAND

NEWS TRAVELS FAST IN THE north. It was always so. On the Kaipara one morning, a flight of fantails flickered round the doorway of the whare of Te Mate Manukau, and then, although he and his wife tried their best to stop it entering, one flew inside. Te Mate Manukau said to his wife, with bitterness, there is trouble in the south.

The land above the Ruawai plain seaward of the hill, Ngati Whatua land, once belonged to the chief — but when his daughter gave birth to the first of her children, he gave it to the man who would be his son-in-law. That was what he believed. The chief continued to believe this when more children were born. He was proud that the man would marry his daughter. The man himself was a chief, a prince among men. Or so he considered then.

He no longer believes that the marriage will take place, although sometimes a lingering hope stirs within him. The fantail entering his house is not a good sign and, since he gave over the land, his thoughts always turn in that direction and how he has come to lose that which was precious to him. The man who would have wed his daughter has changed his mind, had more children already by another woman, and left them behind too, one of them already dead.

His thoughts fly to his grandchildren, but he can see them at play, not far away. It is simply the death of hope, he thinks then. It is a knowledge being borne to him that what he most desires will never happen.

In the distance, he sees his daughter and, from the way she stands, he sees that she knows something already. Soon enough, he will find out the details for himself. He watches her walk across the paddock, head bowed. When she reaches the river he calls sharply to her mother.

Her eyes travel the path their daughter has taken. They take in her stance at the edge of the water, up to her knees in the mud, the mangroves closing around her, despair in every line of her body.

'Stop her,' Te Mate commands his wife. His wife can run faster than he can with his stick.

'She'll come back.'

Te Mate is gathering himself, urging his wife on.

'In a minute she will be all right,' she says.

'How can you say that?'

'She knows he is gone. She knew long ago. Don't startle her.'

So it is as he thought, although nobody has told them; it is about the man.

After a time that seems to go on forever, although really it is just a minute or two, their daughter straightens herself, returns the way she went, wiping a mud-stained sleeve across her face. The oldest of her girls runs towards her, pulls at her hand.

Aroha, my darling, my darling, be happy.

It is true, she has thought of slipping into the river, letting it sweep her along out through the mouth of the Kaipara. Of course, her father had been angry. He had given the land. Beautiful land, still clad in bush, tall trees, dark furled ferns, a stand of totara.

But what good had his rages done? Gordon wouldn't change his ways. He didn't for her, nor for Annie Ngapo, with whom he has also had children. At the store this morning, the ferryman told her: he is married, it is in the newspaper. The Pakeha girl with a face like whey who stayed here a little while, you know the one I mean? And she knew straight away that it was true, and what she had been told did not surprise her. She had always sensed the ambition in his barrel chest, the one that covered hers so many times, her nipples brushing against his skin. They have known each other since they were children. Through and through. The smell of each other when they lay together. Mussels and eels, whisky and tobacco, their dark mingled musk close to the earth. She could hear the sound of him thinking, in the stillest moment.

So that, when he asked her, that last time they were together, 'What is it that you want?', she had known that he trusted her not to tell him the truth, not to say the words that would have kept him. It was in her power to tear his heart apart, but she didn't. What use was half a heart to her? She didn't say, 'Just you, just you for always', because that would have been to hold him when he wanted to be set free.

Instead she said, 'My darling, my darling, be happy.' And another baby stirring in her womb.

POSTSCRIPT

LONG AFTER, YEARS AND YEARS on, when the old people are gone, Gordon will come back to the Kaipara, his power faded, the dances and parties over, and also the money, of which there was never as much as one might have thought. He will want to give the land back. When the people say, No, it is too late, it cannot be put right now, he will suggest that one of his daughters marry into the family, so that they will be linked with the land. The daughter herself will seem not to be against this.

But her mother is English. It will not do, she will say.

The Trouble with Fire

When his baby's stools turned to water, Frederick told his wife they must go to the hills. The town, although pretty, was no longer safe. It boasted gas lamps and paved streets in its centre, and drinking fountains and churches where they might pray to God that their child would be delivered from his illness, but nothing would do except that they take him to the clean air of the mountains. They were living in a boarding house with all manner of guests just off the ships. If it was too late to save the boy from the spread of disease, it was surely not too late for a cure.

Annie demurred at first, for the house was not ready. 'I can bear any discomfort,' she said, 'but surely the baby won't survive the elements if we don't have shelter.' Already she had seen the construction of the house, its floor resting close to the ground on foundations of stones piled one on top of the other. 'I'm afraid of the wind,' she said, 'the nor'wester might blow us away. I can see myself putting rocks in the baby's cradle or he'll vanish.'

But Frederick knew that it was the hot nor'wester that brought flies to town, where the drainage was still in its planning stages. At this time of year, you could feel the wind hovering beneath overcast skies, creating a heat that drove people close to a feeling of madness that the gale, when it did arrive, failed to ease. Annie said she felt the wind not just in her nose and eyes but even beneath her fingernails. Although it was not her husband's practice to tend the baby, servants were hard to come by in the new colony, and in the close confines of the rooms they shared, it was difficult not to see what was happening. He had noted the trail of mucus and a shadow of blood in the baby's stools as if, at each breath he drew, something — a membrane, a tiny vein perhaps — ruptured within him. The smell was enough to make him want to vomit, too, a rank sickly sweet odour such as he had noted in ports where families lived in one-room shacks and burned incense to mask the rot in their bodies. The baby's thin penetrating screams both infuriated Frederick and filled him with grief. He felt his own large body contract as if bearing his son's suffering. He put impotent fists to his eyes.

'Haven't either of your boys had an illness?' he asked his wife. A moment of anguish flickered over her face. At once, and too late, he remembered that one of her children had not drawn breath at all. But the others back in England were sturdy. When he had spoken, he was hoping she might have had some experience, some memory of what to do that would rescue the baby. Although this was the fourth son she had borne, it was his first child. He couldn't believe how much he loved him, how much he saw his own image in the face of the boy, who at birth had appeared so healthy, with long limbs that would grow to be like his, and an unexpected mat of dark hair he was sure was the colour of his own.

Annie rang a bell and a girl no more than sixteen, wearing a white apron over a dark dress, appeared and took the baby from her arms. They had rented an extra room for her after Annie's lying in. Herself the second child in a family of eleven, and already promised to marry in the spring, the girl handled the baby more easily than his mother. All the same, her lip was sticky with sweat, her hands coarse and slippery. There was nowhere to escape the oppressive heat that threatened still more wind.

'Come here, Frederick,' Annie said, when the door was closed. He dropped to his knees, burying his face against her, feeling her arms around him. She caressed his hair and stroked the side of his face.

'My wife,' he said, 'my dear wife.'

'I'll do whatever you say is for the best,' she said. 'We have to be brave or we'll never come through this.'

He promised then to find her a better place to stay. Some people he knew would welcome a titled lady into their home. Meanwhile, he would go to the house in the hills and quickly make some rooms ready for their arrival. In his absence, she could walk by the Avon, a river that meandered through the stately garden at Ilam, smell the sweet honey-like scent of the red flaxes in bloom, eat fruit picked fresh from the orchard, read and play croquet, just as if she was at home.

'Thank you, dearest Frederick,' she said. When he released her, straight away she called the maid back and ordered their travelling cases prepared.

In the night the hounding wind rose to a gale, slamming through the sky, shrieking at the eaves of the boarding house. The walls seemed to bend in on them, the rush and howl drowning out the infant's crying. Annie turned to him in the bed. 'It will be all right, my love,' she murmured, 'all right.' Comforting him again. In the morning they left the boarding house.

ANNIE BROOME, OR LADY BARKER as she is known, fell into conversation with me at a ball when we were both quite danced off our feet. 'Well, Miss Scott,' she said, 'I feel for those poor young men. I'm far too old for them to dance with, and married at that, but there aren't enough of you girls to go round.'

'I'm sure they're very happy to dance with you,' I said, for something polite to say.

She burst out laughing at that. 'No they're not, for one of them has already expressed his disappointment when I was foolish enough to remark on his having nobody to dance with but me. One should never go fishing for compliments.'

'They'll all end up marrying the maids,' said my mother, who had hurried over to ensure a formal introduction had taken place. 'You see it more and more out here in the colonies.'

'I wouldn't say there were many young women here who qualify for the description of maid,' Annie said, tossing off the remark in a way that made it hard to tell whether she was being unkind or merely to the point. 'Of course it's good for one's own education, for I've learnt more about the art of cooking and baking in New Zealand than I would have learnt in a lifetime in London.'

When my mother moved on, Annie and I fell to talking about station life, and some of the catastrophes that had taken place in her kitchen: like the day she made bread and the yeast brewed up so hard that it exploded like a pistol shot, scattering foam all over the ceiling of the kitchen and none left for bread but she cooked the dough anyway, even though nobody could get their teeth into a corner of the loaf. She laughed so hard when she described this that I found myself wanting to experiment in the kitchen at home, both for the fun of it, and so I could have something to tell her about my own adventures the next time I saw her. And before long she had invited me to visit.

'But first you must tell me which of the young men you prefer to dance with,' she said.

When I assured her that so far I had no preferences at all, she raised her eyebrows in mock disbelief.

There is no end of young men I might fall in love with, and I fear I could end up having to choose between two or three. My mother is perpetually anxious about 'my situation', as she calls it. Alice, she says, if you don't fill your card at the balls, how can you ever hope to find the most suitable man?

But, Mother, I say, I can tell without dancing with them that some are not men I will marry. She thinks this unreasonable, on account of the woman shortage so, like Lady Barker, I am bound to a quadrille or two, even with the plainest of them. Besides, my mother says, you don't really know until you've made their acquaintance whether you'll like them or not. But I do know, that's the difficulty. There's the man with big teeth beneath his hairy moustache that I don't want close to my face at any price, and another whose bad breath follows in a trail behind him even when he has passed to the other end of the room, and yet another who has smooth skin and a girlish face that somehow I don't trust, even though he is a great flirt with the young ladies, and keeps kissing the hands of the older women, bowing and scraping as if he were in the most elegant of Europe's ballrooms.

'Always remember that you're the daughter of a major,' my mother says. 'If you keep that in mind it won't be so difficult to make a choice.' To which she might add that my father owns a very large sheep station worth a vast sum of money, but she remarks on that so often that neither I nor any of my suitors is likely to forget. Neither she nor my father would understand the freedom I feel when I am at Broomielaw with Annie and Frederick, how different everything is and, fortunately, they don't know how we carry on.

I couldn't work Annie and Frederick out at the start. Annie is older than Frederick by eleven years and has been married before and has children back in England. I wouldn't call her exactly beautiful, rather handsome, with dark eyes all the more striking for being deep-set, her hair parted with some severity, like a fine slice of sallow peel down the centre of her head. (Frederick parts his hair in exactly the same manner so that they look more brother and big sister than husband and wife.) The set of her mouth can be a little sombre, slightly drawn down at the corners, so that you glimpse sorrow, as if she is only partly in this present time where she appears otherwise so perfectly happy. But you forget that as soon as she speaks, her wide mouth trembling with laughter, her lips as if made for kisses. Oh, forgive me this, but of late I have been worrying about kissing. Mr Forsyth, a young naval lieutenant, has been after me for a kiss and I have thought once or twice that I might give him one. But I have no idea how one goes about it. Do you offer him your cheek and allow him to brush his lips there? Or does he put his mouth upon yours? All of this alarms me. I have almost made up my mind to ask Annie what to do.

Some years ago, when I was still not twenty, Frederick Broome was a man I might have considered, had he shown the slightest interest in me. But he never seemed impressed by any of us girls in the years before he brought Annie here to live, though he was gallant enough. He was a splendid athlete then, but I did hear a rumour that he wrote poetry as well. I wasn't sure that a poetry-writing farmer would be a very good bargain; there was no knowing where his thoughts might stray. What's more, it was said there was some connection with the Greeks, though I had no idea what that was at the time. I thought it might explain why he seemed absent in his manner. I've learnt since that he spent his childhood in Greece, where his father was a chaplain with the British forces. The vicar, it seems, had too many children to support in any style, and decided to dispatch his son to the colonies to follow farming. That has turned out rather well for Frederick, for his school friend, a man called Philip Hill, has joined him, and his father did have money, so now they are in partnership and own their own sheep station. Philip seems shy, not often seen at social gatherings. He is tall and thin, already with that weathered look of a man who toils in the Canterbury weather — hard bright sun in the summer, and driving snow and cold in the winters.

IT WAS, IN FACT, THE immense light of the sky that had sealed Frederick's fate with Annie. Frederick had intended to marry a younger woman. In spite of the shortage, several local women would have accepted him, and might have done well enough. He was tempted more than once. But an English-born woman was what he wanted, young, educated and, with luck, good-looking as well. A woman who read and understood literature, and the nature not just of passion but of the mind, in a way that women who had lived most of their lives in the colonies could not. Poor things, they were raised to hear nothing but talk of sheep and horses and the price of wool, as they dined on mutton chops. Preferably, too, someone who had travelled and would not be discontented, once she had settled far from England and the great centres of Europe. This ideal woman would have read the novels of Anthony Trollope and the poetry of Robert Browning, and could talk about the issues of the day yet still be prepared to live in a country where the landscape was vast and empty and the sky as blue as that above the Ionian Sea.

So he urged his body on, running and hurdling, riding his horse at full gallop for mile upon mile across the Canterbury Plains. Scourging himself, like the martyrs of old. He is the finest boxer and wrestler in the colony, boasted the gentlemen of the Christchurch Club to the newspaper. Not only that, but he is an athlete as well, who can run two hundred yards on a grass track in a mere twenty seconds.

When his friend Philip had gained enough experience, Frederick set out to England to find a wife, leaving his partner in charge of the farm. As he travelled, he began to think how impossible it might be to find the woman who fitted his ideal in the few months available to him.

This turned out not to be difficult at all.

On his arrival, Frederick made his way to Prees Hall in Shrewsbury, the rambling red brick house where Philip's family lived, and where he would stay in England. There, that first evening, he met another of the Hills' house guests, a woman with a long strong face that seemed solemn when he first looked into it. Although she was dressed in a high-collared mourning dress, he noticed that her throat was slender, and the colour of an arum lily. She turned to him and said, 'I've heard so much about you, Mr Broome, that I could hardly contain my delight when I heard you'd be visiting at the same time as me.'

Later she asked him if he enjoyed viewing paintings, to which he replied that, although it was a long time since he had seen any of quality, given that he had lived in the colonies since he was a mere boy and might not be the best judge, he was eager to improve his education. He felt clumsy and out of his depth, because he had arrived so confident in his knowledge of books and literature, and straight away was shown to be lacking in the simple art of looking at a picture.

'Do you know the work of Mr Joseph Turner? He is a great modern master.'

When he admitted that he did not, she said dreamily, 'I love his work more than that of any other artist. He paints light with perfect clarity. Some of it reflects skies like you see here in Shropshire, but some remind me of my girlhood in Jamaica. He mixes pale sea green with deep turquoise blue, purple with crimson and orange, so that I think of light before a storm strikes. Such savage storms we knew in Jamaica.'

'Why that sounds like the sky over Canterbury before a nor'wester sets in,' Frederick exclaimed.

'Really? Then you and I will go to London, and I'll show you some of Mr Turner's work.' With that, Lady Barker placed his hand beneath her elbow, so that they glided together into the dining room.

Later in the evening, they found themselves briefly alone in the drawing room, where a fire glowed in the grate. She stood as if mesmerised, the flames reflected in her eyes, and held out her hands with an odd hungry gesture. 'I am so very glad we have met, Mr Broome,' she said.

After that, they walked often in the foothills that rolled towards the Welsh border. One day he took her hand, with the same confidence she had shown, tucking it palm to palm in his pocket with his, oblivious to eyebrows raised at such uninhibited behaviour from those they encountered. When he glanced sideways to see if this was acceptable to her, he saw a look of deep happiness in her expression. Rapture.

THE FIRST TIME I VISITED Annie and Frederick Broome's station, my mother sent my brother along as a chaperone. I knew there was gossip but that was something mothers did and really none of my business. All the same, I couldn't help overhearing my mother and her sisters when they thought I was absorbed in some sewing. This was not long before I was due to leave for my visit to Broomielaw.

'Why on earth would Mr Broome have taken up with a woman of such mature years?' asked my Aunt Lorna. I thought that was a fine thing coming from her, who had never managed a man at all. My aunt has fine grey eyes and a sharp tongue but her chin is too strong by far, and she forgets to pluck the hairs that stray along her upper lip.

'It's not for her money,' my mother replied. 'I've heard the woman is penniless.'

'But she has a title,' retorted Nancy, another of the aunts, summoning a wise and knowing voice. This is her habit, to sound informed about things that are as clear as the nose on your face, as if she were the first person to think of them, even though she is generally the last. She talks so much that she didn't notice her husband, my uncle by marriage, choking during dinner on a piece of gristle that lodged in his windpipe and felled him to the floor, his face purple, his heart stopped. If only he had told me he was choking, she would say, I might have been able to save him, but that was so like him, not to complain.

'Well,' my mother said, in a brisk and reproving tone, 'Sir George Barker, her first husband, was by all accounts an immensely brave man. He received his title after the fall of Sebastopol, you know. And she lived in Calcutta with him, so she must have some pluck. I've heard she faced up to tigers, not to mention the natives in India. Possibly she doesn't wish his memory to die with him.'

'But this is New Zealand,' murmured Nancy. 'Didn't we come here to be equal? I mean, really what room is there for titles in this country? Unless, of course, you've earnt it yourself. But Sir George is dead and gone, and surely now she should be Mrs Frederick Broome?'

My Aunt Lorna spoke darkly. 'In that case, perhaps we should ask why she married him. Now that he owns a sheep station. And he's a very fine figure of a young man, an excellent physique.'

My mother glanced round quickly, hoping that I had not heard this. 'Hush, Lorna, you know nothing about the . . . the physique of men.'

'The baby arrived rather early, I heard.'

'Lorna, are you not well? The child is with God.'

'Besides,' Nancy said, stepping in swiftly, 'Mr Broome is hardly wealthy yet.'

So, although Mr Broome and Lady Barker were husband and wife, there was indeed this air of slight scandal about them, the titled older woman with the young handsome husband, which made my mother insist that I must not visit them unaccompanied. In the end, quite a party of us set out, and, because my brother George was with me, Mr Forsyth was able to accompany us on our ride. My mother was most encouraging; she was increasingly concerned that I might turn out like Aunt Lorna, whose eyes I have inherited but, mercifully, not her chin. We left at dawn, on one of those sharp spring mornings, the air as crisp as a ripening pear, clear and achingly bright. We fell silent as we rode, only the sound of the horses' hooves crunching the tussock to remind us that we were truly alive, not just part of a picture. The lieutenant rode up beside me and wanted to talk, but I turned what I hoped was a withering stare on him and soon he dropped behind.

A magnificent lunch awaited us at Broomielaw. We started with champagne, then proceeded to tender young goose, and a sirloin of beef and the new season's asparagus. The mysterious Philip Hill, who lives a mile or so away in another house on the station, joined us and I must say he was better company than the lieutenant. Philip has read many of the books that overflow the shelves of the house; he is deeply interested in the work of the famous author Mr Charles Darwin, who comes from Shrewsbury where his parents live, so they were all talking about him as if they were on familiar terms, if not with the great man in person, at least with his work. Frederick was somewhat worried by his theories on the origin of the species because they appear to go against the creation story, and Annie and Frederick do believe in God's will. But Philip argued vigorously in favour of evolution, and the conversation became heated, especially after we'd opened a second bottle of champagne.

The meal was cleared away by an Irish maid named Mary, who kept her eyes averted, as if the conversation might somehow be avoided if she didn't look. In an effort to steer the topic away from science and religion, my brother enquired after a second sheep station that the Broomes had recently bought near Lake Wanaka. My father had snorted when he heard the price Frederick paid. My brother should have known better than to ask. A silence fell around the table.

'The lake is very pretty,' said Annie, after a spell. 'A beautiful spot.'

Frederick folded his linen napkin several times, making a little concertina from the hem. The gentlemen coughed and my brother complimented our hostess on such a splendid lunch.

'We must all take a rest,' Annie said briskly. 'Alice will certainly need one after her ride.'

I was a little saddle sore and weary yet I felt so exhilarated and, I suppose, rather drunk. I didn't want to rest, rather to look through all the books. The small house was so comfortable and pretty, with many prints on the walls, and some trophies of Indian swords and hunting spears hung over the fireplace, and bouquets made entirely of ferns in tall white vases on the side tables. I came to a writing table that I understood to be Frederick's. Some reference had been made to him working there most afternoons. It seems he really is a poet. I noticed a folder containing loose sheets of paper and before I could stop myself I lifted the cover. Scribbled on the front page was a verse that began:

Oh dear little son, born like Perseus
Out of a rain of gold fire, I saw how you fought
In vain. Your memory is like stars that pursue us
From hemisphere to hemisphere . . .

The end of the line was scribbled over, the ink laid on in thick slashes, as if in frustration at not finding a rhyme. But I understood then what had befallen them, the matter my aunt had alluded to. The death of infants is a common enough story here in New Zealand. I was about to turn the page when I heard Annie's footstep, and I hastily replaced the folder, steadying myself in the hope that she had not noticed.

'Where have the men gone?' I asked. The house had become very quiet.

Annie was watching me with a faint smile. 'The gentlemen have all gone to the swimming hole to cool off,' she said.

'Oh, where is that?' I cried. 'Can we go and watch?'

Annie burst out laughing. 'I think not. The gentlemen have laid private claim to it, so they can strip off. They like to swim without their clothes.'

'Oh,' I said, blushing. 'Forgive me.'

She was studying me intently. 'Do you have a taste for danger?' she said.

I was taken aback, because my question was innocent and nothing about my demeanour could have suggested that I wanted to view the gentlemen without their clothes. 'I think we should read for a while,' she said, appearing not to notice my discomfiture, and handed me a book taken at random from the shelves.

In the evening, we danced on the verandah in the cool night air. I said I wouldn't dance with the men if they wore their boots, to which Annie heartily agreed, so these were exchanged for slippers.

She produced several sets made of purple velvet embroidered with gold, acquired from India. The Broomes called in Mary and a young farmhand to join us. I was surprised that they were part of the entertainment, but they looked as if they were used to it and, after a while, even Mary seemed in a good mood. The music was made by my brother and the farmhand, who whistled together and clapped the top and bottom of some silver dishes as if they were cymbals. But although I danced and danced with Mr Forsyth, I looked in vain for Philip Hill, who had not returned with the gentlemen after their swim. Somebody had to do some work on the farm, I supposed. By the time the evening was over I had decided that this would be the last evening I danced with the lieutenant.

NOW THAT THE LAMBING WAS over, Frederick could take up his daily habit of writing again. Like the novelist Anthony Trollope, whose work he so deeply admired, he set himself the goal of beginning a new piece of work as soon as he had completed the one before, so that writing was one seamless occupation. His collection of poems had mounted day by day. But for some time he had been stuck in the same place.

He found himself gazing out of the window, watching his wife and Alice Scott walking in a fast, determined manner towards the hills. There was no keeping Annie and Alice apart, now that they had discovered the joy of burning tussock together. In the spring, the sheep farmers' habit was to burn off the land in order to encourage fresh new grass growth. The earth was laid bare and desolate when it was burnt over but soon tender young shoots transformed it into pasture for ewes and their lambs. He and Annie had set many fires together, setting out with matches and a bundle of flax sticks to use as impromptu torches. They began their line of fire, setting one large tussock blazing, and then, starting from this head-centre, dragging the sticks one to the right and one to the left, and before long a whole hillside was ablaze with racing fire.

Frederick knew the danger, for if the lines of fire were incorrectly laid and a nor'wester sprang up too fiercely, the fire-lighter could be engulfed. But when Annie lit fires it appeared they took hold of her, causing her to discard all caution. One day they had been joined by Alice. She visited often now, and alone. Philip Hill would sit down to dinner with them more often than not. Frederick wished that this were not the case, even though he still enjoyed the company of his friend. They had endured so much together, snowstorms and floods and the loss of so many thousands of newborn lambs. It was simply that, from the line of figures in the accounts book he kept in a locked compartment of his writing desk, he knew how impossible it would be for the station to support another family. Soon one or other of them must leave.

'I love lighting fires,' Alice had declared after her expedition in their company. And Annie had agreed with her, describing it as 'an exceeding joy'. 'Oh, I wish the tussock was still as long as it used to be,' she exclaimed. 'Farmers have told me that in the early days it was six feet high. Imagine the fire that would have made.'

'I'm not allowed to light fires at home,' Alice had confided, and so they had taken to calling it their 'mischief', setting off to the hills on their own, coming back late at night looking like eccentric chimney sweeps, their dresses black and ragged, their eyebrows singed. They seemed to Frederick barbaric, even wicked, in their appearance. He remonstrated with Annie more than once, for enough fires had been laid for one year. But she laughed that off, almost as if he were childish. That hurt. Her thirty-fifth birthday had passed. In other circumstances, he reflected, she might have seen herself as looking a little ridiculous.

The truth was, he missed her in the house, finding it difficult to write in her absence. He had been working on a poem that seemed to go nowhere, toiling over images thrown up by the Greek legend of Perseus, as if he might find comfort for them both, remembering the way their child had been conceived in what seemed, back in England, like a bright flame out of control. Instead, he found himself in a familiar state of agitation, opening a cupboard door, the one where the baby's clothes were kept in a container, wrapped in fine tissue, mothballs laid over the top. He paused, averting his eyes from the box. Back at his desk, he laid his head on his arms and wept.

SUCH FIERCE GAIETY NOW TOOK hold of us. As dusk fell, the fires raced up the surrounding hills. Every now and then they met with a puff of wind, striking a great surge of heat that sent flames rushing uphill to divide into two fiery horns like a crescent. That's the trouble with fire, you never know which way it will turn. The breeze changed and the tips of fire met again, creating a solid wall. The air cracked as the fires collided with exploding green bushes. We try not to burn stands of ti-ti palms, but now and then one gets in our way.

Last evening, I stood and watched a sweet swell of fire, fire looping and curling, swirling higher and higher, sleek fire, orange and blue fire, cardinal fire. I shouted and ran, as a line snaked back down the hill and chased me, but I outran it.

'Alice,' called Annie, 'you need to be careful. Are you not afraid?'

'Not at all,' I cried. But when I looked at her, I felt a sudden caution. From where I stood, I saw her transfixed as the wall of flames raced towards one of the palm trees. Even before they reached it, I could see its *long delicate leaves trembling piteously before the wind of fire. Then the old dry leaves at the base of the palm caught the first spark, and the whole tree was ablaze, a pillar of fire.* Streamers of fire erupted, curtains of fire raining down, torrents of flames. I heard Annie groan, the back of her hand held to her mouth. *The palm tree bent and swayed, tossing its leaves for a few seconds like fiery plumes before all was consumed at the heart of the furnace.* This, later, was how she would describe it to others. As for us, we've stopped the burning here at Broomielaw. But when I read her words, I see that tree awaiting the onslaught, the last soldier standing on a murderous battlefield.

Annie walked towards the tree as if she wasn't going to stop, breathing deeply, as if she would march straight into the fire itself. I knew that if she inhaled another gasp of fire, the inside of her lungs would turn the colour of rust. As a whisper of flame caressed her neck, I raced after her, seizing her by the arms and throwing her to the ground. Her eyes were fixed and staring, her hands moving up and down in useless fluttering little motions by her side. I was truly afraid then, for her, not of the fire.

She shook herself and rolled over on her hands and knees before standing up. She dusted herself down, her expression seemingly normal again.

'It was beautiful. Wasn't it beautiful, Alice?'

'Yes,' I said. 'We should go home now, Annie.' Darkness had fallen. We had walked for miles and miles, and I had no idea how far we had come.

'Home.' She sighed, and brushed her hair from her forehead. 'We'll be going home soon.'

'Yes, yes,' I answered, 'of course we're going home.'

'Back home,' she replied. 'Back home to England.'

In the distance, I saw the figures of men outlined against the still-glowing firelight.

'Frederick is coming to find me,' she said, her eyes following mine.

'They're all looking for us,' I said. I knew one of the men would be

Philip. Perhaps it was the heat but something inside me had melted. I felt like a grown woman at last. At our feet lay a cauldron of embers where the palm tree once stood, thick fire reduced to a porridge of glowing dust. I took my stick and prodded it this way and that as we waited for the men.

In the morning, I saw a cloud of seagulls in the distance. They had moved inland to pick over morsels of roast lizards and grasshoppers among the ashes and last tendrils of smoke. I listened to the low murmur of Annie and Frederick's voices in the next room. Some things had been resolved. I was happier than I had ever been and inescapably filled with sadness. Soon I would live here, and they would be gone.

Acknowledgements

THIS BOOK WAS WRITTEN DURING my tenure of the Creative New Zealand Michael King Fellowship, for which I extend my grateful thanks.

It is hard to imagine completing a book without the input of my editors Harriet Allan and Anna Rogers. Harriet offers unfailing encouragement, and Anna has provoked and challenged me to think more deeply about my work for many years, always with kindness and patience. I cannot thank either of them enough. Thanks, too, to Alexandra Bishop for her skilful input into the editing process.

For early reading of some of these stories, advice and comments, I thank Ian Kidman, Michael Harlow, Mary McCallum and Alison Kember. Special thanks to Alison for introducing me to the basics of Vietnamese, and for support when I needed it most. I am grateful to Dr Margaret Sparrow for her advice. Amelia Herrero-Kidman reminded me of Jack Kerouac's novel *Dharma Bums*. And, I have never forgotten a lunchtime reading, in 1990, when Richard Ford read from his novel *Wild Life* and talked about his fascination with fire, something I share.

Some of these stories have been previously published in *The Best New Zealand Fiction 4* (ed. Fiona Farrell, Vintage, Auckland, 2007), *The Best New Zealand Fiction 5* (ed. Owen Marshall, Vintage, Auckland, 2008), *Second Violins: New Stories Inspired by Katherine*

Mansfield (ed. Marco Sonzogni, Vintage, Auckland, 2008) and *Lost in Translation: New Zealand Stories* (ed. Marco Sonzogni, Vintage, Auckland, 2010).

The first lines of 'The History of It' come from notes towards an unfinished story by Katherine Mansfield. A brief extract from 'The Trouble with Fire' (italicised) appears in Lady Barker's *Station Life in New Zealand*. I acknowledge Dick Scott's book *Seven Lives on Salt River* for information about Gordon Coates's background.

Fiona Kidman